If I Could
Turn Back Time

If I Could Turn Back Time

Beth
Harbison

ST. MARTIN'S PRESS ❧ NEW YORK

IF I COULD TURN BACK TIME. Copyright © 2015 by Beth Harbison. All rights reserved. Printed in the United States of America. For information, address St. Martin's Press, 175 Fifth Avenue, New York, N.Y. 10010.

www.stmartins.com

The Library of Congress Cataloging-in-Publication Data is available upon request.

ISBN 978-1-250-04381-8 (hardcover)
ISBN 978-1-4668-4219-9 (e-book)

St. Martin's Press books may be purchased for educational, business, or promotional use. For information on bulk purchases, please contact the Macmillan Corporate and Premium Sales Department at 1-800-221-7945, extension 5442, or write to specialmarkets@macmillan.com.

First Edition: August 2015

10 9 8 7 6 5 4 3 2 1

To my children, Paige and Jack Harbison. I would not turn back time for anything if it meant I wouldn't have you. You both mean the world to me!

ACKNOWLEDGMENTS

Thanks so much to Katie Ware for all of your help. You will never know what a difference you have made and how grateful my family is to yours. Much appreciation to Kevin and Melanie Ware as well. God bless Orion Triple R: Rescue, Rehab, Rehome!

To my mother, Connie Atkins, for so much more than I can say.

To my sisters, Elaine and Jacquelyn—Mommy and Daddy did a great job to raise three girls who never really got into too much trouble. Daddy would be so proud of us all, I know, but especially you two: so wise and witty and strong.

To my girlfriends who have continued to help and bolster me (and pour the wine) as I vent, I love you: Connie Jo Gernhofer, Jami Nasi, Carolyn Clemens, Denise Whitaker, Dana Carmel, Kim Amori, Tris Zeigler, and Chandler Schwede. I couldn't do without you guys!

Deb Levy, I don't even know what to say—you are the coolest of the cool. Drinks soon. And often.

Marlene Roberts Engel, your kindness and strength inspire me.

Lesli Alison LeJeune, I *so* want to be just like you. ☺

To Cinda and John O'Brien, for our enduring friendship, which I value so much, and which has carried me along more times than you know.

To Greg Rubin, for wise counseling and positive energy.

Mike Scotti, thanks for a weird collection of good things and fun moments that are probably best left unspecified. Also, for the hours of great reading your books have provided—I truly cannot wait to read more.

Paul Minchoff, thanks for "manning around the house" for me. ☺ You probably stopped me from killing myself, or electrocuting myself trying to install the doorbell.

Mr. Bigosi, you will never know how much I love you. It's been lifetimes. I wish the best for you.

Annelise Robey, you have been so much more than an agent, and that was not in the contract for you! Thank you for years of friendship, laughter, and support. You are one of the strongest and wisest people I know, and your counsel always makes me feel better.

And to all the readers who have contacted me privately or posted on Facebook with such kind comments and for sharing your own stories—"thank you" just isn't enough, but it's all I've got!

If I *Could* *Turn* Back *Time*

CHAPTER ONE

THE NIGHT BEFORE MY EIGHTEENTH BIRTHDAY, I WAS THIRTY-seven years old.

Not the first time. The first time I was seventeen. Just like you'd expect of an ordinary person. Because I was an ordinary person. I really couldn't pinpoint what put me over the edge, but something did.

So, when it came down to what I want to tell you about today, yes: The night before my *second* eighteenth birthday, I was thirty-seven.

Doesn't really make it all that much clearer, does it? I'm sorry.

I'll get there.

Meanwhile, let's start someplace else. The day before my thirty-eighth birthday, I was on a boat—a yacht, really—off the coast of Miami, Florida, drenched in the kind of blue-water, sunny-day perfection you see on the cover of *Condé Nast Traveler* and other luxury magazines. It was absolutely, stunningly, *breath-takingly* beautiful.

By all accounts, mine was a stunning, beautiful, absolutely breathtaking luxury life.

I hadn't grown up that way. No one who grows up with over-the-top luxury bothers to appreciate it or describe it in detail. They take it for granted, while the rest of us either dream about it or—as in my case—are perfectly contented until someone swoops us out of our easy anonymous life and plops us down into the middle of some political existence, major or minor, literal or figurative.

But I'm getting ahead of myself.

In my youth, I'd enjoyed a happy, Charlie Brown–landscaped, middle-class life in Potomac, Maryland, close enough to the D.C. border that you could ride a bike there (if you were ambitious). Summers were muggy and smelled of hot pavement and beer at a field party down River Road; fall was always cool and crisp, underlined by the sounds of fiery red and gold leaves (matching the ubiquitous Redskins jerseys) skidding across sidewalks and streets; winters crunched with snow and carried the scent of wood smoke that drifted lazily out of brick chimneys until the inevitable flat and depressing gray stretch that was February and March, when everyone drew into their homes and stopped any festivities, holding their breath for the relief of anything other than the long dark winter of the D.C. suburbs.

But then spring burst forth in a pastel fireworks show of azaleas, daffodils, cherry blossoms—the trees that lined my side of Fox Hills were cherry blossoms, until they all died off, and the other side of the neighborhood had Bradford pears, which I think lasted longer—and the burst of whatever spring nature gave brought the happy smiles of residents who hadn't quite believed it would ever warm up again.

Ours was not a neighborhood of rose competitions or any other attempts to outdo each other's optimism; it was a place where everyone did their best to nourish cheer and no one sought to outdo another, because the point was to hasten the gray winter along as best we could, as best we *all* possibly could.

The rich in our town had old money and horses and bridal paths; the rest of us had bikes and neighborhood pools and solid American cars to take us to the mall or dinner out at Normandie Farm or, on really special occasions, the Peter Pan Inn in Urbana. It was a half-hour drive through the dark but it always ended in a deep-velvet-red dining room and the best Shirley Temple drinks I ever had.

I was a math kid, always loved it, always excelled at it. I couldn't understand how anyone had trouble with math, when it was the most straightforward thing in the world. To me, that would be like not understanding how to breathe. Nothing else in life is so dependable: you plug the right formula in with the right numbers, do the puzzle, and get the answer right every single time.

My dad was a banker and he loved that I shared this quality with him. Early on he taught me sums using coins. When I was five years old he began to teach me about the stock market and how to track a portfolio. He taught me to invest in things I liked, not just things that "made sense." Our first real purchase for my future was one hundred shares of Apple's IPO at $22 a share, because he and I loved to play *Alternate Reality* together. I saved that stock and added to it for the thirty years that followed, through three splits and a high approaching $250 a share.

Thanks to Dad, I had a nice little nest egg for myself long before I hit it big working with Whitestone, one of the top private equity investment firms in the country.

Believe it or not, I'd never actually been financially ambitious. At least not in the greedy sense. I loved to get it right, to invest well, to have my intuition richly rewarded with high growth and big margins, in short to be good at my job. But I'd never felt like I didn't have what I needed until the little enclave that had been my home since I was born became a very popular metropolitan suburb for bigwigs and the prices escalated well beyond what I or 99 percent of my school classmates could have afforded.

Until Dad died unexpectedly halfway through my college education, that is. Well, I say unexpectedly, but when you smoke three packs of unfiltered Pall Mall cigarettes a day, a sudden and devastating stroke can't exactly be characterized as "unexpected." *Unfortunate*, certainly. *Unendurable*, very nearly.

But not *unexpected*.

It was definitely the most formative experience of my life, though. I was twenty years old, and it wasn't what *I'd* expected. I'd fully expected him to be there for me forever, to fix doorknobs in my first shabby apartment, to advise me when the market wobbled, to walk me down the aisle if and when I found someone I wanted to marry, and, most importantly—and most vivid in my imagination—to be a grandfather to my kids: to throw them up in the air and catch them; to make games of "fishing" with homemade poles held from the second floor of the house for treasures he'd hidden in his shoes.

That was the dad he'd been to me, and that was the grand-dad I was sure he'd be to my children someday. And, damn it, it was really something to look forward to.

But it was never to be.

My mom later told me she'd feared it for years. So strongly, in fact, that sometimes she had a sneaking suspicion that she'd caused his death by focusing so much attention on that specific dread. But that was nonsense. He smoked, he enjoyed his Irish coffees, he spent his evenings in his easy chair in front of ESPN, and he died.

And life changed. Even though the house was paid off, Mom had a hard time paying the taxes along with all her other ex-penses, so I had the most important investment assignment of my life: to profitably invest the life insurance payment in a bad market so that she could comfortably live off the dividends.

It's worked out pretty well.

So I was able to sit on the bow of that yacht the day before my birthday, soaking up the sun without many cares in the world.

I was with my best friend, Sammy—whom tackier people would probably call my "gay husband" and which probably gives you a fair idea of him and our relationship—as well as two couples we weren't actually that close to but whom we'd known for a decade and who tended to show up every time there was a party, and Lisa and Larry Springston. Larry was my associate at Whitestone, and Lisa was his wife. She and I had gotten partic-ularly close in the past five years or so, and everyone called us "partners in crime," thanks to a few better-left-unmentioned wine-fueled party antics.

"It's time for *champagne*," Sammy announced, shortly after noon and a few nibbles of cheese dictated that it was reasonably five o'clock somewhere. He came out of the galley with a tray containing eight glasses, and a silver bucket with the distinct flower-painted bottle of Perrier-Jouët poking out of the top. Each delicate Waterford flute had a slender straw in it—a nod to the brief period when I'd been obsessed with Pommery Pops, small bottles of fine Pommery champagne in blue bottles with little blue straws.

That habit had ended quickly—it just wasn't economically responsible, and I was nothing if not economically responsible—but we figured out it was really the straws that drew us in, so we always tried to use them for special occasions.

Sammy's theory was that every birthday with an *eight* in it was an anniversary of my eighteenth birthday, and thus qualified as a *very* special occasion.

He set the tray down on the table and held up the bottle. "Your *favorite!*"

"Thank you so much!" I made my way over to him and gave him a hug. "You know me so well."

"Honey, anyone here could have come up with your favorite champs. But when you see the present I got you, you'll know who your daddy is."

Sammy was not, and would never be, a who's-your-daddy guy, though he'd dated a few.

But it gave me a moment's pause, as that sort of thing still did, to think about my own daddy and the fact that he *wasn't* here. That he'd never be here. And the fact that I still hadn't managed to find my way completely over that fact.

This wasn't the time for mourning, though. This was a fun

occasion, a party. I wasn't going to let myself slip into the maudlin.

Sammy poured expertly into tilted flutes so the foam didn't rise over and spill any precious liquid gold, and handed them to me one by one to distribute. One for Kristin, one for Melanie, one for Ray, one for Ronnie, one for Larry, and one for—

"None for me," Lisa said, holding up her hand, her diamond wedding ensemble glittering madly in the sun.

"Oh, come on." I laughed and held it out to her. "Since when do you not want champagne? Particularly when it's the good stuff!"

"Nope. I'm serious. I . . . I'm just going to have water." Her face went a little pink.

Slow to the punch, I grew concerned. "Are you sick? You're kind of flushed."

"Oh, no, I'm fine. Better than ever."

This still didn't register at all. Dumb, right? "Okay," I said slowly. "If you're sure. . . ."

She met my eyes and smiled. "I'm drinking for two now," she said in a stage whisper, then patted her board-flat belly with her hand. "Or, rather, *not* drinking for two."

Ding ding ding. "You're *pregnant?*" I was so shocked I didn't bother to keep my voice down, so of course everyone turned their attention to our conversation.

Lisa didn't seem to mind, though. She reached her hand out for Larry's and said, "We are."

Good lord. Not only was Lisa—*Lisa!*—pregnant, but she was also suddenly a *we are* sort of person. This wasn't the woman I'd been hanging out with at all.

"Well . . ." I didn't know what to say. "Well. Congratulations!" I raised my glass to them, and everyone else followed suit.

"Congratulations!"

Then, of course, everyone crowded around the couple to ask how had this come about, had they been planning it, did they know yet if it was a girl or a boy, and did they have names lined up. All those things everyone always asks in situations like this.

Honestly, it seemed to go on forever, though, and Lisa seemed to tell the "Free Bird" version of the story about peeing on a stick, then another, then another, and so on, until she ran to Larry, who was on his stationary bike, holding six positive pregnancy tests with, presumably, urine-covered hands, though she didn't mention that part. I don't know why, though, since she seemed to go on about every other detail anyone could possibly come up with, right down to, and including, the fact that one of the little red lines was pink and that threw the other five positive tests into doubt for them, so they went to the doctor the next day for a blood test, and . . . blah blah blah. The story was endless. Seriously. The extended dance version of the oldest story on earth.

I felt an embarrassing little ping of irritation that my thirty-eighth birthday eve—so horribly close to forty—had been overshadowed by toasts and congratulations for Lisa's unexpected pregnancy, but I squelched it immediately. What a self-centered jerk I was being! A total baby, feeling proprietary about people's attention when, really, it was just another day like any other. Lisa and Larry had wonderful news, a life-changing event, and I wanted . . . what? To be patted on the back for the magnificent feat of not dying by age thirty-eight? It was shameful.

Though, seriously, no matter when she *got* pregnant, was this really the time and place to announce it? Could she not know that her previous partner in crime—me—might feel a little weird about being ambushed by this news of her total acquiescence to domestication?

Because it was clear that this was not the end of the story; Lisa was never going to go back to being the fun person I remembered. Now she was a mother. A hugely proud, almost cocky mother. And as great as it was that she'd gotten what she evidently wanted—it was apparently a dream come true for her— how could I be anything less than supportive?

I told her how happy I was for her, of course. What a great mother I knew she'd be, based on what a great friend she'd been. How strong their family would be, because of her incredible bond with Larry, though privately I thought they'd fought and occasionally broken up over the dumbest things on earth. So how on earth could any sane person think this union would last and get stronger in the presence of a small being who wailed like a harmonica played by a first grader, pooped and peed in their pants, *could not* be ignored without calling attention to child protective authorities, and needed constant attention for more than a decade before they could even be counted on to go to bed when instructed, and even then you only had like two years before they snuck out six hours later . . . ?

No, I wasn't exactly jealous of Lisa. But I already missed the times we'd had—the times we'd never have again—and more than anything I missed imagining that a baby would come along and turn two people into a wonderful family. I hadn't believed that in years, because I had never seen evidence that it happened.

No super-happy families around me!

Not that I was in the business for it. Finance professionals at my level barely had time to breathe, much less form relationships. As long as the market was open, there was no taking my eyes off it. I could see that the guys I worked with always ended up screwed if they formed close relationships. Inevitably they started feeling stifled and, eventually, suffocated.

How could I feel jealous?

Yet, undeniably, I felt left behind. And I felt like I was suddenly being faced with questions I had to ask about the decisions I'd made in my life. The sense of a ticking time bomb was indisputable.

I'd made a lot of mistakes in my life. Was this the biggest one?

CHAPTER TWO

AS THE GROUP CHATTERED ON, I FELT SAMMY PUT AN ARM around my waist and say, loud enough to be heard by the others, "Come on, chickie, let's go catch us some rays, eh?" He took the bottle and signaled a deckhand in the kitchen to bring more out.

No one really noticed as we walked away, but the announcement had been a nice gesture anyway.

"That selfish cow," Sammy said scathingly. "She didn't need to bring that up *now*, of all times."

Of course, this bit of cattiness was completely validating for me, as he knew it would be, even though I said, "I did put her on the spot by insisting she have champagne."

"Oh, please." He settled his blue eyes on me, and even though what he was saying was tacky and uncalled-for, the sincerity was truly written all over his face. Which made it almost worse. He felt sorry for me. "She could have taken the glass and set it down after the toast. She *wanted* this. Next thing you know, she's going to be opening your presents!"

I laughed outright. It was a funny visual, and even though *obviously* Lisa would *never* do such a thing, in a way it was kind of consistent with her personality. Her shallow party-girl personality was exactly what I'd always found fun about her; how could I expect her to turn it off now that she really *was* going to be the belle of the ball for nine months?

"You're being an asshole for me and I love you for it."

We clinked glasses and lay down, turning our faces to the sun.

"This is nicer than having another euphemism-filled conversation about golf with Ray anyway," Sammy said. Then, as an afterthought, he added, "Did I tell you he made a pass at me at the Memorial Day party?"

"What?" I gasped. "No, you did not! There is no way; he and Kristin have been together for like three years now!"

"So? I've turned straighter men than that before."

"I don't believe it." But I did. Sammy could almost coax *me* into bed if he wanted to, and I knew his habits better than anyone.

This was a different crowd than I'd grown up with. Once upon a time, life had been simple for me. Full of what you'd think of as "normal" people, not characters out of central casting.

All that had changed, though. When you enter a world of big stakes, there are big personalities with big lives and, more often than not, big differences from the population at large. Honestly, I wondered sometimes why I had any popularity at all, because inside I felt like the same suburban girl I'd always been, counting coins with my father and hoping to someday have a four-bedroom brick house with one-sixteenth of an acre and box-woods, azaleas, and a viburnum bush under my bedroom window, just like when I was growing up.

"Ohhhh, he wanted it bad," Sammy continued, oblivious to the leaps my mind and memory were taking. "But he gave up fast. Chickenshit. As soon as I brushed him off, he began doing that dance where he was pretending that anything I'd rightly inter-preted as an advance was a misunderstanding."

I smiled and nodded and took a long gulp of champagne. "I know that dance. I got it from Bill Whitestone himself once." President and CEO of the company. Turning him down could have lost me my job.

But taking him on almost certainly would have. Eventually.

Sammy laughed and pointed at me. "I *knew* it! I always sus-pected he had a hard-on for you. Ever since that company picnic you made me go to with you on Roosevelt Island that time. I could just *tell* he had the hots for you."

"He has the hots for everyone."

"Especially the women he can't have."

"Yeah." I took another sip of champagne. "It's really pretty icky, isn't it?"

"Yup."

A few minutes passed in silence. I looked at the rolling swells of the sea in the distance, thinking how this was a dream-come-true for so many people—even just a day on the water like this—yet I was bored. Unfulfilled. Already thinking about going home alone.

Even looking forward to going home alone.

Once upon a time, I'd thought money could buy everything

to make me happy. Well, not *everything*, I guess—we all know the clichés—but I did think that it could buy a lot of things *I* wanted. For instance, when I was a kid and had a modest $5-per-week allowance, that was enough for two Bonne Bell Lip Smackers (the large ones). Or *almost* a week's worth of Good Humor ice cream at the pool. (Inevitably, Saturdays I'd be out of money and disappointed, scrabbling for a place on the white lines of the hot black parking lot, with just enough to buy some horrid Laffy Taffy.)

As I grew older, I learned even more the power of retail therapy, hitting the department stores for good makeup when things went bad, and then—glory be!—Sephora opened.

It was hard to feel like anything was wrong in my world when I was sitting on the sofa with a bunch of new products to try out.

But, as anyone knows or could guess, they weren't actually all that fulfilling. I'd had real tragedy in my life and I'd decided very early on that it wasn't worth it to suffer and anguish over things. Much better to skim along the surface, enjoying the simple pleasures.

"You seem down," Sammy said. And for once he wasn't on the edge of a punch line. There wasn't a joke in his eyes, ready to come out and lighten the mood. He was just serious. And very, very correct. "Really down," he added with a sobriety I wasn't in the mood to face.

"Oh." I gave a laugh. "I'm just trying to picture Lisa as a mother. All the little Kate Spade purses she's going to have to find." Annnnnd, truth be told, I was picturing *me* as a mother. If there was a Kate Spade diaper bag to be had—and there probably was—sure, I'd probably want that as well. But when I thought about babies, I thought about chubby cheeks, and hands, and feet, and gummy smiles, and bright eyes, and the promise of love forever. The promise *to* love forever. That's one part people don't often think about, though it's important: those who have been disappointed, or even fickle, in love aren't necessarily happy for their solitary existence. When you feel like the world has let you down time and again, and at the end of the day your friends all return to their own lives, a life without love can be devastatingly lonely.

I'm not sure that every childless person feels that way. I suspect that *that* is the feeling that separates those who *know* they don't want children from those who *say* they don't want children.

I was, more than likely, in the latter group. Though I was trying like hell to convince the world I was in the former.

Sammy wasn't buying it. "You were like this before her big announcement. Though I definitely take your meaning on the little Kate Spades and Ralph Laurens. Though they'd be pretty damn cute."

"I know."

"Not that you want that."

"Of course not." Our eyes met.

A moment passed. "Seriously"—he put his hand on mine—"what's up, Tiger Lily?"

It was impossible to answer. I'd been feeling down lately, no question about it. No explanation either. The Dark had come over me unexpectedly, without obvious explanation or reason. Was thirty-eight too young to be going through perimenopause, in my family? I needed to ask my mother. I hadn't spoken to her in about a month anyway, so it was a good excuse for me to call. It would give us something to talk about, since normally all we did was *not* talk about her jerk of a husband or my *lack* of a husband.

I was glad she'd found someone, finally, after my dad died so young, but did the guy really have to be such a domineering asshole?

"Who's a domineering asshole?" Sammy asked.

"What?"

"Who are you talking about?" He poured more champagne into my glass. "Jeffrey?"

"I didn't realize I said that out loud."

Sammy lowered his chin and raised his brows, lifting the champagne bottle pointedly. "Have you had enough to drink?"

"Not today." I took a big gulp and held the glass out for more. "Fill me up, buttercup."

He hesitated, then poured. "So . . . ? Who is the domineering asshole in question today?"

"I was thinking about my mother's husband."

"Your . . . father?"

"No, no, her current husband. Jonathan."

"You know, it's weird, you almost never talk about your parents."

"Mother. My father's dead." There was that twinge I always had. The coil of nerves that ran from my heart and never let me fully get used to the fact that my father was gone.

"That's right," Sammy said. "I did know that. I'm sorry. I gather you're not a huge fan of her second husband."

I shrugged. There wasn't a lot to say about Jonathan. Not *Jon,* by the way—woe be unto he who called him that!—just *Jona-than*. Yes, I thought he was a jerk. I knew he was bossy and dom-ineering. But he wasn't abusive in any technical sense, so if Mom was happy, there was no reason for me to be miserable about him. But, man, I had such a hard time acting like a grown person when she brought him up in conversation.

"I'm just being a baby," I said, and meant it more sincerely than I wanted to let on. "I don't like him, probably mostly be-cause he's not my dad, so I'm being a twelve-year-old about it in-stead of an adult."

Sammy nodded, but I could tell he didn't understand.

I barely understood, myself.

I was not just an adult. I was an Adult with Issues.

"If he'd lived, my dad would be sixty-five this year," I went on, floundering a little because I didn't have a firm grasp on my feelings. "*Sixty-five*. That's still young by today's standards. It's not even retirement age anymore! I know—I just *know*—he'd have held off on collecting Social Security because it made more sense to draw more later." How like me to move off into a tan-gent instead of elaborating on the important point at hand. "But he's been gone eighteen years now."

I pictured him, as I often did, in the ground, all these years on. It was a game I played with myself even though I hated it. To my mind, that was the best argument there was for cremation; no one could picture you rotting. Or, thanks to embalming, maybe *not* rotting. Maybe just lying under six feet of dirt in a suspended lack of animation forever.

Sammy looked at me carefully for a moment, reading into my expression and gestures every bit as much as he was reading into my words. "So this news of Lisa's, starting a new family, fired those thoughts right on up."

"No!" Yes, of course. But how bitter and small that was of me, taking her good news and twisting it into my own angst, so strongly that I was yards away from her, getting drunk and feeling sorry for myself, rather than putting my palm on her belly and talking about baby names and nursery décor.

"No . . . ?" Sammy prompted.

"Okay, yes. I guess so." Involuntarily, I pictured Lisa's next few months: growing bigger daily, the bloom in her cheeks, the small—superior—maternal smile. I pictured the baby shower, the birth, the first visits, the over-the-top first birthday party. . . . And, more poignantly than that, I pictured the baby aisle at the grocery store, a place I'd had to cut through now and then and which always gave me pause.

Did I do the right thing, not having kids?

Did I make the right choice?

Or did I make the wrong choice so long ago now that there's no way to rectify it?

These were torturous thoughts. Questions I didn't have the answers to. Pains I didn't have the medication for. A person can spend a good percentage of their early life playing with the angst of, *Did I do it right?*—because there was still time to rectify the wrongs. Twenty, twenty-five, thirty, even thirty-five—and all the many years in between—were still young enough to change directions.

Then suddenly you're looking forty in the face and realizing that some of those choices you had forever to make are gone, or at least going so rapidly that you can't possibly have enough time to make a good and trustworthy decision about them.

So Lisa's news, rather than making me happy for her (though to be *totally honest* I wasn't at all sure this wasn't simply another acquisition for them), had made me feel stupidly sorry for myself and for all of my lost opportunities, crushed chances, and wilted dreams. Regardless of anyone else's character, I was a jerk.

I held my glass out again and Sammy refilled it wordlessly, but this time there was a new darkness in his expression.

"Tod and I have talked about having a baby," he said, then quickly added, "Adopting, you know."

I looked at him, agog. Was everyone doing this? Was the whole wide world coupling off and starting families *now*? Did this really have to come down like a big old waterfall on me *now*? "Since when?"

He pressed his lips together, considering, then said, "We talked about it on and off for a couple of years."

I was shocked. I mean, really, I felt like I'd been punched in the stomach. "You never told me." Had I been such a crummy friend that I hadn't even seen that he was headed toward this? Had I just expected him to be my little gay sidekick forever, the second half of my *act*, without taking into serious consideration his *real* life?

"Eh." He gave a dismissive wave of his hand, a gesture that would normally be reassuring. "You're not into that kind of thing."

And there it was. I'd been so selfish and blind that I hadn't even realized anything like this was going on. Truth be told, I often forgot he and Tod were married, because he was always available to be my plus-one at events, so I kind of thought he was *mine*. But no, I'd completely missed this whole other life of his. I was *such* a jerk! "Why would you feel you couldn't share that with me?"

"Oh, I don't know . . . you know."

It was a vague nonanswer, yet I *did* know. And it wasn't even just him. No one wanted to talk about this stuff with me. I'd even seen the little glint of nervousness in Lisa's eyes when she'd made her announcement. Everyone seemed to think I was cold to warm, fuzzy stuff.

And, actually, I was.

Now that I thought about it, they were right. I *was*.

I'd traded the warm, fuzzy home stuff for success. It had served me well, because I almost never had moods or undefined depression.

But was that really working for me? "Sammy, you know you can always talk to me about anything."

"I know." He looked a little doubtful. Maybe that was a trick of my imagination. "But . . . do you know you can always talk to *me*?"

"Sure!" I said it quickly, with certainty, but the truth was I didn't talk much about my inner self. I didn't like to face that stuff, think about it. What was past was past, and I never saw much point in reexamining it, as there was no changing it.

"How come you never do?" he asked. "You hardly ever talk about yourself."

"What do you mean? I talk to you all the time!"

He gave me a look that called bullshit on me. "You *never* talk about deep, emotional stuff."

"I don't have any!"

His look called me out. "Everyone has some. Listen, girl-friend, I don't even know if you've ever been in love."

"Oh, come on, I——" I stopped.

"Yes . . . ?"

A rush of feelings came to me, memories, thoughts, longings I hadn't had in so many years. It was the champagne. I held my glass out for him to top me off. "I don't know, honestly. Which I guess you'd take as a no. But I remember thinking I was. Way, way back with my first boyfriend. I remember *wanting* that and believing that I would grow up to have the gleaming suburban life I thought my mom had."

I remembered the warmth I felt when envisioning that future.

It was a stark contrast to the cold I felt right now in the blaz-ing Florida sun—I who had everything.

Yet nothing.

Sammy snorted. "The past is rough enough. But first boy-friends are killer."

"*All* boyfriends are killer," I said, erasing the discomfort of my thoughts. "That's why I prefer to avoid them altogether." I stood up, a bit unsteadily.

"You say that now, but when the next Hottie McDreamy comes along, you'll give in."

"No, I won't."

"You will. I've seen it before."

"No!" I threw my hands in the air dramatically, then laughed. "I take that as a personal challenge. I will *not* fall in love!" I started walking unsteadily toward the diving board off the side of the yacht. "I will *not* start thinking about knitting baby booties!" I felt the eyes of my friends on me and knew I shouldn't have said that. "Sorry!"

"Ramie," Sammy said. "You don't mean what you're saying. And, believe me, if you keep talking, you're going to regret it."

"I *never* talk," I said. "*That's* what I regret!" I could have gone on, but didn't. But I thought it. I thought about how often I wanted to say some truth or other, but held it in because I couldn't let people get the wrong impression of me. Or I couldn't let them get the *right* impression of me. Hard to define which. I just had to be careful, neutral, all the time, so that people would take my financial advice without a feeling of prejudice.

But I didn't have to say all that for Sammy to get the gist.

He sobered quickly. "Ramie, come back. I don't think you're in any condition to—"

"I will *not* need anyone else, *ever!*" I stepped onto the rough surface of the diving board and walked out, one foot in front of the other, as if I were on a balance beam. I used to do that, you know. Gymnastics. I was damn good on the balance beam, as a matter of fact. My body remembered exactly what it felt like to tip over into a cartwheel and land perfectly at the end of the beam, then do a backflip off.

And before I knew it, I was doing it. Even though it had been twenty-five years, I didn't even stop and think; I just planted my right foot, dove down onto the board, right hand, left hand, then made a perfect landing with my left foot, then right foot. I stopped and put my hands up and laughed at the amazed face of Sammy; then—habit? drunkenness? just plain thoughtless idiocy?—I went to flip into the water, but I didn't even glance at the board, the clearance, anything. I just threw back like the drunk moron I was.

The last thing I remember was the impact against my head (the board? the boat? I'm not even sure), and the split second of, *Oh, shit*, and pain that surrendered instantly to oblivion.

CHAPTER THREE

THE BEEPING WAS DRIVING ME CRAZY.

It cut through the thickest part of sleep, leaving about one blissful second for me to drift back away into oblivion before *beep!* again. Funny how sleep can be like that. So delicious, so comfortable, so *necessary* that even one and a half more seconds of it feel like heaven.

I would have given anything, absolutely *anything*, to stay in that deep, black unconscious state.

If that was what death was, bring it on.

But no—*beep . . . beep . . . beep . . .*

I batted my hand out in the direction of the sound—break it! stop it!—but the movement felt heavy and went without contact or landing.

Wait, where was I? This didn't make sense; the puzzle pieces were slow to slide toward each other. Alarm clock? I didn't even *have* an alarm clock! I used my phone now, a gentle piano trill to pull me back into the world, not some old-school LCD alarm.

I tried to open my eyes. God, it was hard. Like they were glued shut with Krazy Glue. That happened to me once. I was trying to put a mug handle back on and got a sudden, violent eye itch and went to touch my eye without thinking of the glue on my fingertips. You think it's annoying when you glue your thumb and index finger together? Try your eyelids! Nightmare!

I tried again, and slowly light and color filtered into my brain. My head was pounding. God almighty, I hadn't been this hung over in *years*. My head hurt, everything was achy to the point where I felt like I couldn't move, my mouth was as dry as cotton, even *the top of my hand* hurt—what did I *do*? How do you hurt the top of your hand?

Drunk. I'd gotten drunk. Anything can happen when you're drunk. All kinds of dumb, embarrassing things, in fact, *do* happen when you're drunk. So . . . what? I'd been on the boat. Now I was in someone's bedroom somewhere—please, god, their guest bedroom—and someone had set an alarm. Great. Thanks a lot.

The beeping started to fade. Thank god. Got to love an alarm clock that gives up.

I blinked and squinched my eyes and the room began to come into focus. There was a red LED readout across the room that read 7:04. The room was light, so it must have been 7:04 A.M. But where the hell was I, that I—or *somebody*—needed to set an *alarm*?

My eyes rested on the door.

I knew this place.

The beige door. The familiar full-length mirror on the back

of it, reflecting the familiar dresser, with many instantly familiar colors and patterns on T-shirts and clothes that were hanging haphazardly out of the drawers.

I blinked again. And again.

What? This wasn't possible. A dream. A drunken dream? It seemed too sharp to be ethanol-induced, but maybe my brain had energy where my body did not.

I closed my eyes, breathed deeply, tried to quiet my pounding heart, and took another deep breath before opening my eyes again. I looked to the left. I was expecting—fully expecting—to see the red walls, the black accent paint, the simple lines of the hotel room I'd left before going out on the boat with my friends—but instead I saw the little rose-print Laura Ashley wallpaper of my youth.

And there on the bed next to me was the achingly familiar, sleeping, gray-muzzled face of my long-gone golden retriever Zuzu.

My exclamation roused her; those sleepy brown eyes, with what my mother always called "Cleopatra eyeliner" around them, opened for a moment, took me in, and closed again as she stretched her front legs straight out, groaned, and relaxed immediately back into a deep sleep.

"Zuzu . . ." The word drifted from me, and the dog didn't move. She was used to me. I'd sighed her name so many times in teenage angst that she usually waited until the third or fourth repeat before actually believing me and responding.

I wanted to reach out and touch her, but I was frozen. This was a dream, obviously, but it felt so real that I didn't want it to end. Reaching for nothing would end it. I wanted to look around and memorize every detail, I wanted to take in the smell, the sound of the neighbor's lawn mower in the distance.

So I rolled over onto my side and watched the dog breathing for I don't know how long. It seemed so real. Tears burned my eyes. Zuzu was the last dog I had. After she died, when I was twenty-one (seventeen years ago), I was too busy with my career to take care of a dog, even though I was every inch a Dog Person and wanted one badly. I was a Real Dog Person; I liked big, bouncy, happy retrievers, and those were not easy to tote to work at the brokerage firm.

Since I was the third generation of my family in a career having to do with finance, it had never even occurred to me to do something else. It's an awful lot like being a third-generation psychic or something, because my family has a weird gift for predicting the market. When my grandfather was able to do so in the thirties, naturally people took notice. That gave my dad, and then me, a leg up on the reputation part of the job.

Not everyone liked my style, of course; it's risky to put your money down on someone else's hunches, particularly when those ideas don't appear to make good fiscal sense, but over and over again I was right, and I made my own nest egg as well as that of more than a few of my clients. The problem, if you want to call it that, was that I wasn't willing to play it safe. I wouldn't stop anyone else from playing things safe, but the comfortable stalwarts were easy to find and identify; no one needed me to recommend stock in Proctor & Gamble, which routinely rises and splits, rises and splits. My job was to eyeball the high-growth risks and assess them.

I didn't know how to assess this.

I was lying in what seemed for all the world to be my old bed
and looking at the crystal-clear dream room of my past. I couldn't
think of what to do with the emotions of the situation. All I
could think was that if I really *were* time-traveling, to just about
any time in which I'd be lying in this bed with this pup, this
would be a really excellent time to invest in Apple. And to start
watching out for Google to come along in a couple of years. Those
two stocks alone could have turned a token IRA contribution
into a fortune in two decades.

I had to smile at the very idea.

But this was a dumb time to think about work. My mind was
playing a cool trick on me; showing me my past with unusual
clarity. This was obviously a time for remembering. Briefly "reliving" a carefree, happy time. I saw my perfume bottles sitting
on the dresser—the dark red square bottle of Lauren, the thick
sphere of Dior's Poison, the tall rectangle of etched glass with
old-time White Shoulders in it. Did they even make that anymore? I hadn't thought about it in years. Each one of them carried specific memories. I wondered when I'd last had them and
what made me abandon them so completely. If nothing else, they
could have made interesting aromatherapy. Though, come to
think of it, I didn't think they made that Lauren anymore. If I
could take that bottle out of my dream and sell it, maybe I'd get
a pretty penny from some collector.

Well, maybe twenty bucks.

Staying still, so as not to break the dream, I surveyed the rest
of the room, and even though it had been twenty years since I'd
last inhabited this space, I was surprised how well I knew every
inch of it. I knew what the closet doorknobs felt like in my hand,

with their cool, thin brass, knew the tiny, hard-to-reach switch inside the reading light by my bed, and even knew the way my bed squeaked every time I rolled over.

As a teenager, I'd had to be *very* careful about those squeaks sometimes when my boyfriend, Brendan, was over.

I sighed at the memory and rolled over to go back to sleep. Or, rather, to wake up. It had been a pleasant dream, but I had things to do. Only two more days in Miami and then I had to go home and get back to work. I was determined to rest as much as possible before that. Everyone I knew was telling me I was stressed beyond capacity and was acting like a bitch, so I wasn't going to give them any more ammunition.

I yawned and stretched, hitting something sharp with my upper arm. I reached up and retrieved a book, *Shanna* by Kathleen Woodiwiss. Ah. Good one, dream mind. I hadn't thought about Kathleen Woodiwiss and her historical romance novels in years. Man, I loved those. *Shanna* was my favorite. I remembered that much, though I couldn't reel in the details. Something about an island, and water all around, and a handsome, tanned romance hero. . . . Maybe this was a portent of good things to come. Maybe, when I woke up and went back out on the boat, my own romance hero would finally come to me. Just as Jeffrey, my most recent ex, was on his way, rather forcibly, out.

I rolled over and floated back into a comfortable, warm relaxation. It was like going under anesthesia, pleasantly counting the moments as they grew slower and heavier until I was out.

I don't know where I went during that weighty sleep, but when I woke again, it was not to the perfumed breezes coming in my

Florida hotel room, but to the smell of Endust and my mother bursting in the door.

"Ramie, what in the world is wrong with you? I've been calling you for ten minutes! You have three days of school left. *Three days.* You're not skipping!"

I watched, amazed at the realistic details of my dream, as my mother—from a couple of decades ago—bustled through my room, yanking the closet doors open and digging through clothes I remembered even from across the room.

Crazy.

When I woke up, I was going to have to Google this detailed phenomenon.

My mom's dress was familiar too, though I hadn't thought about it in years. A straight pink linen shift. I remembered it. She'd sewn it herself, as she had most of her clothes as well as mine, after she'd found the fabric on sale at G Street Fabrics. It was still more than she'd wanted to pay, but she said she'd "never seen a more perfect ballerina-pink" and she couldn't resist it. With her lightly tanned skin, it really did look great.

That made sense, I guessed. She said there were three days left of school, so that would mean it was May.

Dream May.

Memory May.

"Do you hear me?" She turned to look at me. "You are *not* missing another day. Do you really want to risk not getting credit for your senior year because of yet another unexcused absence?"

That was bunk, of course. I knew it now. She always used to make those threats when I wanted to stay home. Summer school, being put back a grade, not graduating, and watching all my friends go off to college while I stayed home and began a scintillating career in fast food. . . .

I vaguely wondered what would happen next, what I'd say to that. Probably something sulky like, *Okay, I was just* tired, *and wanted to get some sleep. I don't have to be there for half an hour!*

But I said nothing. That is, Dream Me said nothing.

Dream Me did not take over and read her lines, like in a play, as she was supposed to.

And Dream Mom glared at what felt, for all the world, like Real Me.

"Can't be bothered to answer?" she asked.

I tried my voice. "Me?"

It worked. I mean, of course it worked, but I guess I thought maybe it wouldn't, since I'd never had to actually *try* to participate in my dreams before. No dream person had ever stood there glaring at me, waiting for me to take a more active participation in my unconscious.

Leave it to my mother.

She drew back and looked at me. "Yes, you. What kind of a question is that? Do you see someone else in here?"

"No." It was weird enough to see *her*. But I looked around, because *was* there someone else in here? Was Jimmy Stewart holding a crushed flower in the corner? Was Leonardo DiCaprio looking longingly at my door and murmuring, "There's room for both of us on there . . ."?

"Ramie!"

Me. I was onstage. "I . . ." I *what?* "I'm just having a really weird dream."

Any minute a giraffe would poke its head in through the window or the kid who delivers Chinese food in my neighborhood would walk by wrapped in a towel, and I'd say something in Dutch and then wake up in my own bed, more than likely with a nice big lump on my head.

Meanwhile, Dream Mom looked concerned. "Ramie?" She came over to me and put her familiar cool hand on my forehead. Even when I was sick, that always made me feel a little better. "What's going on? You're not making any sense."

"Well, of course I'm not making sense, an hour ago I was thirty-eight and on a yacht in Florida and suddenly I'm in my teenage bed, where I haven't slept in twenty years, being yelled at for missing school!" I said this, I didn't just think it. Why wouldn't I say it? It was true.

Her eyes narrowed. "I cannot believe I have to ask you this, Ramie Phillips, but are you on something?" Her voice grew hushed. "Tell me the truth. Did you try pot?"

I laughed. "About a thousand times in college."

Her expression sharpened. "You smoked pot when you were looking at colleges?"

"*In* college." What a stupid, boring dream. What psychological phenomenon was this? I'd never heard of restless, anxious, non-REM dreaming. Maybe I was just supposed to play along. Maybe that was how this would take me wherever I was supposed to be going. "You know, Wake Forest?"

"Okay . . ." she said slowly. "So you're suddenly going to go to Wake Forest and this is your way of . . . pretending it's a sure thing?"

I felt drowsy again. In and out of this world. "It *is* a sure thing," I told her. "I went to Wake Forest, graduated in three years with a three-point-nine average and a degree in finance. You always said Dad would have been so proud, because he only got a three-point-eight."

"Would have been proud? Like he isn't here? Why wouldn't he be proud of you now?"

"Well, you know . . . what with him dying and everything." I hated saying that even still. It never got *normal*. "Though I guess he's proud of me wherever he is." I didn't know whether I really believed that, whether I really thought there was a *wherever he is* or if he was just as gone as he'd felt for eighteen years, but there was no point in quibbling with Dream Mom about something so sad and depressing.

Now she just looked completely flummoxed. "He's downstairs having coffee." She gave me a hard look, then yelled without moving her gaze from me, "Robert? Can you come up here for a minute? We have a *situation*."

Italicized *situation* was what she always said when she was trying to tell Dad I was in trouble.

"Mom, he's not going to—"

There was an answering shout from below. I didn't hear the words, but the tone was unmistakable. And heartbreaking. It had been so long since I'd heard it, I wouldn't have thought I could recall it so completely. A rush of emotion welled in my chest, and expanded as I heard the footsteps I hadn't heard in almost twenty years clomping up the stairs. It never occurred to me before that even a person's footfall could be distinctive enough to identify them.

Then, there he was.

I was speechless.

Dream or not, this was a moment in my life where I got a second chance, of sorts, with someone I'd loved and lost. Who doesn't love that story line in a soap opera, where the death is all one big mistake and the loved one returns until the next time the actor wants a raise? Only this was . . . well, if not my real life, my real father. Dream or not, I was looking at the features I'd once known so well but hadn't seen in such a long, long time. The kind, watery blue eyes; straight, nonjudgmental brows; dimples in his cheeks that still showed as weathered creases when he wasn't smiling; and the blond hair gone gray, but tinged a little yellow in front from the cigarette habit that I knew to have killed him eighteen years ago.

CHAPTER FOUR

MY FATHER.

My *late* father.

How many times had I gotten *so* irritated with him, just for *being*? For *parenting*? How much time had I wasted, when I had him, being pissed off because he tried to stand in the way of fun that could have been dangerous for me? Had I been the disappointment to him that I had once believed he was to me? Had he died thinking he'd failed me because I told him so many times he had?

Had he died *because* I'd insisted he'd failed me?

Was this a chance, somehow, to undo that now, if only in my own conscience?

I almost couldn't find my voice. And I mostly didn't think it mattered, except, once again, nothing happened unless I exerted the effort. "Dad," I croaked.

"What's wrong, baby?" He looked concerned, then shot an uncertain look at my mom. *What's going on?*

"Tell me," I said urgently, hoping this was one of those chances you heard about now and then where you could talk to the dead in your dreams and get great insights, "what is it like on the other side?"

There was absolutely no gleam of wisdom and comprehension, as I'd expected to see upon asking such a profound question. Instead he just screwed up those unruly brows, glanced behind him, then back at me, and asked, "The other side of what?"

"You know," I said, then lowered my voice as if a stage whisper were all it would take to get him to spill the beans. *"After death."*

He looked at my mom and she bit her lower lip and raised her brows. *What should we do with her?* She might as well have said it; that would have been no more obvious than her body language.

Dad put his hand to my forehead and frowned. "I can never tell if there's a fever," he muttered to my mom. "Human bodies are warm all the time."

"I didn't think there was."

"Did you check to see if she has some sort of head injury?" He wasn't really even bothering to keep quiet. Like if I'd had a head injury I'd be too stupid to understand the words he was saying.

"How?" she asked him.

"Feel her head!" He came at me and started palpating my head in a way that would have hurt like crazy if I *had* had an injury.

"I'm right here," I interjected, but they ignored me. And rightfully so, I guess, because I'd proven myself to be a completely unreliable witness of my own mental state.

Dad looked back at Mom. "I can't really tell anything."

"My head doesn't hurt." I paused, then added, I don't know why, "But I do think I hit it when I dove off the boat." And actually it *did* hurt. But for some reason, it didn't hurt at his touch. It was like a cluster migraine on one side of my head, though the feeling was coming and going really fast, and when it was there it was really there, yet when it was gone it was truly gone.

It didn't make sense.

"The *boat*," my mom rasped, a stage aside to my father and to the audience of hundreds who were not watching but needed to hear in the back rows. "Do you see what I'm saying? She's delusional. I say we call Dr. Scruggs."

"Are you sure she's not . . ." Dad paused. "Are you sure it's not D-R-U-G-S?"

"Oh, for god's sake, I can *spell*," I said, but I had to laugh. This was *exactly* how they would have been when I was in high school. "No, I'm not on D-R-U-G-S!"

Mom glanced at me, then said to him, "She said she'd smoked a lot of pot . . ."

Dad's eyes turned to flint. He did not approve.

". . . in college."

"In college," he repeated, the nonsense of the words, to them, becoming clear.

She nodded meaningfully.

"She's been hanging out with college boys?" he asked, his voice hard.

My mother touched her hand to her lips. "Oh. I didn't think of that. Maybe that's what she meant."

I gave a tight laugh. "I haven't been hanging out with college boys. Believe me, that would be creepy."

"I'll say it would." Dad's expression didn't lighten. "Tell me the truth, Ramie, have you taken something? Anything at all, even an aspirin? Or did you leave a drink unattended, then return to it, when you were in public?"

I'd forgotten that particular Dad Lesson. Once upon a time, a very long time ago, he'd worked as a bouncer in a bar and his number one lesson about men, bars, and life was to never put your drink down and leave it—not even for a second—because someone could, and likely would, easily slip something into it.

Resulting, of course, in rape, pregnancy, and a permanently ruined life.

No one else took over the dream conversation, so I said, "No, Dad, I didn't do anything like that. I'm telling you, I was on a boat off the coast of Miami and I dove off the board, but my foot slipped at the last second and threw me off. I hit something. I don't know what. But something hit my head and I can feel it now. Here." I pointed to the left side of my skull.

He reached out and touched me, but it didn't hurt. The pain was still inside, not external.

"There's no lump at all," he observed, then met my eyes. There was a smile in his that I didn't quite understand. Then he said over his shoulder to my mother, "I don't think there's an injury to worry about."

"And no boat," my mother added, "and no water. Come on, Robert, we need to get her to the doctor. Maybe to the ER."

There was an urgency to her voice. "If she's taken something, we have to hurry so they can pump her stomach."

How far was this dream going to go? I still felt a weird sense of floaty lack of concern, because I'd been lying in bed the whole time, observing my memories from a fairly comfortable distance (of a few surreal feet and a couple of very real decades). Yet, at the same time, everything so far had been so ridiculously sharp and real that if I didn't wake up soon I was going to experience some nightmarishly vivid version of stomach-pumping, and I didn't want that. The subconscious mind always amplifies our fears ten times.

This dream was weird enough; I didn't want a full-fledged nightmare to plague me for the rest of the day.

"Okay, okay, I'm sorry, I was kidding," I said, my voice the stiff plastic version of a sincere tone. I swallowed and tried to soften my words, even while I knew it was dumb to have to work so hard to manipulate the trajectory of my own dream. "I'm just not myself today." That wasn't true, of course. I was exactly myself. Just the *wrong* self. "I had some weird dreams last night and I don't feel good. Could be that flu that's going around." A flu was always going around, wasn't it? "Maybe I could just go back to sleep?"

My mother looked doubtful. "I don't know—"

"That seems like a good idea," my father said, putting a reassuring hand on her arm. "You know Ramie's always had vivid dreams. Remember when she was three and she was convinced she could fly down the stairwell instead of taking the steps?"

Man, I remembered that dream still. Soaring down the stairway like a feather, drifting. And I well remember the certainty I had when I woke up that it *hadn't* been a dream, that it was entirely possible, and a good idea, to boot.

I remember sitting at the top of the stairs, daring myself to do it when I was still mostly sure I could. I thought I did it all the time. But something in me must have known it was a dream, so that thing stopped me from taking the leap.

Kind of made me wonder what would have happened if I'd confidently taken the chance.

Did we miss out on a lot of opportunities because we were afraid they weren't real?

"Oh, goodness, what a memory you have," Mom said to Dad, and she looked rattled at the very thought I was having. *What if I'd tried?* "That was fifteen years ago!"

Thirty-five, actually.

"Ah." He shrugged. "What is time? Just yesterday she was a baby. Fifteen years is the blink of an eye in the grand scheme of things. Could have been last week to me."

Well, *that* was the thing, wasn't it? It was so weirdly spot-on that I half thought he was believing me. But that was madness, or at least it would seem so to him.

"She looks like she's fading," Mom said, but she didn't sound worried anymore. "Let's just let her go on back to sleep."

"Daddy?" I forced my voice through the fog of sleep. "Dad? Can you stay for a minute?"

My mother shot him a look, but he fastened his eyes on me. "Sure. I don't have to be at work for a bit. One of the privileges of being my own boss."

"Lucky you." Mom shook her head. "Sometimes it feels like you're *my* own boss too. I don't like it as much as you do."

He chuckled. "I'm a very benevolent boss."

She made a sound of derision, shot me a commiserative look that quickly turned back to mild suspicion, and left, clopping down the squeaky stairs to what I knew was probably a bunch of ingredients set out on the counter to make something for dinner. She was very June Cleaver that way once; less so now. I think she'd genuinely liked having a husband and family to take care of, and things just weren't like that now.

"What's going on with you, princess?" he asked, sitting down on the bed. It didn't squeak the way it used to with my every move (something that had generally kept boyfriends out of my room when my parents were home, though there had been exceptions). My dream self was making repairs, I guess. Even though it was throwing me into a confusing situation.

Whatever was going on, I knew I could trust my father to help me. "I feel really weird, Dad. I'm . . . confused. I mean, I don't think I'm confused, but I must be."

"*I* am. Please elaborate."

I smiled. I could try and explain my story again, but it was going to sound as crazy as it had the first time, and where would that get me? "I'm scared of losing you. I'm dreading it."

He raised his eyebrows. "I'm not going anywhere!"

"But . . . but *someday* . . ."—*October 15 when you're forty-seven years old*—"someday you *will* be gone." I felt weird saying even that much to him, because it would have freaked me out if someone else were to say it to me. Yet, at the same time, how could I not? How could I just hedge and play along when I had a chance, albeit a distant one, to somehow connect to my father through this weird nether-region of sleep?

He took my hands and learned toward me, looking intently into my eyes. "I will *never* be gone. I will always be around, looking after you. Just like Mims and Pop are with us now." Mims and Pop were his parents, long gone. I didn't remember either one of them. In fact, I didn't really even remember talking much about them with Dad, though I was ashamed now, realizing how much they must have been on *his* mind, just as he was, so often, on mine.

"But don't you miss them?"

He sighed and considered his answer. "I did," he said. "Very much at first. Of course. But we always fear the unknown. Death seems like such a scary, dark place. I can remember being afraid to go to sleep for fear of not waking up. Or maybe for fear of everything I knew and loved disappearing, like it was all a dream." He lowered his chin and regarded me. "Are you feeling something like that now?"

I suddenly felt choked up. He'd hit the nail right on the head. "I'm confused about everything. I feel like I've wasted so much of my life, and I'm practically the age when you . . . Nothing is certain. Even now, I feel like I should ask you something incredibly profound so I can get an answer I will remember and be comforted by forever, but I don't know what!" I was getting really upset, my voice sliding up into near-hysteria, my eyes burning with unshed tears.

"Shhh." He patted my head, awkwardly like he always did, and I could smell the cheap but comforting Aqua Velva mingled with nicotine on his fingertips. Those damn cigarettes. "There is nothing to be afraid of. You are safe, always. Love goes on forever, and just because you don't know something doesn't mean it's bad. In fact"—he smiled and looked out my open window— "I can't think of anything scary in the great unknown. And believe you me, I have given it a lot of thought."

I wanted to grab that, to believe it forever, to never worry about it—or him—again, but it was almost too perfect. It was just the kind of Hallmark sentiment that my brain would come up with to comfort me.

I wasn't really all that creative.

So I couldn't answer him. All I could do was bite my lip and try not to cry.

"Get a bit more rest," he said. "Things will make more sense when you're rested."

That seemed like as good advice as any—and it was certainly what I wanted to do—so I nodded. "Thanks, Dad. Will you be here when I wake up?"

"No, no."

"No?" I squeaked. My heart lurched. He knew. He understood. This was a rare moment and this was good-bye.

He looked surprised at what must have registered as surprise on my own face. "I'll be at work, princess. Unless you plan on sleeping until dinner. Hmm?"

"Oh. Right. But you promise you'll be back?"

"I promise. I'll always come back." Before I could take that as a piece of greatly profound insight from *beyond*, he added, "God knows what your mom would do with all that meat loaf if I didn't."

"God knows," I said. It had been years since I'd had it, but I was *still* sick of the stuff.

Exhaustion started to take over, mercifully, and I watched him leave my room, his scent going with him like a ghost. Then I rolled over and stared at the wallpaper, studying the detail of the roses that I remembered so well, until I finally drifted off to sleep.

When I woke up, everything would be back to normal.

Or so I thought.

CHAPTER FIVE

I WOKE UP TO THAT STUPID BEEPING AGAIN.

Bad sign. The dream wasn't over.

I opened my eyes, and this time I was not completely surprised to see my teenage bedroom bloom again before me. The
clock, which had stopped beeping as suddenly as it had started,
said it was 4:17 and the bright sun outside made clear that it was
afternoon. It took me a moment to comprehend this. Then I
remembered: in my dream, I'd gone back to sleep. So now I was . . .
awake. Ish. Awake without actually waking up.

I'd just slept late in my dream.

That was a new one for me.

But what could I do, except go with it? Play along and hope
that whatever meaning was supposed to come out of this would
come, sooner rather than later.

I stretched and sat up. I'd gotten used to having a dull ache
in my lower back—I was afraid to see a chiropractor, even though

my old friend Tanya swore she knew just the one to put me back in alignment—but in this incarnation, I had no back pain at all. I felt strong and light. I wished I could take that back into reality with me.

I glanced around. The room looked the same as before I'd last closed my eyes. Same old room. Same old life. No reality whatsoever creeping in. What was I supposed to do now?

What was one supposed to do when trapped in a dream that wouldn't end? I would have Googled it, but I didn't have my phone.

Or the Internet.

So I was absolutely lost as to what to do. I mean, everyone *thinks* they know what they'd do if they time-traveled, if such an impossible thing were even possible, but it's one thing if you climb into some machine and suddenly find yourself in Ford's Theatre next to Abraham Lincoln; it's quite another to find yourself a bored teenager in the middle of nothing-in-particular.

So what was this, if not a dream or nightmare? Not time travel. There's no such thing. I had long since rejected the metaphysical theory that time was a circle, or a bunch of parallel lines, or off-ramps you could take or leave, or *whatever*. In college I'd had a boyfriend who was a philosophy major (Hans! what sweet eyes he had!) and we'd spent many alcohol-fueled nights having hot sex and cold arguments about "reality" and his theories on quantum metaphysics.

This didn't fit any of his theories.

Since at least some part of my logical mind was clearly still at work, I could only conclude that I must have had a psychotic break. Something had triggered guilt, or maybe regret, that was traceable to this time, and I had to undo it—if only in the deep recesses of my memory—in order to return to normal.

It was a flawed theory, I realized that. I wasn't entirely convinced that my logical mind would be on duty at all if I'd had a psychotic break, and I wasn't at all sure that people had psychotic breaks in order to *fix* their psyches, but what did I know? Oliver Sacks's *The Man Who Mistook His Wife for a Hat* and other bestsellers about weird phenomena had sat, unread, on my shelves for years while I instead studied the more interesting (I thought) *Wall Street Journal* and *Financial Times.*

Which left me here. Seemingly time-traveling, but having decided I was in the safety of my own mind and I just had a few things to work out. It wasn't really that hard to buy—I'd had some rough years. There were definitely regrets.

Hell, maybe it was even Lisa's news on the eve of my birthday that had lit a fire under some heretofore-unexamined desire to be Donna Reed. It wasn't *impossible.* I'd had baby dolls as a kid. I remembered playing school with a little chipped blackboard and some stuffed animals in the basement. I'd had deeply traditional and sexually stereotyped ideas about my future once upon a time.

But I was turning thirty-eight—in fact, at this point I must *be* thirty-eight—and I knew the odds of getting pregnant had dropped tremendously since my late twenties. They drop every year. That doesn't mean anything concrete, obviously, doesn't mean it was impossible, but maybe I'd taken the statistics as comfort, even as justification for my not having a family. Was that really such a bad thing? More to the point, did I, somewhere inside, believe it was?

Now maybe my inner Donna Reed was screaming at me for equal time. Maybe Inner Donna Reed was pissed that Inner Mary Tyler Moore and Inner That Girl (aka Inner Marlo Thomas) had better wardrobes and hair and had, thus, won my allegiance.

Or . . . maybe part of me was just deeply, deeply tired. Maybe—and this seemed likely—part of me just didn't want to spend my whole life doing it alone. I'd succeeded, certainly, but that didn't mean it was easy. At the end of the day, I still had no one to count on besides myself. Very often—and on a conscious level—that was a really heavy burden.

So—time travel. What if I went back in time and did things differently? I already knew I could succeed and have a very comfortable career and financial life. I knew, even, that I could do just fine without a husband or longtime significant other. I knew I *could* manage very well on my own, thank you very much.

But at the same time, maybe I'd ignored a happier alternative.

In fact—I knew I was reaching into crazy, yet what about this *wasn't* crazy?—maybe everyone went through this. Maybe this, which seemed like an eternal dream at the moment, would turn out to be a blip somewhere undetectable on my timeline that changed the course of my fate.

For better or worse.

In any event, I decided that the only thing I could do with this . . . *circumstance* . . . whatever it truly was, was to go along with it. To live and breathe through it and to play it out, as crazy as it was. If it *was* a psychotic break—and that continued to be the only thing that made sense—it was still angst in search of an answer. Fighting it and trying to figure out the science or psychology of it was clearly getting me nowhere. It felt, very realistically, like many hours had passed with me pondering the question, with no answer. I'd never had a dream like this before.

So, instead, I had to figure out whatever I was supposed to figure out from it.

And that began with orienting myself to this memory.

That was, at the very least, a concrete problem to be solved. And concrete solutions were my forte.

From what Mom had said it was the week of my senior graduation. That was May. I turned eighteen two days before graduation, and my birthday was May 19, so that meant today was May 18. Wednesday.

Once again, I wished I had my phone so I could just look at it and confirm the day and date (and year), but that wasn't happening, so I had to rely on my memory and logic. It was Wednesday. High school was almost over.

What had happened in the week before graduation? What was coming up in the next few days? Even the next few hours might be relevant. Who knew?

I searched my mind, but nothing important, nothing even remotely important, stuck out. Which wasn't to say something important hadn't happened, but only to say that I hadn't committed it to memory when it *did* happen. Often, life-changing events are only recognized as such in the rearview mirror. But twenty years on is quite a long distance to see in that mirror.

All I could remember of this time was Tanya (my best friend) and me going to the pool and trying to get as tan as possible for the rounds of graduation parties that were coming up. Easier for her than for me. She had that tawny skin that always looked golden and tanned easily. Brown hair that got bright golden high-lights in it from the sun. Hazel eyes that really could look green or brown, depending on the light.

I had to work a lot harder to get tan. Even though I was fair, with dark blond hair and light blue eyes, I didn't tend to burn. But neither could I hold on to a tan to save my life. Two days after looking like a sunscreen ad, I'd look blotchy and pale again. So I *really* needed to work on my tan. I had a perfect green sun-dress all ready to go, while Tanya was opting for the more obvious turquoise. We were also going crazy with the Close-Up tooth-paste, hoping for perfect Christie Brinkley white smiles with our tanned skin and highlighted hair.

And only then did it occur to me to wonder what I actually *looked* like at this point. I got up and made my way to the mirror on the door.

The first thing I noticed, even just getting out of bed, was that my body didn't ache. It always did lately, either because of the muffin top I was constantly working to get rid of or because of the workouts I was constantly doing to get rid of the muffin top. It seemed like *something* always hurt, not just my back.

Not today, though. Today I felt as light as a ballerina. It was uncanny. Almost zero-gravity stuff. Just for fun I bent down to touch my toes—in my thirties my hamstrings had gotten as tight as banjo strings, so I didn't think I'd get past my knees, but to my surprise I went all the way down easily and touched the cool wood floor.

My first thought was: *Sex would be SO great with this body!* Seriously.

What a fool I'd been to hold out all through my high school

years, being such a high-collared prude instead of enjoying the hell out of this thin, tight body.

Next thought: Brendan.

Naturally.

Brendan Riley was my boyfriend in high school. From the tail end of tenth grade through twelfth, which I guess made him my boyfriend right now. I laughed out loud to myself. I had an eighteen-year-old boyfriend. Typical black Irish, with dark, wavy hair and light blue eyes. The lightest sprinkling of freckles over his cheeks and nose. He was beautiful, honestly. He'd set my standard for male beauty at a young age, and he was still the yardstick for my "type." Hopefully I would be able to wrangle this dream to see him, but either way, he was out there somewhere. Wait till I told Sammy.

Assuming Sammy would believe anything I said and not just have me committed right away.

And assuming I wasn't *already* committed, and this wasn't just a manifestation of whatever I might be being obliviously treated for. Which seemed pretty possible.

This was the problem with spending a lifetime imagining different outcomes and scenarios: it was all too easy to imagine things that were too tough to really contemplate.

Back to now, I reminded myself. Whatever *now* was. Back to the present thoughts. Back to the thing I was wrestling with above all else. Back to the past.

I looked in the mirror.

It was a shock. It doesn't seem like it should have been: waking up in my high school bedroom, talking to my parents about my last week of high school, and knowing, therefore, that this was a dream about being in high school should *certainly* have prepared me to look in the mirror and see my high school self. *Or* my present self. Or J. Lo, or a Martian, or just about anything. *Nothing* should have been a shock.

But when I saw the smooth skin, the fuller cheeks and lips, and the bright, clear eyes, something cold ran down my spine. Previously I'd thought I hadn't really changed that much from high school. I was definitely holding up all right, thanks to a lot of work and good genes, but, wow, it turned out I really looked quite a bit different. I honestly felt like I was seeing an old friend whom I hadn't seen for a very, very long time.

And, obviously, in a sense I was: I was definitely seeing a face I hadn't seen in twenty years, but wasn't it so completely embedded in my subconscious memory that seeing it should have felt natural on some level? Why didn't the part of my brain that knew exactly what was in the closets and drawers, and that knew exactly where I'd taped my Jon Bon Jovi pinup, know my own face as well as the material echoes of that time?

I can't say, but I stood there, frozen, looking at my reflection until I realized I was holding my breath, and let it out in a heavy flow. My heart was pounding, racing. It was uncomfortable and scary. Not really *fun*, like you'd expect, but terrifying.

Was this what crazy felt like? Being trapped in a false "reality" and unable to break through to the other side? It was like floating around in a soap bubble that wouldn't break. I could see, or remember, everything from my *real* world, so part of my mind was completely intact and logical, yet everything I looked at— the gauge I'd usually call the most trustworthy one—defied every single thing I thought I knew.

Time travel doesn't happen. There are no time machines. And spontaneous time-hopping is a ridiculous notion, best saved for children's books and sci-fi enthusiasts. Fun? Sure. In a movie.

But this was madness.

I was trapped, surely, in my own mind, and I couldn't get out.

And who would believe me? No one who wasn't experiencing the exact same thing could possibly understand. No scientist or doctor who hadn't been there could treat this, unless the "treat-ment" was strong sedatives and a straitjacket.

This was the most alone I had ever felt in my life.

I took a bracing breath and looked back in the mirror, hoping—I don't know—hoping I would morph back into myself or something.

Now, I'd never even *wished* to go back in time and be younger. I wasn't one of those people who was constantly lamenting the past. Admittedly, when I'd gotten out of bed with no aches and pains, that had been pretty nice, and not something I'd really expected. But looking at my reflection made me feel, more than anything, like time had passed without my realizing it.

People drop out of our lives all the time, we all know that. Friends come and go. People join you for *a reason, a season, or a lifetime*, as the saying goes. But you never really stop and think about all the *selves* you lose on the way. I wasn't the same person I was in high school anymore, obviously, but there were things about her I had liked. Qualities she had that I was sorry to have lost. A certain optimism, an absolute faith that everything would be all right and that I'd have everything I ever dreamed of, a se-curity that came with having no real responsibilities and both parents, loving and present and comparatively young.

I saw all of that in the face in the mirror. Crazy or not, I saw truth there. All of those thoughts and confidences and dreams. And that, perhaps, was the biggest difference between my eighteen-year-old face and my thirty-eight-year-old one: A lot of the dreams had gone out of me. There were too many things I didn't believe in anymore. I'd lost a lot of my optimism.

Yet there it was in the face in the mirror.

Physically, the differences were to be expected: My eyes were completely without crow's-feet. There were no faint ghost lines where I raised my eyebrows. My mouth was fuller than I'd ever realized it was, though I could recall being embarrassed by my pillow lips because they definitely were not "in" back in those days. Now I saw it was flattering, though. Youthful, you might redundantly say.

It was still going to take a decade or so for that to be considered desirable.

My hair was a ridiculous mess of layering and strawlike high-lights from the sun and chlorine. Now I knew how to fix that with some good conditioner, a blow-dryer, and throwing out my old lavender curling iron, which smelled like burning rubber when it was turned on, and which had left countless burn marks on my wood dressing table. But then I'd been doing my best, and my best left a lot to be desired.

So perhaps the most surprising thing of all—no matter what had brought me to this dark old corner of my mind—was that, more than envying the girl I once was, I kind of felt sorry for her.

I looked at my youthful face in the mirror and saw my eyes shift—"smize," Tyra Banks would call it in a couple of decades on *America's Next Top Model*—with the secret knowledge that I was being given a second chance to *enjoy* my history and relive those magical make-out sessions of youth without being a cougarish creep.

Because, make no mistake, Brendan was really cute. My days with him had been sweet and romantic and exciting and in so many ways wonderful. I know every generation looks at their youth as a time of so much more innocence, but I think that is particularly true for the pre-9/11 generation. There just wasn't as much *fear* in the air, back in those days. There was a hope and positivity, at least for me, that I didn't fully realize I'd lost until the very moment I was standing in my old room, surrounded by my old stuff, looking at my young face.

Somewhere along the way I'd stopped wanting to be the happy homemaker and had made a new decision to be strong in the workforce. I was proud of how I'd succeeded and there had been a lot of rewards along the way, but there had been some niggling doubts along that path as well. Lisa's news wasn't just a huge bolt from the blue for me, it was the icing on the top of a tall, precarious birthday cake I'd been assembling for thirty-eight years now.

If I had the chance, if I could turn back time and have the chance, would I do anything differently?

That was the question, obviously. That was the only question that made sense in this situation, no matter what *this situation* actually was. I was here for some reason, so if this was a fork in the road, and I had the chance to go a different direction, should I?

Did I *really* have the chance now?

It was a heady thought. I went to the bed, sat down, and picked up the phone receiver. Because that's what eighteen-year-old me would have been doing, she would have been talking on the phone to Brendan. And didn't it make sense for me to do what eighteen-year-old me would have been doing?

I still knew the number, having dialed it so many times.

So I picked up the phone and dialed.

It didn't go through. There were three tones, then a recording telling me to "check the number and dial again."

I'd forgotten that back in the day we didn't need to include the area code.

I lifted the receiver again and started to dial. Then stopped. What was I actually going to say? What did thirty-eight-year-old me have to say to an eighteen-year-old guy?

Hey, kid, like cougars?

He'd think of the animal.

And he'd probably say yes because he really *did* like animals. He probably even actively liked cougars.

Brendan and I had been together on and off for two years, but in senior year we really started to get closer. I think the deep-known realization we both had that we were going to go our separate ways for college made us cling even harder to one another.

Then—oh, it made me sad just to think about it—then, as I'd thrown away the stuff of my childhood and packed up my stuff to go to college, I'd thrown him out, along with most of my pictures and souvenirs of junior high and high school dances and anything else that made me feel like a baby instead of the grown-up I'd really wanted to be. I'd thrown away the only tangible evidence I'd ever have of this life I'd grown out of.

I regretted *that*. Profoundly.

Not just Brendan, though ending things with him in such a harsh, abrupt manner was something I had come to regret more and more as I got older, more successful, and emptier. I'd been so determined to yank on my Big Girl Panties that I had thrown out all the stuff of childhood. Including my last days of it.

Including people.

That's not a commentary on the life I eventually chose, because my life had been happy for the most part, but I definitely see that I lost my grip on the life I'd *had* at the time, a life I'd never be able to get back.

Except, well, now . . .

I picked up the phone and, without letting myself stop to think anymore, dialed his number.

CHAPTER SIX

FUNNY, THE FEELING OF THE SQUISHY NUMBERS, THE SOUND of them, which mobile phones tried to emulate but, I realized now, missed the real mark on. If you pressed the 7, 8, and 9 together, then the 4, 5, and 6 together, then the 1, 2, and 3 together, and so on, you could play *Mary Had a Little Lamb*. You couldn't do that with a cell phone.

Naturally, I did take a moment to do that. I also called the old weather number, which was 936- and whatever other digits you cared to add; then the time number, which was 844- and whatever other digits you wanted to press. Small things, but even hearing those old recorded voices—"At the tone, the time will be . . ." and "This is the Bell Atlantic weather service with today's forecast . . ."—gave me a kick.

Done with my games, I finally dialed Brendan's number, and held the phone to my ear. While it rang, I distracted my nerves by wondering why we'd ever decided tiny little flat phones, which obeyed the commands of your cheek and hung up on callers minutes before you realized you were talking to no one, were better than the old technology.

He picked up on the third ring, just as I was calculating that in two more rings it would have gone to the machine, which he probably didn't have yet. "Hello?" No caller ID, no familiar greeting, no way to gauge mood.

"Hey," I said, like I was trying my voice for the first time. That's what I would have said then, so that's what I said now.

"Hey." His tone gave me a complete picture of him, smiling and relaxing his shoulders, maybe leaning against the kitchen doorframe, since the phone was tethered to the wall. No question at all who he was talking to. "You just about ready?"

Ready? Ready for what?

"What, uh . . ." I searched for a sufficiently generic question to prompt him with. "What did you have in mind?"

He gave a laugh. "Come on, Raim, we're supposed to leave in like ten minutes and you're *always* late. Hop to it. Get your ass in gear, I'll be there in fifteen."

"But—"

"Get moving!" He hung up.

Well, shit, what was I supposed to do now?

Plans, plans, plans, what plans did we have around my birthday, right before school ended? I just couldn't remember. There were so many things going on at that time, graduation parties and so on.

I went out into the hall and down the stairs. "Mom?"

No answer.

I started down the stairwell and called again, my voice echoing in a way I would never have guessed would register yet another memory for me. "Mom!"

"What?" She was in the kitchen.

I went the rest of the way down, another six steps. That old green carpet was still on the stairs! Only now did I realize this was the first time I'd left my room since I'd been back, and somehow I hadn't even thought to tour the house.

I touched the textured wallpaper behind the banister. Getting rid of it had been a good idea; it was tacky only a few years after it was "in," yet it had lived a long obsolete life on the wall anyway. But at this moment I was glad to see it again. How many Christmases had I come down these stairs in the semidark of six A.M., waiting while Dad got the Super 8 movie camera (and eventually camcorder) ready? I would inevitably be sent back up a few steps to start over when he forgot to put the light on . . . which he did pretty consistently.

I could almost feel the anticipation of Christmas, Easter, the first snow of winter, all of the wonderful things I came down this stairway to find. I found myself smiling as the anticipation rose, unbidden, in my chest, even though I was headed for none of that. What *would* I see? What forgotten corners of life were about to bloom before me in full *Wizard of Oz* Technicolor?

I got to the bottom step and put my bare foot on the cold slate floor of the front hall. It was always cold, I remembered suddenly. No matter the season. I loved that in summer; running in, wet from the sprinkler, squinting against the absence of sun, and slipping carefully across the cool floor to go to the kitchen and get a snack. Pop-Tarts from the cupboard, Jeno's Pizza Rolls from the freezer, kiwifruit in the fridge, Mom got it all. Even

Carnation Instant Breakfast, which I'd shake up every morning in a Tupperware cup with milk and drink with it still bubbly on top.

How had I not realized how *easy* I'd had it then?

Why had I always been in such a hurry to grow up?

Maybe now I had my chance to get at least a small snippet of those carefree times back. Maybe not Santa Claus; I was still on top of things enough to know that was a myth. But some of the last days of a teenage summer?

I could really use that now.

"So, Mom?" I went into the kitchen and smiled at the bright, sunny, familiar haven. I went straight to the cereal closet. Lucky Charms. "Yes!" I couldn't help a private little fist pump. I mean, honestly, who doesn't love sugary, colorful breakfast cereal? Especially when they have the metabolism to process it?

"What's that?" my mom asked.

"I'm starving suddenly." I passed her and went to the closet to take out one of the little Corelle bowls she'd had for decades. White with that seventies gold/wheat-colored border. It was horrible, but it had been horrible since before the time I could tell, so to me it just felt even more like home. "I'm totally in the mood for this."

"Junk food," she muttered and shook her head, returning to the task of peeling hard-boiled eggs at the sink. "Apart from adding a few calories to your bony frame, it has no nutritional value."

Totally right. I would *never* have this in my place now. I'd have organic pineapple and banana—neither of which would last longer than like two days—and organic oatmeal that tasted like paper, extra-protein almond milk, and unsweetened Kashi. Which made me realize, all the more, how much I missed the simple pleasure of Lucky Charms. It wasn't broccoli, but it wasn't *quite* candy canes either. I got the milk out. "Hey, you're the one who bought it!"

"It was supposed to be a *dessert*, remember?" That was the rule in our house. Those sweet cereals were *only* an after-dinner treat. Never allowed as the one-and-only breakfast food, because Mom knew—as anyone does now—a bowlful of sugar would not lead to good memory and mental sharpness, but a sugar coma about the time I'd have gotten to school. And of course I knew this because of the number of times I'd crept downstairs and had "dessert" for breakfast.

I remembered eating it for breakfast before school, while watching *General Hospital* after school, and more often than I should have, taking a bowl up with me at bedtime, which was gross because I always forgot to bring it down for a few days, and since I didn't drink the milk after eating the cereal (that always seemed a weird practice to me, drinking crumb-filled milk), it tended to become a nasty science experiment. "Anyway, I was wondering about tonight—"

The phone rang and she pushed the faucet control down with her forearm. "Hold on, I'm expecting a call from Mr. Henckle."

That was a blast from the past. Mr. Henckle was her sewing machine repair guy. She went to the family room to answer it, wiping her hands on her apron along the way.

"And I'm still wondering..." I said to myself, then listened as her voice went from the cheerful singsongy greeting to a sudden tense undertone.

"Yes," I heard her say. "Yes, I understand. It's fine. I'll be right there."

Every muscle in my body tightened. Over the years I had gotten enough bad news on the phone to hate the sound of it ringing, even though over the years the sound of a telephone ringing had gone from the actual banging bell sound of the phones in my childhood home to strains of Beethoven or Jack Johnson or whatever the holder wanted to tell the world about their psychology every time someone rang them.

She came back in, looking a little rattled.

"What's wrong?" I asked, setting my spoon down. Three magically delicious marshmallows floated off it into the milk.

"It's your father."

I almost threw up right then and there. Seriously, my throat went tight suddenly, and I felt whatever I couldn't recall putting into my stomach threatening to come up. Was it time? Had it happened again? Had my coming back made it happen sooner than it was supposed to? Tears sprang to my eyes and burned like acid.

"Is he okay?" Stupid question. She hadn't come in looking like that to report that he'd had a nice lunch. *Just one dirty martini, nothing to worry about.* "What happened?" I said, almost expecting to hear that he'd had a cerebral hemorrhage while he was out somewhere, and no one had been there, so we'd never know if he could have been saved.

I knew that wasn't how it happened, but still I could picture it in horrible graphic color.

No one was there.

He died alone.

No one should die alone.

But that didn't have anything to do with today. His death came to him at home, like a ghost in the night, and took him without warning, without accusation or the chance for penance.

My fists were clenched, my nails digging into the soft flesh of my palm. "What happened?" I asked, harder and more urgently than the situation called for. I didn't need to make things worse by freaking out before she said anything. "What happened?" I asked again, trying to make my voice gentler.

Mom drew in a breath. "He was in a car accident."

CHAPTER SEVEN

THE WORDS *CAR ACCIDENT* HAD LONG SINCE STOPPED MEANING *fender bender* to me. No one talked about little bumps, so I was instantly on alert, bracing myself for the worst news. Which was ironic, since I'd already gotten the worst news about my father and processed it and grieved, yet here I was again, about to relive it all, one way or another.

"It was on the American Legion Bridge," my mother said, sounding more hassled than upset. How was that possible? He could have died! "Someone cut him off and he overcompensated. He said the Chevy is totaled."

He said. So he was okay, he was the one who called. This wasn't a case of his number being up around now, one way or another. No wonder she was so calm. I took a deep breath and let it out in a long, shaking stream. "Wait, so he was in an accident but he's okay."

"He's not going to *die* or anything, but he said his arm got hit pretty hard." She was hurrying about, collecting her purse, her keys. She stopped in front of the hall mirror to check her reflection, a reflex, I'm sure, as she did it literally every time she went out the door. "I have to get there."

This was coming back to me. The car accident on the bridge. So minor in retrospect that it hadn't really registered in my memory. He'd had a dislocated shoulder and had wrenched his back, but when it first happened his shoulder had hurt so badly that he hadn't even realized about his back, which slowed his recovery.

It was New Me who panicked every time there was an unexpected phone call or any sort of bad news. It took years to build up that kind of paranoia. How interesting that this, which must have been a really scary moment for me at the time, had been whitewashed away as soon as I knew he was fine.

"He's at Sibley Hospital?" I asked. God, I could smell the antiseptic hospital scent just saying it.

She stopped. "How did you know?"

"I—" This was definitely not the time to add confusion. "It makes sense; it's closest to that spot. Do you want me to go with you?" Instead of keeping whatever plans I had with Brendan? Good lord, he was going to be here any minute. Where were we supposed to be *going*?

"No, no, I'll go," Mom said, and I recognized her lifelong trait of wanting to be the heroine, the Florence Nightingale who swooped in and saved everyone. Alone. Sharing credit was not her style. "It's not *that* bad, for heaven's sake; he called me himself. He's just not careful enough, your father. He's never careful enough." She clicked her tongue against her teeth, then added, "You go have fun with Brendan and his folks."

Brendan and I were going someplace with his *parents?* Another event that hadn't ultimately registered in my memory. I guess I could take that to mean there was no trauma and thus nothing to worry about. That's who I am now: a person who assesses risk and worry 100 percent of the time. "O . . . kay. Call me if you need anything, though."

"Right, I'll just call you at the restaurant and have them page you," she said with a laugh.

I automatically gave an exasperated sigh. Page me. Please. Like that had *ever* worked efficiently. "I meant call my cell phone."

She rolled her eyes and shook her head. "We're not having *that* argument right now. You absolutely do *not* need a car phone. Who do you think you are, Donald Trump?"

"God, no."

She opened the screen door. It creaked in a way I'd never before realized was distinct. "Have a fun graduation dinner." She took a step out, then stopped and turned back to add, "Aloha!"

Aloha?

Oh, *yes!* Yes, yes, yes, we were going to a graduation dinner at the Kona Kai Restaurant in Bethesda, which closed not too long afterward and never reopened. In fact, there is a huge dearth of Polynesian restaurants in this world, as far as I'm concerned. Given the number of tiki decorations at Party City, and the sheer volume of tarantula nightmares people still experience from the tiki episode of *The Brady Bunch,* I'm absolutely amazed no one has picked up the Trader Vic's idea and run with it. I'd invest in that, for sure.

But I remembered tonight now. Not well, but I remembered the creamy piña coladas (virgin, alas), and the guy who came over and pulled a slab of dough into hundreds of noodles before our eyes. I also remembered, of course, the pu pu platter, which was both delicious and embarrassingly named. And bananas fried in butter and rum and served with vanilla ice cream.

I did *not* want to miss this revisit to the Kona Kai.

But I had to offer. "You sure you don't want me to go with you, Mom?"

She looked back at me with a frown, and she was right: this wasn't like eighteen-year-old me. I seldom offered to go out of my way more than once, and certainly not in an easily heard tone. "Well, now that you mention it . . ." She must have seen the panic in my eyes, because she genuinely laughed. "I'm kidding, let me go get Dad and bring him back. You can come in and do your duty later, catering to him hand and foot, as I'm sure I'll have to."

"Will do!"

"Have fun, sweetie." She went out to her Oldsmobile Cutlass and I watched her get in, close the door, put on the seat belt, adjust the mirrors, and basically do everything you had to do for a driver's test but never again. Mom was so safety-conscious that she did every check, every single time. She was still like that.

Dad was not so vigilant about anything like that, which was probably how he'd managed to sideswipe someone while trying to switch the radio to *The Chris Core Show* when he was driving on the Beltway.

I went to the door and watched her taillights fade down the road, then took a moment to absorb the change of scenery. It was one thing to return to your childhood school and note how small the bathroom stalls are, or how big the trees have gotten in the decades since you left, but quite another to "return" to how things were, from a place of more maturity.

The Japanese cherry trees that lined the street, many of which had since died and been replaced by a heartier variety, were all intact, and at the end of their bloom. The shutters on the house across the street were powder-blue, almost the color of the sky on an especially fine day. New neighbors had come in almost twenty years ago and changed the blue to black, which still looked cute against the white brick house, but there had always been something so cheerful about the blue.

I was about to turn and go back inside, hoping to find some of the old junk food favorites I'd long since stopped indulging in, when, from the other end of the street, Brendan's car caught my eye. The old red Dodge was as familiar as a person to me, and I caught my breath, instantly and fully recalling the scent of it and the feel of the leather (or vinyl?) seats. Whatever they were, they were sticky and hot in the summer and I could remember the smell of them when we'd sit in the backseat and make out. Good lord, I was going to be able to ride in that car again!

I watched him pull up and park in the same spot he always parked in, joggling in and out to straighten the car.

It's funny how sharp old memories are. I think it's because the things that happened to us, and that we saw and felt and heard, when we had the freedom and inexperience of youth, were much bigger in the basket of our experience than later things that had to be squeezed in among job interviews, apartment applications, meaningless boyfriends, and dull, unmemorable holidays.

I can't remember my twenty-seventh Christmas at all, but I sure remember my tenth Christmas, when I'd learned, a week before, that there was no Santa Claus, so the entire day was one of denial and angst for me, as I wanted to keep believing. I could probably recall every detail, from waking up in the morning to going to sleep at night, yet I couldn't recall the same number of details from ten subsequent Christmases together.

And so Brendan parking his car was like that tenth Christmas in a sense. Something I'd thought of many times since our breakup and since making other choices in my life: how often, on a summer day, my mind had returned to this very ordinary scene in my past because the comparatively few days in which this had happened amounted, in my mind, to an entire history.

He put the car in park and got out, the tremendous bang of the old car door heralding his arrival as it always had. Good old American car. My dad loved that and commented on it every time he saw Brendan. He started to walk up the yard and I stood transfixed, watching him like I was watching a movie I couldn't rewind. I already wanted to rewind it, to see the step up the curb again, to see the cursory glance at his wristwatch again, but this was live.

He got to the front stoop and only then noticed me standing on the other side of the screen door watching him.

"I'm being creepy," I said, reading the surprised expression on his face. "I know. I just saw you coming and . . ." I shrugged. "Watched you walk up."

He gave that quick smile of his and raked his hand across his dark brown hair. "I've watched you sleep before," he said. Oh, that voice. If not for this, would I have ever heard that voice again? "When you've fallen asleep in my car on the way home."

I laughed. "Creeper." At this point in history, we'd never had sex together, so that was the closest he'd gotten: making out with me in the car until I sank into an easy, relaxed sleep. Boy, those days were long over; I hadn't had a good night's sleep in years.

Probably not since those days.

He smiled, then moved in and kissed me on the mouth. The smell of Ivory soap drifted around me, and I leaned in to him instinctively. Habit? After all these years? I don't know, but rather than feeling improper, like I guess it should have, it just felt *good*. I didn't want to stop.

And however old *I* was, *he* was already eighteen, so there was no compelling reason to stop myself, as far as any technical "ickiness" yardstick went.

It was so nice. My body came alive in his embrace. Nerves danced wherever he touched my skin, and I felt warm all over. There's no beating chemistry. As an adult, I'd dated men who "made sense" on paper. Jeffrey made sense on paper, and obviously that hadn't gone all that well, just like it hadn't with those before him. It had been ages since I'd been with someone just because he was physically irresistible.

Brendan was irresistible.

It made me wonder if it was really all that bad to base a relationship on sexual chemistry. I knew one couple, friends of my parents who had famously gotten divorced twice and gotten remarried each time. They were still married today. If that was chemistry, the "working" seemed to be overriding the "not working," though I can't say those divorces are all that appealing.

Still, kissing Brendan, feeling those soft lips against mine, feeling his tongue and that taste that was so uniquely him and pleasant and *right*, made my heart race and every part of my body heat up as if touched by fire. I felt tingly in a way I hadn't felt in as long as I could remember.

Had Brendan actually been the last guy to make me feel this way?

Was that possible?

"Come in," I said, taking his warm hand in mine and pulling him all the way into the house. I closed the door.

"Where is everyone?" he asked. That had to be the number one question of hormonal teenagers.

I slid the chain lock into place. "My dad had an accident." I saw his face grow alarmed, and amended, "A fender bender. He's fine, but the car is smashed, so my mom went to get him. Come upstairs with me." I tugged on his hand to pull him toward the stairway.

"My parents are waiting for us," he said, holding back. "If we start something, we're not going to want to stop."

For one hugely disappointing minute, I thought he was going to wimp out, tell me he couldn't have what I was about to uncharacteristically offer, because his mom and dad were tapping their toes and looking at the clock. Instead he said, "Let me call them." Then he disappeared into the living room and I heard him dialing the landline. Seven digits, not ten. That might be one of the hardest things to get used to here. The mark of simplicity represented by not having to dial an area code.

I waited impatiently, feeling a lot like a person in a plaster cast waiting for a stick to reach in and scratch with, but he was back quickly, leading the way up to my room. "I just bought us forty-five minutes," he said. "How long till your parents come home?"

"Longer than that." I had no fear. As I recalled, it had been a very long night, as the cop who was taking the report was a rookie who didn't understand English very well and he kept making everyone repeat their stories till he got it all down, rather than letting someone who understood the language take it down. My father had complained about that for ages afterward. *We had better things to do than sit in a waiting room repeating the story louder and louder. Hell, he could have looked at the cars and seen exactly what happened!*

We got into my room and closed the door. Both of us reached over to lock it at the same time, then laughed and kissed each other. It was tender at first, tentative, like Brendan had always been, but things heated up quickly. They always had, but this time I was on fire, kissing him hungrily, as if my survival somehow depended on it.

"Happy birthday," he said to me between kisses.

"Thank you." Eighteen. Yup, I lost my virginity a couple of months later.

Now I was about to lose it again. No sense in waiting this time.

CHAPTER EIGHT

NOT MANY PEOPLE COULD SAY THAT AND MEAN IT. THAT THEY were about to lose their virginity for the first time again.

Again.

But I was.

"Happy my birthday to you too," I said to Brendan, and reached for the buckle of his jeans. It was cool to the touch, and I fumbled with it for a moment, trying to remember how it opened.

He shifted his weight, making my access easier, and I pulled the belt off and dropped it to the floor. Then I went for the button.

He exhaled harshly and reached his hands inside my shorts, sliding easily along my abdomen and down between my legs. It had been a long time since my stomach was that flat. When he reached the spot he sought, he sucked his breath in sharply.

"You are so hot," he breathed.

The words lit me on fire. "So are you."

I ground gently against him. It wasn't a move I'd ever used on him before, and when his finger slid easily into me, he responded with enthusiasm. "What has gotten into you?"

"I'm about to turn eighteen!"

"Who knew that was all it took?" He laughed, but he did not stop working his fingers.

"I certainly never dreamed it," I said, sliding his jeans down over his hips, then kneeling before him and taking him into my mouth.

He moaned and I looked up at him, using that Jenna Jameson eye contact trick everyone talked about (decades after this) but which I'd always felt self-conscious using. But it drove men insane. That's why everyone talked about it, because it was the trick we'd all learned later (much later), to giving the perfect blow job.

Funny thing was, I was surprised to find he was already as hard as a rock before I even did anything. This was another thing that didn't happen anymore. Grown men had more control or less sensation, I wasn't sure which, but it took more time to get a grown man excited. This was a very heady compliment.

I flattened my palms on his abdomen and worked him, pleased at the way he responded to every stroke.

"Babe." He put his hand on mine and curled his fingers to hold me tight. "Get on the bed."

"Not yet." I kept going, enjoying the power of controlling his desire. He couldn't stop if he wanted to, and part of me wanted to just finish him off against his will. Why not? He'd be able to get it up in another ten minutes anyway.

It had been so long since I'd felt quite so desirable.

But this was my virginity we were talking about. I wanted to get it right this time. Originally, he'd tried to get me into the backseat tonight after dinner, but I was too scared. Not that I remembered that specifically, mind you; that's just pretty much how all of our dates ended. It had originally taken me another two months after my eighteenth birthday to give in to him.

Not this time. As long as I was here, I was going to enjoy every minute of this that I could.

I stepped out of my shorts and pulled my tube top up over my head easily. It was nice to be able to take off *anything* easily; there was so much binding and *securing* these days. I don't know if that came from age or garment technology, but I *do* know that I couldn't simply slip out of my clothes like I used to. And I definitely couldn't get away with putting my T-shirt on without a bra after Brendan and I were done, as the sagging today would be all too apparent, and the tightness then was as taut as could be.

Brendan kicked his shoes off and reached down to pull his pants off over his feet. Normally he laid them across the back of my dressing table chair, so he'd be able to find them and put them on quickly in case of parental interruption, but he didn't take the time for that tonight. In my current mind-set, I took that as another badge of honor.

I lay back on the bed and pulled him onto me.

Every woman knows that is one of her better angles, lying on her back with her skin smoothing back over her bone structure, but it is ten times better when the face in question is only eighteen. To say nothing of the body—stomach and hips without stretch marks; a neck that bears no resemblance to a turkey in any way, shape, or form; arms that are tight and strong but still look like pipe cleaners. . . . I couldn't help but feel great about myself. I had confidence that was brand-new to me, as I had not had it at the time, and it took the cruelties of age to make these simple pleasures obvious.

He eased onto me in a way I could tell was more practiced for him, as we were in his "now," than for me. But I still yielded to him. Just as I always had.

I was coming to find that my consciousness wasn't purely the disembodied future mind to this body of the past, but a combination of my teenage thoughts and reactions and my older self's thoughts and knowledge that came with experience.

Honestly, it didn't leave a lot of room for thought in my brain, since I was playing so many subconscious roles, but, in this moment with Brendan, I decided to let go of all thought and logic and anything like it. Because the truth was, I didn't have any control over the situation anyway. I could have the most salient, logical thoughts anyone had had since Einstein, but I couldn't do a thing to understand or change these strange circumstances I was living in.

So instead I went with the flow.

And I liked it.

Actually, no, I *relished* it. I relished the feel of his body on mine, his mouth hungrily working mine, his cheek, smooth to my touch, save for a little bit of youthful stubble. No errant ear hairs, no stray nose hairs, no gray in the beard (or, god forbid, dyed beard!), just maleness in what must have been its purest and, in our basest history, most masculine form.

So there was nothing wrong with this.

Everything felt *right* about this.

And I told myself that several times as he kissed me, then worked his hand under the waistband of my underwear and straight on down to the hot spot, where I was dying to feel him.

He moved his hand down in a way I remembered as he went along. I remembered those fingers and the way it felt when he got what he was reaching for.

It was good.

Really good.

I knew it wasn't skill or experience as much as love. His love for me and—harder to define—my love for him. I don't know that it was pure and meaningful love, in the *The One* sense. But it was the pure, untarnished affection between two people who hadn't yet had time to go out in the world and figure out how hard it was to find love and, more, real self-acceptance over time.

This was just uncomplicated. And that made it hot.

I was responding to him on every level, attracted to him on multiple levels, feeling the physical sensation, yet much more turned on by the timbre of his voice or the little things he said that showed he knew who I was, knew, apparently, who I'd always be.

This wasn't just sex. It wasn't exactly *making love* either, a term I'd always hated. But there was a subtle level of connection that I didn't even remember ever having had with another person.

Had I misunderstood its value because I never knew I'd already experienced it? Because nothing else had ever felt quite like this to me, regardless of all the other perks of subsequent relationships?

I didn't know. I couldn't know. I may never know.

But what I *did* know was that this was perfectly all right for me to do, because I'd already done it with no ill effects; and it was perfectly all right for me to explore it and feel it and dive straight into it.

It's hard to describe what it felt like to get a second chance at first love. But the main thing I can tell you is that it wasn't *dirty*, like me hitting on a kid in a bar, and it wasn't *beautiful*, like I'd found my way into my own personal heaven.

It was *raw*. It was *honest*.

It was cathartic.

And on top of all of that, it was *delicious*. No wonder I'd spent such a huge percentage of my teenage days thinking about this guy: the chemistry was amazing. It would have been harder to ignore the thoughts than to just let them run in the background, like some slightly annoying sound track, and go ahead and muddle through school and classes and chores and regular home life despite them.

But I remembered that I filled every spare moment I possibly could with him; I tapped my toes impatiently when he was at work, waiting for him to check out and come over; I saw him in the morning before school, in the afternoon when I got out of school, and on weekends in between his work shifts. And most of the time we were together, we were together like this; touching, kissing, exploring, even just *hugging*.

I hadn't had that with Jeffrey. I didn't even have to think about that juxtaposition to realize it. Jeffrey had been handsome and interesting, if only because of his position with Deutsche Bank (perhaps more than for any in-depth conversations we'd had), and our sex had felt movie-worthy. Not porn, mind you, just two people with specific looks and specific proportions joining together in a sort of dance that would have looked pretty with hazy lighting and a soft-focus lens.

No passion, I realized, feeling the light graze of Brendan's teeth on my neck. No words said that could not leave the moment, yet could not leave my mind either, making me tremble later in memory. There had not even been the wet results, inside of me and spilling slightly beneath me, with Jeffrey. He always had a dry washcloth at the ready. With Jeffrey everything had been NASCAR-fast and whip-clean.

No evidence.

In a way that was lucky for me, because it gave me absolute clarity about the breakup. Wherever I was, past or present, in my mind I was very clearly at the end of *yet another* failed relationship, and I had no sadness or regret whatsoever about walking away.

Here, in my eighteen-year-old self, I felt like I had nothing to lose. I was reclaiming a small feeling of confidence and optimism, thanks to the echoes of thoughts from long ago.

Losing my virginity was painful, just as it had been the first time around. Another advantage of my strange vantage point, however, was that I knew and understood the mechanics of it; I knew the pain would stop soon and I remembered the rewards that lay in store.

I wanted to do this. I wanted to experience this again, consciously. I wanted to enjoy every lingering moment of it, because this time I had the chance to commit it to memory forever.

So I did.

CHAPTER NINE

DINNER WITH BRENDAN AND HIS PARENTS WAS SERIOUSLY weird. They were not much older than I really was, yet I still felt like such a child in their presence. I guess it's true that you react to the way people treat you and, naturally, they treated me like an eighteen-year-old girl. Of course, why wouldn't they? I was just an eighteen-year-old girl to them. Fresh-faced, a bit immature, optimistic, more than a little foolish (though I'd only add that in retrospect, and I know it wasn't what they were thinking).

And I slipped comfortably into that role.

I've got to say, one thing that isn't normally mentioned in the conversation about time travel, quantum metaphysics, psychosis, or whatever this was, is food. The Kona Kai Restaurant had been closed for years in real time—I think it went under shortly after this graduation/birthday dinner, in fact—but it was incredible to be sitting here, eating the pu pu platter again, leaning my back against the elaborate peacock chair.

"So what do you see yourself doing in college?" Brendan's father asked me.

Easy question, right? I could literally recall everything I did in college. Well, except for those nights I couldn't recall. Everyone has a few of those.

"I'm going to study finance," I said, though I realized this wasn't a decision I had made by this point. Still, it was easy to recall and recite the blueprint. "And then do a year at the LSE before becoming a broker."

"LSE?" Suzanne, Brendan's mother, echoed, then glanced at her husband. "Is that down in Louisiana?"

"Oh, no, that's LSU," I said, "Louisiana State University. I'm going to the London School of Economics. LSE." I could feel Brendan's eyes on me and I knew this was *not* a decision I'd made or declared before our breakup. I glanced at him. "Mick Jagger went there."

Like that explained it. If Mick Jagger went there, I was obviously going to go. Even though, if forced to pick, I'd go Beatles over Rolling Stones any day.

"I actually know that," he said, his expression inscrutable. "Weirdly enough."

"You want to be a musician?" Suzanne asked. "I can see you fronting a band in town."

Brendan laughed. "Have you heard her sing?"

I shot him a look, though he was right, and said, "I'm not very musically inclined." I loved listening to the car radio—I was a total fanatic about finding my favorite songs and driving Brendan absolutely crazy by cranking them up—but I wasn't exactly great at singing along. "I'm better with numbers than with notes."

"Sooo." Mike, Brendan's father, leaned back in his chair. "Where should I be investing right now?" He asked me that now and then, and I could never tell for sure if he was patronizing me or not. I always answered seriously, but there was no way for me to ever know if he followed any of my advice.

"Well, you should always invest in companies and products you believe in," I said, giving my usual disclaimer. Probably quaint coming from a kid, in retrospect, but it was how I began every consult with a new client. "Don't invest in something just because you *think* it's going to 'take off' because other people like it. When you invest in a product or company you yourself enjoy, you're much more likely to hold on and have faith in its resurrection."

Everyone looked at me silently.

"I mean, obviously, right?" I went on. I couldn't tell why no one else was talking. Mike, at least, nodded and looked more interested than usual. Suzanne looked straight-up puzzled. And Brendan just looked like he always did: sort of bemused and besotted at the same time. He probably hadn't really heard anything I said.

"Good advice," Brendan said, then picked up a chicken wing and gnawed on it thoughtfully. "Sound."

"But what are you thinking is a good investment *right now?*" Mike persisted, and suddenly I knew he was taking this more seriously than usual. Had they been having money troubles? I'd never noticed back then. If so, I don't think they lasted long. Last I'd heard, the family was still living in the same house in the same neighborhood and Mike was still working for the same company.

"Microsoft," I told him. It was a sure thing. I couldn't feel bad about recommending it.

Mike furrowed his brow. "There are so many computer systems out now, how do you know which one is going to stick? It's like Betamax versus VHS. Which one will win in the end? Why Microsoft instead of, say, Atari, or Commodore?"

Atari or Commodore! They were so popular at one moment in time, but if he were to invest heavily in those companies, he would drown. "They all work on similar platforms," I told him, though I had absolutely no idea what I was saying. I didn't know squat about computer systems or programming; all I know is who ended up on top when all was said and done.

"Then why that one?"

"Because Microsoft has more versatility and room to grow." I was floundering. My father had told me a long time ago to speak with confidence even if I had none, and people would believe me. I was giving that my very best attempt right now. "Trust me, that is the direction that businesses all over the world are going." And that much, I knew, was true. "My dad told me that," I added, since he'd take me more seriously if I'd heard it from a grown man.

"You and your dad have really been working on the old portfolios, huh?" Brendan took my hand in his. "Pretty impressive."

I felt my face grow warm, though he'd given me the perfect excuse. "You know Dad."

"He's really into this stuff." Brendan looked at his own father earnestly. "He really does know what he's talking about. You should take it seriously."

"I will, I will," Mike agreed. He looked thoughtful. "Thanks for the advice, Ramie."

Our waiter came over with our entrées and set them down in front of us, and we were, mercifully, allowed to stop talking for a bit while the sweet scents of coconut and chicken and grilled pineapple filled the air between us.

Still, this whole experience was just too weird. People were looking at me in a way that I'd never even noticed, and therefore that I'd never noticed had stopped. I felt as self-conscious as if I were wearing a rubber Reagan mask. How could anyone be fooled into thinking I was really eighteen when it seemed so obvious, to me, that I was a fraud?

The answer was obvious, of course. How could they believe anything but? *That* was the part that sounded so patently unbelievable.

I was still having trouble believing it myself.

We made it through dinner with small talk, and I tried to let everyone else lead so I could just follow lightly and not say too much or have my behavior stand out as odd. Every word I said sounded self-conscious to my ear, but listening to these voices I'd once thought I knew by heart was like a whole new experience for me.

It was really nice. That's the part I haven't really pointed out yet. We were in a great restaurant with great atmosphere, and everyone around us was dressed like they were auditioning for a bit part in *Magnum, P.I.* The only worry I had, apart from the small matter of what had happened to the whole rest of my life, was whether or not I'd get home in time for my curfew. I had two days of school left, which would probably be pretty cool to revisit, and then, if I was still here, I was going to be a jobless, responsibility-free teenager in summer.

This wasn't really that bad.

We plowed our way through dinner, and then, because it was my birthday tomorrow, Suzanne had asked the waiter to do something special, so he brought over a sliced pineapple and a bowl of dipping caramel, and presented it to me while he and the rest of the servers sang "Happy Birthday." I always hated that, by the way. Still hate it. Hate being the center of attention like that. It's so embarrassing.

However, it's a little less embarrassing when you're getting your eighteenth birthday celebration. Particularly when you're thirty-eight and getting your second eighteenth birthday celebration. Basically I got to sit there and know I looked *super*-young for my age.

So it ended up being pretty fun, and I was growing more and more at ease with my youthful self-identity until the check came. That's when years of reflex took over.

"I'll get that," I said, putting my hand over the little book with the gilded palm trees on the outside.

Mike had reached for it at the same time, and withdrew his hand when it touched mine, as if he'd touched a snake.

"What are you *doing?*" Brendan whispered urgently. "*Stop* it. Come on." It looked like I was making a joke of their generosity, I guess. As soon as I realized my mistake, I took my hand off the check and put it, shamefully, in my lap.

"Sorry," I said. "It was just such a wonderful dinner, I didn't

want you to have to . . ." I searched for an explanation, but nothing came to me. "I didn't want you to have to pay for my portion."

"Ramie, we asked you to come and celebrate your birthday
and graduation!" Suzanne said, and it was clear that she didn't
think anything more of my gesture than that. The self-conscious
action of a girl. It was obnoxious of me, but at least it wasn't re-
vealing of anything. "We are *delighted* to be able to treat you. I
can't imagine why you'd think we expected you to pay."

I'd really insulted them. I'd taken an ordinary situation that
would have been—and once was—completely forgotten, and
made it into something hideously awkward for all of us.

Further explanations were only going to go badly so I gave
up. "I just really, really appreciate all you do for me," I said honestly.

"We are happy to have you!" Suzanne cried.

"This celebration was for you," Mike added. "You and Brendan. What a milestone, getting out of high school."

That returned the point where it needed to go. This happened
to be my birthday, but soon Brendan and I would graduate,
and that *was* a big deal at this time.

Finally the conversation drifted back into the mundane—our
favorite classes over the years, our best memories, our worst
teachers, and so on—and the bill was settled, so we got up to go
back out to our cars.

As permanent as my state of suspended teenage-hood felt, I
knew that I probably wouldn't be here for long, so when we
walked outside onto the sidewalk in front of the restaurant, I gave
Suzanne a big hug. "Thank you so much for everything," I said,

close to her ear. She had always been good to me, even after Brendan and I had broken up. She was one of those adults you could count on to always be normal, and pretty sane, if not super-wise and all-knowing. "You'll never know how grateful I am for you."

"We love having you around," she said, giving me a squeeze. "Thank *you* for celebrating your birthday with us."

We drew back, and I turned to Brendan's dad. "Thank you," I said to him. "It was a lovely dinner. I'm totally stuffed."

"The sign of a good meal. Glad you enjoyed it!"

"I did! Almost as much as I enjoyed the company. And remember"—I lowered my voice but hardened it meaningfully— "Microsoft. It's on NASDAQ." The shares were probably under three dollars right now. "Trust me."

He gave a hearty laugh. He didn't trust me at all. Who could blame him? "I'll look into it."

I wondered if he'd remember this moment in the future and look back on it with regret, or maybe wonder at my "psychic abilities." If I'd pushed the Google or Apple points, he could have made a fortune, but I knew those stories would only make me seem fanciful or, in the case of a name like "Google," maybe like I was making stuff up entirely. Plus, he wasn't going to hear that name for another few years and trust his memory enough to overinvest.

I kissed him good-bye on the cheek and we waved them up Old Georgetown Road until they turned into the garage where their car was parked.

Only then did Brendan and I head back to his car and talk to each other, alone, for the first time in what suddenly felt like ages.

"So now you're a real financier," he commented, hooking his arm lazily over my shoulder. "A financial whiz kid."

"Actually, yes. And a very good one."

He laughed. "I think Dad got a real kick out of that."

"He also got some really good advice."

"Okay." He turned the corners of his mouth down and shrugged. "We'll see."

I stopped on the sidewalk. "Excuse me, are you saying you don't have faith in my opinion?"

He was unfazed. "I'm saying you were completely not your-self tonight, so I don't know *what* to believe."

That was reasonable. He was right, I *wasn't* myself. Or at least I wasn't the self he'd expected to see. Why on earth should I be giving him grief for not taking my teenage professional advice seriously?

I needed to get a grip. I know it sounds crazy, but it was as if my teen hormones were mingling with my adult sense of pride, and the result was a real mess.

I tried to find a way to soften this and make it more reason-able. Or less hysterical-seeming. "Well, Dad and I were going over some new long-range options yesterday, so I happened to be thinking about that stuff anyway."

Brendan nodded. "What's this about going to London?" he asked. "Last I heard, you were going to Flagler in *Florida* to study art. What happened to that?"

It was true, I did my first year at Flagler, thinking I'd study art, but the more fun I had, the more I worried that I was pur-suing a major that would be too challenging to make into a career. If there was one thing Dad had taught me, and taught me well, it was to eliminate risk, particularly when it came to finances. So I'd gone to Wake Forest for my undergrad work, then taken a year at the London School of Economics and finished my master's back at the University of Maryland. Sincerely, to this day, one of my favorite reads is the *Financial Times*. I may be a geek, but it's to a good end.

Brendan and I got into his old station wagon, and he started the engine. My Marti Jones mix tape started blasting out over the speakers. *It was the chance of a lifetime* . . . Yes, it was. Whatever it was, this was the chance of a lifetime. I sang along with abandon. What a weird feeling: with no job to go to in the morning, nothing I did mattered right now, at least not in a losing-your-job sense.

Brendan turned the dial to lower the volume.

Then he leaned across the seat and kissed me.

This was routine for us, I realized. My body remembered it, even while my mind lagged a little behind, asking questions I didn't want to ask, and giving warnings I didn't want to heed. *I shouldn't! I'm so much older! This hormonally driven eighteen-year-old body could get pregnant so easily!* All of that warred with, *This feels incredible.*

Try and guess which impulse was stronger.

The kiss was delicious. There is something about making out as a teenager that absolutely beats every other experience. Nothing feels better. Sex isn't far behind, of course, if the kissing compels it, but I'd still have to say that the best part of it all is the kissing.

This was where I'd learned that.

This was bliss.

Chalk it up to those teenage hormones my body was feeling.

I sank into it, willfully feeling every bit of the experience. It had never occurred to me how much I missed this, but I did. I had. I *loved* this. I could do it all night.

And that was the best part, I *could* do it all night.

Why had I been so determined to grow up when I was a kid? I just couldn't wait to be twenty-one, to be legal, to be finishing school, to be moving out into *the real world* and starting my life properly. Why hadn't I enjoyed these halcyon days of carefree, jobless, stress-free heaven a lot more?

This was what people dreamed of when they looked back at their lost youth. All that possibility ahead, everything seeming like a good idea, every road well paved and open. There was so little fear of the unknown back then because I, at least, had absolute confidence that no matter what I did, I'd succeed wildly.

And I had, I guess, but I'd learned pretty quickly that it took a lot of work and a lot of worry and a lot, a lot, a *lot* of setbacks and knockouts and getting back up again, to finally make it.

Right this moment I was reliving the time right before I had to find out all those hard lessons for myself.

On top of everything else, I got to enjoy free, unbridled passion. I had never known how really good I'd had it.

We drew together, ever closer even though that didn't even seem possible. And soon we were peeling our clothes off, first my shirt, after which he spent a long time and a lot of attention on my breasts. No one did that anymore. Not like this.

He moved down, pushing my pants out of his way and moving his mouth down where everything inside of me wanted him to be. I closed my eyes and just let it all happen, felt it all, enjoyed it all, every second, until finally he moved on top of me and entered me.

We both moaned with the relief of it.

I arched against him, meeting him move for move. God, this was awesome. I hadn't even remembered just how good this was. When Brendan and I had broken up, I'd moved on so determinedly that I don't think I allowed myself to think about him until I'd all but forgotten the details. Certainly I had taken my time before I got involved with anyone else, and then romance was all mixed up with overloaded college schedules, early morning exams, part-time jobs, and all the things that were the first steps toward the unforgiving schedule I was setting myself up to have for my career.

If I could have had this all those years, would that have been enough? Would I have forgone some of that intense career determination?

For so long I'd been proud of the fact that I'd never *needed* a man to take care of me, I'd never needed a man's income, I'd never needed anything from a man. Or, to be less specific, I'd never really needed anything from another human being at all as far as personal relationships went.

Now I wondered if I'd totally missed the most important mark.

Now I wondered if all those years I'd needed the one thing I had so casually pushed away: love.

CHAPTER TEN

WHEN I GOT IN, AROUND MIDNIGHT, MY FATHER WAS UP, AS usual, watching TV from the sofa in the living room. His left arm was in a sling and his posture suggested his back was not quite up to par either. Just as I'd recalled.

"Hi, Daddy."

He pushed the mute button on the old Zenith remote and struggled to sit up straighter and turn to see me. "Hey, princess, how did your night go?" His voice was thick with pain, from the car accident and maybe a little bit of bourbon for pain control.

I sat down on the end of the sofa by his feet. "Weird. It was really weird."

He picked up the remote again and committed to *off*, then turned back to me. "Weird? How so?"

I sighed dramatically. "You wouldn't understand. I can't even understand. It's crazy."

"I understand a lot more than you think," he said, and when

I looked at him, he went on: "There isn't that much that separates us, you know. A few years seems like everything when you're young, but when time moves on and you see what it really is, it's meaningless. I was a kid just like you not too long ago." He hesitated, then shook his head and added, "Not too long ago, and way too long ago."

I knew what he meant, though he couldn't have realized it. This throwback was all too familiar, all too easy and tempting to dive into, but at the same time, it felt like so long ago that it might have been someone else's life.

"Daddy," I began, then paused. How could I ask him all the things I wanted to without freaking him out about either my sanity or his own death? Could I possibly just be subtle and get answers without indicating my fear/dread/certainty about the future?

Then, as if reading my mind, he took a cigarette out of the pack and lit it with his old gold lighter. I'd thrown that thing away when he died. Never wanted to see it again.

Now it almost looked like an old friend.

Almost.

I watched him take a long drag and hold it in for a moment before blowing it out, bluish smoke surrounding us both. I hated it. "How come you keep smoking, even though you know it's terrible for your health? Even though you know it's *dangerous*."

He didn't hesitate. "Because it is a stupid choice I made a long time ago and at this point it makes no difference."

"But it *does!*" Something like hope surged in me. Did I have the chance to get him to stop right here and right now? If I did, could I save his life? Was *that* why I was here? "If you'd stop and get into shape, you could live a long and happy life."

He shook his head, and I could tell by the resignation in that small movement that there was no way he was going to change one damn thing. "It takes years to reverse the damage," he said, and I thought he sounded regretful. "I know that. Don't you?" Yes, I did. Unfortunately. "I don't have that kind of time."

He was right.

Tears filled my eyes immediately, and burned like they were acid. He was giving a nod to his own death sentence. Did he *know*? Had he already had pangs that indicated he was on his way out? "Why are you saying that?" I asked, verging on an ugly echo of hysteria. "You're not even fifty years old!"

"Ramie." He sat up and reached for my hand. His was cool. A little rough. "Is this really what you want to talk about right now?"

"Yes. This is about the most important thing we possibly *could* talk about." Obviously. "Isn't it?"

He looked me in the eye for a moment, then shook his head. "I don't think so. Sometimes things are written in the stars. And we don't like them. You know, when I started smoking, it was prescribed as an antidote to stress?"

Stupid stupid stupid medical community. How had minds trained in any sort of health care *ever* thought it made good sense to draw smoke into your lungs? *Lucky Strike will calm your nerves. Doctors prescribe a good smoke after a bad day.* Did those same doctors think it a good idea for a person to remain inside a burning building? "I know, but we've known for a long time that wasn't true. It's all bad."

"You just need to sleep," he said.

I frowned and rewound that, but it didn't make sense. Was he sending me to my room for having an uncomfortable conversation? "What?"

"I said it didn't stop me."

"Oh." I tried to rewind our words again, but they were gone and I knew what he was saying mattered more anyway. "Why not?"

He shrugged, but his gaze was penetrating. "Dumb, isn't it? I heard the news, same as you, about the dangers of smoking, but I kept doing it. I made a choice. I kept making that choice for many decades, always thinking I'd quit *later*."

But you didn't and then you died from it! I wanted to say. But I couldn't. You can't look your loved one in the face and predict his impending death. "So you're saying you will willingly do this until the day you die?" I asked angrily, but tears slipped down my cheeks, because there was so much more grief in me than anger.

"Yes," he said simply. "Me and many, many others who should know better and do better. Maddening, isn't it?" It would have been a good time to punctuate his question with a puff on the cigarette and I was glad he didn't.

"Yes," I said, my voice hard with the knowledge that my mother was going to be widowed, that I was going to work my way through school by myself, that my father wouldn't be there to walk me down the aisle, though it didn't seem likely I'd get there anyway. "It's very maddening. And seriously selfish."

He sighed. "This is not the time for me to sit here and lie to you, though, is it? To say I'll stop and then have you surprised all over again by the truth?"

Given that the truth was he was going to die, I supposed he was right. But still, *he* didn't know that he would die so early, so this was a bullheaded position to take when his daughter was sitting before him, crying, begging him to live.

"Why can't you even just *try*?"

A long quiet stretched between us.

"You know."

"What if something happens to you?" I asked carefully.

"None of us gets out alive."

I frowned. "I know, but we don't all have to die at fifty."

He stubbed the cigarette out. Even though I hated it, the tiny crunch of the burned leaves in the ashtray was nostalgic. I watched as all the tiny orange bits of flame extinguished, then looked at him.

"What do you really want to talk about?" he asked.

I sank back against the edge of the couch and felt tears come back to my eyes, fast and hot. I wiped awkwardly with the back of my hand. "I don't know. Something so messed up is going on and I don't know why or how to explain it. I don't know what to do."

"There are a lot of times in life when you're not going to know what to do," he said. "We never outgrow that. What you need to remember is that, at those times especially, you need to slow down and just put one foot in front of the other. There's no faster route to madness than to try and take everything in at once and figure out your whole path in life from one blind vantage point."

I gave a dry laugh, without a touch of humor. "I kind of feel like I'm there right now."

"You can always change the future," he said. "Always. Given enough lead time," he added, probably anticipating my retort. "I'm not so sure about the past." He met my eyes and gave a soft laugh. "Many have tried and failed."

We'd see about that.

We sat together in an uneasy silence.

"Do you believe there's a heaven?" I asked at last. I don't think we'd ever really talked about this before and I wanted to know his feelings on things like this if he really did have to go.

Once again, he stopped to consider before speaking. He reached, reflexively, for the cigarette pack in his pocket but stopped and drew his hand away. "Yes."

"And . . . ?"

"And that's one hell of a relief, eh?" He gave a genuine laugh, but I didn't join in.

I'd been expecting more. Something philosophical, maybe. Some key to everything that was happening right now, even something I could read into as the reason for it all. But that one single word—that yes, he believed in heaven—was an immeasurable comfort to me.

"Listen to me," Dad went on gently. "You're looking for answers. We all are. That's what we do in life, we try and find our way through every stage, day after day, year after year, and we look to others for guidance. It's natural. But the thing is, when you come down to it, the answers are all inside of you."

The tears came on full-force. "That scares me," I said brokenly. "I don't feel like a grown-up and I don't know if I ever will at this point." He let that slide, even though it must have sounded childish coming from my eighteen-year-old mouth. "I'm scared of being entirely in charge of my own destiny. What if I do it wrong? A bad marriage, no kids, too many kids, the wrong job, the wrong career . . . so many things can go wrong!"

"That depends how you define *wrong*. You learn something from all of that. Remember that yappy little dog we had when you were in fourth grade? The one that bit you?"

I reached up to my lip, where a faint scar still remained. "Oh, god. It was third grade. Binky. That horrible little rat. That's a perfect example of what I'm saying—what was the point of having Binky at all when all he did was spend one miserable month pooping all over the place and then bit me so I had to get twelve stitches and a facial scar that would disfigure me forever?"

He laughed. "Disfigure."

"Okay, maybe not *disfigure*, but it's there!"

"Be that," he said, raising an eyebrow, "as it may, what happened when we gave Binky to Aunt Pat?"

"I'm pretty sure he destroyed her house."

"That's her lesson." Dad smiled. "What happened *here*?"

I shrugged. "We adopted Bailey, who we should have gotten in the first place! See? Binky *was* a mistake."

I could tell he was itching for a cigarette. I was annoying him, but I was right!

"When we went to the shelter and got Bailey, what did we learn about her?"

"That her horrible previous family had given her up because

she got too big. Once she wasn't a cute little puppy anymore, they didn't want her. Jerks."

He nodded, too patiently. "And she'd been in the shelter for how long?"

I thought about it. "A few days. Three, maybe?"

"Right. So you see my point?"

"No."

"If we hadn't gotten Binky first, we never would have ended up having Bailey."

I wasn't so sure. "Or we could have just waited and gotten Bailey in the first place, and then we would have saved all the trouble of the Binky Month."

He shook his head. "You were not waiting one more day to get a dog, much less a month and three days. Everything on our path led us to that day, to that shelter, and to that dog. And so it will be with all the Binkys of your life, whether they are bad jobs, nasty bosses, even, god forbid, a dud husband. Whatever happens, as long as you're doing your best and putting one foot in front of the other, you will live your destiny."

"Are you sure? *Really sure?*" My voice sounded small, embarrassingly childlike.

"As sure as I'm sitting here." He patted my head. "This is one thing I know to be the truth."

I was crying again—or had I never stopped?—and reached over to hug him. "I miss you so much, Daddy."

"I'm right here."

"I know, but . . . I don't want you to ever go away."

"I never will," he reassured me. "I'll always be here when you need me."

It was eerie how wrong he was about that. In less than two years he'd be gone forever, and he had no idea.

AFTER TALKING WITH my dad, I made a cup of hot raspberry herbal tea and took it up to my room. It was a cool night for May, and my windows were open, blowing in the glorious scent of viburnum and magnolia. The magnolia tree had gotten out of control, growing up taller than the roof of the house, and when the wind blew, it scratched on the screen like fingernails. It was really creepy, but when it bloomed it made all of that worth it.

I went to my bookshelf and pulled out a book. *Illusions* by Richard Bach. I hadn't thought about it for years but as a teenager I remembered thinking it was incredibly profound. I stood and flipped through it for a moment, then creaked into the old canopy bed, and snuggled down comfortably against the pillows.

Crickets chirped outside, and in the distance I could hear the Henley family laughing on their porch. That was the sound of summer to me. They had a straight-up legitimate screen porch— one season—and they spent virtually every summer night out there, playing cards, drinking, and telling anecdotes, whatever. Sometimes my parents went over and I could hear my father's booming laugh rising over the trees and floating down to where I lay in the dark in my bed, safe and sound in the knowledge that my parents were just a few steps away if I needed them.

It has to be said, I have never slept as well again in my life as I did as a teenager. No great tragedy had yet befallen me, nothing weighed heavily on my mind or conscience. My body was light and efficient and worked all day and slept all night. I was looking forward to that tonight. Many times I'd cited my wonderful memories of reading well into the summer night, then waking up and picking the book up off the bed next to me and starting where I'd left off, no cares or responsibilities in the world.

The little brass reading light next to my bed was really mis-named. My thirty-eight-year-old eyes couldn't have stood the strain, but my eighteen-year-old eyes had no problem. I wished *that* were something I could take back with me.

Then again, I had no guarantee I was *going* back. And, natu-rally, that thought was constantly with me. It was hard to just let go and enjoy the fantasy a little bit, because I was always aware that this was an unknown phenomenon and it could end, abruptly, at any moment.

Or not at all.

I'd *wanted* to talk to my dad about it, but I knew it would have just been alarming to him. Not the death part, I never would have mentioned that at all, but that I believed myself to be a time traveler. What is a sane person supposed to say to someone who announces something like that?

I opened the book and started to read, hoping to let go of the spirographic circles that were going around and around in my brain like madness in print.

I don't know how long I was reading when I came to the pas-sage that struck me:

You seek problems because you need their gifts.

Wasn't that basically what my father had just been telling me? And here it was again, in black-and-white. There was a message there, I knew it. Or at least I *hoped* it. Though I wasn't generally superstitious, I did tend to take signs seriously.

So . . . extrapolating from that . . . maybe the whole reason I was here *was* to dig deeper into some of the mistakes I thought I'd made in the first part of my life. Because obviously I hadn't learned *enough* from them to keep me from wondering.

Maybe now I needed to really dive into this part of my life and see what I could do with it. *Live* it, breathe it, really commit to it as much as my logical mind would let me, and see what happened.

Maybe I could even change some of the things that continued to haunt me into adulthood.

It seemed as good a plan as any at this point.

CHAPTER ELEVEN

THE NEXT MORNING I WAS LYING IN BED READING WHEN THE phone on the bedside table trilled, scaring me half to death.

But I had reached over to answer it before I even had time to think about what I was doing. Funny how reflexes work to cut through all thought processes.

"Hello?" I have never answered the phone with more curiosity. It could have been just about anyone. It was bound to be interesting.

"Why do you sound like you're asleep?" It was Tanya. But, disconcertingly, a much younger version of her than the one I'd talked to a few days ago from my hotel in Miami.

"I'm not," I lied. I wanted to keep the conversation going. To keep hearing this version of her voice. To remember, in such a pure way, the roots of our friendship.

"You totally are." It was going to be hard to get any depths out of this.

I had to laugh. Might as well go with it as she was expecting. "Well, I'm not *anymore.*"

"Get your ass out of bed. I'm picking you up in twenty minutes, I just wanted to remind you to bring my yearbook. Finish signing if you didn't already."

"Picking me up in twenty minutes?" I was completely disoriented. I looked over at the clock. Seven A.M. Where could we be going at 7:20 A.M.?

"You know if we're late they're going to mark us absent and we're going to have to totally jump through hoops to get our credits without having to go to summer school. Mrs. Sykes has it out for me and she'd give anything to screw me over like that."

Oh, yeah. *School.*

Wow.

I was *not* up for this.

"She would," I agreed, because . . . she would. Tanya's guidance counselor seemed to hate her inexplicably. I'd gone on to know a lot of Mrs. Sykeses in my life, and pinning someone with the letter of the law—even something as small as marking a "tardy" as a technical "absence"—was a source of great pleasure for them.

"Clock's ticking, tick tick tick," Tanya went on, for all the world sounding like a small version of her bossy mother self. "Get up. And *don't forget my yearbook.*"

The yearbook. *That* rang a bell and, in so doing, brought back a big heap of memories.

Actually, I *had* forgotten her yearbook when I first went through this. I remembered that now. She'd had a crush on Kenny Singer and she was *absolutely convinced* they were soul mates and they would be together forever. The problem was, he'd barely ever said two words to her. So her plan was to get him to sign her yearbook, thereby basically necessitating that he ask her to do the same, whereupon she would write:

> Kenny, I'm sorry I never really got to know you but it's not too late! My number is 555-5801 so give me a call sometime! Have a great summer!

Lord, I still knew it by heart because she had hammered it to death, trying to make it perfect, changing one word, then another, then changing them back, despite all of my suggestions that perhaps *silence* would be golden.

According to Tanya's plan, Kenny was supposed to read that, realize that he had been missing out on this great thing all this time, and he was going to call her, and so on. Eventually they were going to have three kids. All boys. She thought Kenny would like that.

I thought the plan was stupid at the time, but now, with a lot of years on me, I actually thought it wasn't too bad. Not brilliant, but at least an overture that he could seize or ignore. If he was shy—and I had no idea, because I'd never heard another word about him—maybe this was all he needed. If he was not interested, there was no harm, no foul. She'd still end up in the same place: she'd eventually meet Vince Langston, marry him, and have two beautiful little girls and live happily ever after.

And if she got that opportunity to get Kenny out of her system, she could avoid the entire year of blaming me for screwing up her fate. Given the ferocity of her belief, I wondered if she might still, somewhere deep in her subconscious, wonder if Kenny was the Real One for her.

That was silly, of course. She was a sensible person, not prone to romantic notions about her past.

Still, you never know.

I got up, amazed, as before, at the ease with which I could just spring out of bed. Man, it was nice to be thin, and strong, and young. I went to the bathroom, brushed my hair and my teeth, then quickly did a better job with my makeup than I'd ever done in high school the first time around. No green eye shadow. Throw that electric-pink lipstick away. Get rid of that eternally orange foundation that smelled like medicine. It wasn't fooling anyone, and I was pretty sure now I'd probably always had monkey-face, that ugly line along your jaw where your makeup and real skin collide and tell the world you've been doing your face like an amateur in bad light.

Which, of course, I was.

I went through the drawer and took out the most egregious items just to save me from myself if I should suddenly pop back into the future and leave my poor hapless high school self with all those loud, unflattering drugstore cosmetics.

But while I was digging in there I saw a bottle of Gap Heaven perfume. Oh, my god, I hadn't smelled that in *ages!* I spritzed it on and was immediately transported to . . . well, now. My eighteenth summer. The smell conjured memories of steamy backseat sex, warm summer nights, the county fair, and love.

It also conjured my breakup with Brendan, the hurt in his eyes when I told him and every time I ran into him afterward, and the dull ache it had left in me for longer than I'd expected.

I shouldn't have done it. I'm not saying I would have married him, I have no idea what could have happened, but I shouldn't have ended such a sweet relationship for such a stupid reason. I was going away, moving on. I thought it made sense for us to end things before we were torn apart by circumstance (i.e., the fact that we were going to different colleges, hundreds of miles apart).

The truth is, a college student spends much more time at home than they think they're going to. And I *missed* Brendan, I really did. Sometimes I thought I *still* missed him. Certainly I'd never found anyone I could be quite so myself with, though maybe that was because myself got guarded with age, the way adults tend to. Unless they want to be weirdos played by Will Ferrell in the movies.

But I couldn't help thinking, what if Tanya wasn't completely wrong about that whole soul mate thing? What if our destinies *could* be screwed up by one mistake? Like I said, *Tanya's* life hadn't been a mistake, so I'm not saying she was right about *that*, but what if the whole reason I was back here was because one of the wrongs I needed to right, maybe even the *main* wrong I needed to right, was not to dump Brendan?

It would be interesting, albeit scary, to see how my life might change if I hadn't done it. But was I scared of that? I shouldn't be—I already possessed all the knowledge my career required to get me to this point, so I could have my life back no matter what. What was there to lose? Maybe it was time to see what a reset could do.

But, man, could I really go back into the halls of high school?

It didn't look as if I had any choice.

I went downstairs quietly, avoiding the squeaky stair fourth from the top, and into the kitchen. The cabinet under the counter was the liquor cabinet and it was unlocked, because I never stole anything from it. But today, come on—today I needed a little help.

I took out the bottle of Smirnoff and drew a slug of it. It burned going down, but other than that I felt nothing.

So I took another.

Then two more before I *finally* started to relax a little bit.

I could do this.

I could do it.

I could do it.

You can do it.

You can do it. . . .

Tanya's horn blasted outside, and I started, jerking my hand and spilling vodka all over myself and the floor. I looked at my shirt, and sniffed it. Fortunately the scent was mild, and the shirt would dry by the time we got to school. With a little luck no one would be any the wiser.

I ran to the door and signaled to her that I'd be right out.

Then I dashed back upstairs to brush my teeth and squirt on a little more perfume.

Admittedly it might have been a little obvious to come out smelling so strongly of toothpaste and Gap, but it was better than smelling of alcohol. I rinsed, spat, and took off down the stairs again.

Shit, the yearbook!

I held up a finger to her from the door: *Wait!* Then I ran back up, grabbed the book from next to my bed without even thinking about it, and ran back down the stairs and out to the big gray Buick that was chugging perilously in the driveway.

I got in and she immediately said, "Did you get a new job at the Gap?"

"Too much?"

"Little bit." She backed out of the drive, making a distasteful face. "Open the window."

I did. I cranked it down by hand. I couldn't even think when the last time I'd done that was. "Sorry." I set the yearbook down on the seat between us.

"Hey, you've smelled worse." She gave me a sidelong smile. "You probably smelled worse before you put it on this morning."

"Thanks."

"Always here for ya."

We rode the mile and a half to school in silence. So many thoughts crowded my mind, while I'm sure she was just idly thinking how glad she would be to graduate.

She weaved her way down the road in front of school, looking for a parking space on the car-clogged street. Soon the neighbors would get sick of this scene and demand permit-only parking, but for now it was still a madhouse.

And for me it was fascinating, passing all these long-forgotten faces, like being *inside* an old home movie.

I pointed, like a child at the zoo seeing a panda for the first time. "Good lord, it's Frances Lee!" I cried, seeing the girl whom I later saw running in the Olympics.

"Obviously," Tanya said, screwing up her brows. "It's *always* Frances Lee. She *lives* on that track. Why is that so fucking surprising today?"

"I—" What could I say? "I'd heard she had mono and wasn't going to be back before the end of term."

"Frances Lee."

"Yes."

"You heard Frances Lee had mono."

I knew where this was going, but I had no choice but to stick to my lie. "Yes."

Tanya snorted. "Where, pray tell, would that girl possibly get mono? I seriously doubt she's ever kissed anyone."

"It's not *literally* just a kissing disease," I began, but it was a stupid waste of time to back up my lie with pointless facts. From now on, I just had to be careful not to be outwardly shocked to see anyone. "Anyway, there she is!"

"Yup, there she is." Tanya gave another snort as she parallel-parked her car, and we got out.

I took a bracing breath to steady myself before going in, and wished I'd had a lot more than the four shots I'd had. Vodka was powerless compared to the adrenaline-fueling strength of high school.

THERE IS SOMETHING about the smell of school that you never completely forget. It stays lodged in your subconscious, ready to resurface unexpectedly, when you least need to feel anxious and uncomfortable. I couldn't have recalled it, or pegged any partic-ular characteristics to it, but as soon as I walked in, I knew it well. A thousand, maybe even a million, memories flooded into my head, most of which I couldn't have put words to, but I could *feel* them.

School.

Some tangled combination of old books, xerox paper, heated processed food, and . . . fear? Embarrassment? There was some note I couldn't define and I couldn't say if it was sweet or sour, but it made my heart pound a little faster. Not in a good way. My stress rose like a cat jumping neatly onto a counter.

"What's wrong with you?" Tanya asked me.

"Mm?" I returned my attention to her, trying not to seem nervous. "What do you mean?"

She gave me a what-the-fuck look. "I just totally *watched* the blood drain from your face."

I had to laugh, despite myself. I'd felt it myself. "I'm fine. Just . . . a little sad."

"Why?"

I looked at her. The youthful face that I would watch move through subtle changes, like in time-lapse photography, for at least the next two decades. Through jobs, marriage, pregnancy, kids, dogs. "Because it's almost our last day here. After four long years, we're never going to walk through these doors again. Probably," I amended hastily. "Tomorrow is our *last day of high school.*"

"Thank. God." She did the sign of the cross.

"Someday you're going to feel melancholy about this, believe me. You'll be off in some suburban home with two kids and a job that you're sick of and you're going to remember how nice it was to be in high school."

She screwed up her face. "Okay, *Mom*, thanks for the lecture." She shifted the weight of the backpack on her back and said, "So I'm going to turn all these books in so I don't have to wear this stupid thing all day. See you later."

"Tanya?"

She'd already started to walk away, but she stopped and looked back at me. "Yeah?"

"Can you write me a note and pass it to me in the hall? Just one more time? For old times' sake?"

She looked at me like I was crazy. As well she should have. "If I have something to actually *say*, I will." She shook her head. "You're being weird as shit today. Weird. As. Shit."

I laughed. Of course I was. I wasn't very good at being myself, it seemed. What a bizarre problem to have.

After just a few minutes of wandering aimlessly, I realized I had no idea where I was supposed to go. I'd completely forgotten my schedule. I was, quite literally, living out one of my recurring nightmares: I had to go to class but I'd missed so many of them that I didn't even know where it was, or who the teacher was, and there was no way on earth I was ever going to get caught up.

I went to the office and saw Mrs. Perrow, a smiling secretary with cropped gray hair and always-bright blue eyes, at her desk. "Miss Phillips," she said, as she always did. She had the tiniest bit of a Texas twang.

"Hi," I said. "I was wondering if you could give me a copy of my schedule?"

She frowned. "Your *schedule?* What, do you suddenly have amnesia or something?"

"No, no, no." Though that wouldn't have been a terrible explanation. And it was better than what I had . . . which was *nothing*. "My"—I thought fast—"doctor wants a copy. I mean my adviser. My college adviser. Because I'm thinking about doing a year abroad." I nodded, as if that totally explained why I'd suddenly need a copy of my second-semester senior-year schedule.

Fortunately, I'd managed to spark Mrs. Perrow's interest anyway. "Oh, *abroad!* How *exciting!*" She got up and went to a file cabinet and opened the N–P drawer and started searching the folders. "Where are you thinking of going?"

"London."

"*London!* I have always wanted to go there. I just know Princess Di and I would be the best of friends if I could only get over to Kensington Palace at teatime." She trilled with laughter.

Oh, sad. She'd be horrified to hear that Princess Diana was going to die in a car crash pretty soon. The fairy tale would be well and truly over. No chance of tea with Di in Kensington Palace for Mrs. Perrow, who otherwise probably *could* have charmed her way in.

She was riffling through the files and pulled one out. "Here we are!" It was a thin sheet, almost transparent. I remembered that. "Let me just go and make you a copy." She went over to a massive copy machine, and it roared to life and spat out one piece of paper, which she then brought over and handed to me. "There. Now, you stay in touch with me and let me know if you go to London, okay?"

"Sure," I said. "What's your e-mail address?"

"E-mail?"

I glanced at the ancient PC on her desk and quickly reoriented myself in time. E-mail was *about* to become widely used, but it wasn't there yet, and it would probably take Mrs. Perrow a little longer than kids like me to get interested in it.

"Mail, I mean. Your mailing address. Can I just write to you in care of the school?"

"Of course! I don't plan on going anywhere. You address it to Jacquelyn Perrow."

"Will do." I walked out and thought about that. Did her friends call her *Jackie*? Did she have a vibrant social life when she wasn't in the school office? I wondered how old she was. Probably not as old as I thought. I would have guessed mid-fifties, but she could have been in her mid-forties. She could have been just a few years older than I was! I knew now that gray hair was a liar.

I stopped in the empty hall outside of view of the office and looked at my schedule. English. Mr. McCarthy. Oh, shoot. If I had to come tripping in late one last time, it *would* have to be in that snide old goat's class. I briefly considered just skipping altogether, but I wasn't sure how to do that. If I hid in the bathroom the janitors would inevitably come in and find me and call me out. And I got caught every damn time I tried to leave the campus, even if it was just to go down to Roy Rogers for lunch, so actually *leaving* wasn't an option.

Nope, I was going to have to face Mr. McCarthy's music one more time.

Unsurprisingly, he fell silent the minute I walked into the classroom, and he stood, like a sentry, watching my every step to an empty desk.

"Miss Phillips," he said, but in a very different tone from the one Mrs. Perrow had used. "I suppose it was overly optimistic of me to expect that on one of your very last days of high school you might be able to get yourself into school on time."

It was amazing how small I felt. And how quickly. "I *was* here on time," I said.

He made a point of looking at the clock on the wall. I was seven minutes late. Might as well have been half an hour to him. Jeez, he was just as bad as I remembered him.

"I was in the office," I explained. Truthfully, for once. "Talking to Mrs. Perrow."

"Mmm-hmm."

"No, really!" I started to take out the copy of my schedule to show to him, but he wouldn't buy my ridiculous story nearly as handily as she had. "I lost my math book and had to go pay for it. Apparently I wasn't the only one, so there was a bit of a backup."

He lifted one eyebrow, but I could see his uncertainty in his eyes. It was a plausible story. And suddenly my strength surged. Why was I feeling intimidated by this guy? He was a classic Little Big Man. He didn't want to actually *follow up* or go check out my story, he probably didn't even want to bother punishing me all those times he'd threatened to. He just wanted to feel big by making me feel small, and he'd almost done it.

"You can go ask her if you want!" I said, knowing, now, that he wouldn't. I leaned back comfortably in my chair, raised my chin, and looked at him.

Checkmate.

Boy, it was a *lot* easier to deal with teachers once you had almost forty years of living under your belt.

He shook his head, the only thing he could do even resembling a threat, and cleared his throat. "As I was saying before Miss Phillips's grand entrance, you have learned a lot of things in this class this year. . . ."

CHAPTER TWELVE

I PASSED TANYA TWICE IN THE HALL—LOOKING AT HER PER-haps a bit too longingly, hoping for a note—until finally, on our third and last pass, she slipped me a folded piece of paper the way she had so many times during ninth, tenth, eleventh, and twelfth grades. I opened it eagerly.

> Stop looking at me like a baby bird looking for a worm from
> Mom!!!! I don't have anything to say except it's almost the last
> day of school and I'm so glad I could scream. Satisfied???????

I had to laugh. Even today, Tanya would say the same thing. I'd wanted to revisit one of her old notes, like, *Oh my God, A.H. just farted in class and everyone knew it was him and now they're calling him "Piggy"! I want to tell them to stop because it's mean but it's so funny!* or, *J.M. was moved to the seat right in front of me. I think now is my chance! Also, what do you want to do this weekend? I think my 'rents are going out of town. Party at my house?*

There had been a million of them once. What had I done with them all? Had I, somewhere along the line, been going through my things and decided those precious, irreplaceable tokens of my childhood were clutter and thrown them out? I honestly couldn't remember the last time I'd seen one. Which was weird, because I'd kept track of all of my diaries since I was twelve and you'd think I would have treasured these time capsules from another point of view as much, if not more.

But of course that kind of thing couldn't be done authentically on command.

I wanted to savor my last last week of high school—that is, assuming this weird phenomenon didn't happen again, and how could I assume that?—but it went so fast. The last days of school are not typical ones: Classes aren't about teaching anything. It's just a matter of turning materials and books in and saying goodbye, signing yearbooks and pretending you hoped to soon see people you actually hoped you'd never see again.

But there were a few particularly melancholy standouts. Not just young Tanya, handing me a snide note but in a familiar way; there was Christopher Lotsky, a friendly, smiling, moon-faced guy who had died in a small plane crash just a couple of months after graduation. (It had been hard to believe until there was a neighborhood swap meet a few years later and I bought an ice crusher from his mother and carefully asked, only to find out it was true.) I watched him kiss his girlfriend by her locker... their hands lingering until they were just fingertip to fingertip before they went their separate ways. I'd heard they were still together when he died, but there's no way to tell if that was really true. I sure didn't ask his mom for the most painful, specific details.

There was also Doug Holborn, who was a real pothead and who managed to get hit by a car on his bicycle sometime after graduation and was never quite the same again. No girlfriend there, but a confident, probably stoned (but definitely content) swagger that said all was right in his world, and would be forever.

Forever didn't last so long after all.

Then again, there was Haley Nichols, who went on to be a semi-famous local newscaster for a really long time, and whom I assume was happy; and poor shy Destin Kingsford, his real name, who later came out of his shell and produced one of the most popular HBO series ever. He never spoke of his upbringing, and I think that was because he was somewhat shunned for being a shy, effeminate theater type, but he did go on to build a spectacular life, and I never saw even a hint of shadow in his red carpet pictures in later years.

It was such a strange, emotionally evocative experience. I saw them all, there in the fear-scented halls of high school, eyes a little wide, walking uncertainly into their various futures, no idea what was really ahead of them. It was almost exactly like being on *The Price Is Right*. Destin got the vacation package, the pop-up camper, the Hamilton Beach mixer, the whole shebang.

Doug got the goat and a hasty good-bye.

Better luck next time.

Honestly, it wasn't really a vantage point I'd recommend. I think there's a reason most of us can't see the future: It's sad. Even when it's happy, it's a little sad. Tinged with losses and things, and people, left behind.

But I also ran into Julia Green, whom I'd gone all the way through elementary school with, and then had seen briefly on a layover in Chicago, of all places, and found we really connected. I wished I'd kept up with her, but it was fun to see her teenage self again, since I'd been trying to remember how I could have forgotten her, considering how simpatico we were when we met up. We'd even stayed in touch for a year or so via e-mail, sending our recollections of our shared childhood, like diary entries. She remembered Bambino's Pizza at Cabin John Shopping Center, and talked about how she and her sister would argue over who got to sit in the front of the station wagon on the way home after picking it up, holding the warm box on her lap in the cold of winter.

I also ran into Greg Betz. I'd had the hots for him since we were both at Cabin John Junior High School, and nothing had ever come of it. We'd talked, hedged toward actual communication, but never kept it up.

I remembered this one time when he walked me all the way down Gainsborough Road, from the school to my house on Candlelight Lane, holding my umbrella for me. I'd glanced frequently but—I hoped—surreptitiously at his dark curly hair and bright blue eyes. And when I say curly hair, I mean the kind girls would kill for, not some crazy "rainbow hair wig" you'd get for Halloween. It was wavy and glossy, and he was a few inches taller than me, which was good if I wore heels, and he had these blue, blue eyes.

How was it that I'd never wondered what happened to him? Maybe because he was just that quiet, that understated. Did he ever remember me and that semi-rainy walk home from school we'd shared? It was funny, but it felt silly to think he might, since wistful memories seemed to be the domain of women and I'd have almost thought less of him if he'd thought of it as I had.

Yet I did wonder. If I ran into him on the street, would I have to explain who I was until we both expired in the embarrassed blue silence of his unspoken, *I'm sorry, I just can't recall* . . . ?

At any rate, I did see him that day and, wow, he was really as hot as I remembered. I don't mean that in a creepy way, as a woman talking about a guy twenty years her junior, but we all know what it is to see a kid who's about to grow up into a knockout.

Everyone knew Brooke Shields was going to be gorgeous from the time she was, what, twelve? Younger? I don't know, but somehow no one got the "creepy" label for that, yet I felt kind of creepy looking at Greg and thinking about how wonderfully he'd age.

But why not, right? For one thing, I was his age, technically, here, and for another thing, he was currently, wherever he was, my age *now*, so this was a totally legit way to think about someone.

Not that I was thinking about Greg, because I wasn't, beyond that point.

I was thinking about Brendan.

Or, rather, trying *not* to think about Brendan. The Brendan thing still had me totally freaked out. I realized that, by whatever magic, I was actually eighteen. And it was not in any way oogie for one eighteen-year-old to hook up with another. That was normal. In fact, that was normal enough for someone to travel in time to *do* again, if such a thing were, for some reason, necessary for one's development.

No sooner did I have the thought than he appeared, coming toward me in the hall, and scooped an arm around my ribs and swept me around the corner into an empty alcove.

He kissed me.

And it was fantastic.

Oh, my god, he was young, strong, and wildly enthusiastic. A man hadn't wanted me as much as Brendan *clearly* did for so long.

"Better stop." I smiled against his mouth. "Or you're going to cause a spectacle in public." It was a joke we'd had the whole time we were together; it was so easy to excite him and so diffi- cult to calm him down that he'd invariably end up sitting at places much longer than might otherwise have been proper because he couldn't get up.

"You're driving me *crazy*."

"Ditto." I meant it. I guess the vodka was still in my system a little bit, because I was dizzy with desire.

"Let's skip tomorrow night and get a hotel room."

I laughed. "We can get a hotel room anytime." Now that we were eighteen, that was true. I remember how heady it felt when we'd first realized that.

"Then why don't we?"

Because we're basically just kids, and kids are meant to sneak around and do it in backseats and unsupervised homes. It's what "youth" is.

"Because you're cheap."

He was a little defensive. "Do you know how much it costs to fill my car with gas?"

"No." But I was curious. "How much?"

"*Twelve* bucks."

"*Really?*" I couldn't remember when filling a big car like his had only cost twelve dollars. Even my small hybrid SUV could make it into the fifty- or sixty-dollar range.

"Really," he said, nodding like he had just solidly landed his point. "It's all that driving around looking for alternatives to a hotel."

"So we should move into a hotel."

He flashed that sly grin. "Yes. I think it would be more economical." He kissed me again. And I let him again. In fact, I was ready to just take him by the hand and leave, school be damned. It had been a long time since I'd had to worry about anyone having a stake in where I went or when I did it.

It would have been so nice to just jump into Brendan's car and drive until we were someplace nice and private, where I'd let him do whatever his eighteen-year-old heart and body desired.

Yet in my mind I knew, or felt, I was thirty-eight, and though I knew plenty of women who would have lauded me for that trophy, it wasn't one I was completely comfortable with.

Though there was this place in my mind that kept pointing out I was young; I was even having trouble holding on to my thirty-eight-year-old logic and maturity. Slipping into the life had, in a sense, made me slip back into the mentality. I was easing into it more quickly than I could have imagined, even relaxing about the work I might or might not have been missing back in the "present" . . . whenever that actually was.

So why was it that the judgment and condemnation of my own decisions were the things that held on with the most tenacity?

I was back in time to figure out something, at least one thing, in a maze of life choices. I couldn't dismiss *any* of them as "inappropriate" from the vantage of a thirty-eight-year-old, because I was eighteen again. There had to be a reason for that.

Didn't there?

CHAPTER THIRTEEN

THE AFTERNOON PASSED FAIRLY UNEVENTFULLY, BY WHICH I
mean it was like watching a fascinating movie that I'd never
forget—the characters on the screen had never registered me
at all, much less remembered me.

Actually, it was a bit humbling to see how essentially unnoticed I went in high school. Meanwhile, the really popular kids
were, for the most part, the ones you never heard about doing
anything worthwhile once they got into the real world.

It was an emotional roller coaster, nevertheless. All those
people I knew the sad fate of, or, perhaps weirdest of all,
had literally never thought of again . . . It was strange to think
you could spend years side by side with someone in the same
neighborhood and same school and yet have such totally
different experiences of the same that you never connected
at all.

Vito Vecchio—where was he now? I was absolutely positive he was fine; he'd never shown up on any of the Facebook "In Memoriam" pages for our neighborhood or school, so he was just a guy I saw every day for years and then forgot completely until "time-traveling" twenty years later, only to realize I knew every freckle on his face, the space of the gap in his teeth, and even the very faded lunch stains on his green-and-white-striped rugby shirt.

There were no Tide sticks back then.

How did someone who was in your periphery for so long just blow away like they'd never existed? Honestly, if I'd been on *Jeopardy!* and the Final Jeopardy question was "Ramie Phillips's eighth-grade lunch companions," I would have bet all but a dollar and lost because of Vito Vecchio. Seriously, it made me long for Google more than almost anything else I'd encountered so far.

What ever happened to him?

By the time school was over, my mind was racing. There was too much to comprehend and absolutely no one who might understand. Even if I'd gone to some sort of shrink, who'd be expected to be objective and understanding, the notes he would take would say things like *psychotic, delusional,* and I don't even know what else, because it would all sound, in layman's terms, batshit-crazy.

I wandered into the front courtyard in something of a daze when the final school bell rang for the day. A lot of kids had tears in their eyes, mostly the girls, because they were feeling the *last-ness* of it all. And they were right, that was the thing. I'd already been here and gone. Even now I was aware of being in its echo, not living it for the first (and, usually, only) time. Those days of youth, as much as we scramble to age past them and into adulthood, cast long, cold shadows into the future.

"Want to go to Bambino's?" Tanya asked, suddenly at my elbow and smiling like the Cheshire cat.

I started.

"Whoa!" She laughed and slapped her hand down on my shoulder, startling me yet again. "I'd ask if you had too much coffee this morning if I didn't know I'd woken your ass up and you didn't have time to pee, much less make a coffee."

"I'm a little jumpy," I conceded. Understatement.

"Why?"

I hesitated. I knew it would sound crazy and I shouldn't tell her, but I also knew I was going to. I had to *try*. If anyone would believe me, it would be Tanya.

Not that anyone would believe me.

"It's complicated. . . ."

"I've known you forever. How complicated can you be? If I don't understand, no one will."

Yup. There it was. No one could understand this. "What do you think about getting some beer and going to the lake?" I asked suddenly. That would be the perfect place to have a quiet talk.

She eyed me suspiciously. "What on earth is going on?"

"I'll tell you."

"Is this bad?" she asked, stopping and taking hold of my arm. "I don't want to sit in the car all this time wondering what's going on, only so you can tell me you're dying or something. If you have bad news, spit it out right now."

"No, no, it's nothing like *that*."

She was about to say something and I interrupted, "I'm not pregnant either."

She sighed and I watched her posture relax.

Normally I would have made a joke about her not having much faith in me, but since I was about to make her think I was clinically insane, I thought it would be best to just keep it straight for now.

We walked to her car. I opened the door and it creaked in a way that hadn't registered with me this morning. The smell, too, was the stuff of memories: part old leather, part gasoline, and a very vague whiff of the occasional Marlboro Light 100, though she didn't want her mom to know she ever smoked, so she tried to keep it aired out.

"Where to?" she asked.

"Bambino's." Bambino's Pizza, in the local shopping center, never carded back in those days. Everyone knew that and would come from miles away. I don't know why it wasn't a major hangout for cops. I guess they weren't as interested in underage drinking then as they are now.

She drove and I watched the passing scenery. It was different, kind of like I was looking at life through a Hipstamatic filter. It was odd to see the cars we'd thought of as so modern back then, all looking like relics now. Literally all of them could be registered as antiques now with the Motor Vehicle Administration. But there was Brian Hall's dad, in his driveway, washing his Mazda like it was the DeLorean from *Back to the Future* or something.

Actually, back then it might almost as well have been. I did think it was pretty hot myself back in the day.

Mr. Hall, however, was not. It was suddenly obvious to me why he'd bought a little sports car. Middle-aged, with a paunch, one of the early customers of hair plugs, so it looked as if he had a black rash on his scalp. He was back on the dating scene and he'd clearly invested in this car as his ticket to ride.

I wondered if it helped.

Tanya was singing along with Bon Jovi as she swung into the shopping center parking lot. It took my breath away. I hadn't realized how much the place had changed—how much I'd forgotten—until now, seeing it like this. There was that quirky stationery store with all the funky gift items, a record and CD shop that was about to go out of business, a Szechuan restaurant I used to love but which was going to be replaced by a burger joint in a few years, banks whose names would be swallowed up by others, a Peoples Drug store that would soon be CVS, and a grocery store that seemingly never changed.

Jeez, the parking lot needed fixing up back then; I couldn't believe that the place had grown—added California Tortilla, one of those ubiquitous juice places, a Popeyes Chicken, and a bookstore that only lasted a couple of years before being replaced by a Baskin-Robbins/Dunkin' Donuts—all without ever fixing or expanding the parking lot.

That didn't seem to do the businesses any harm, though the community constantly complained about it. Given that it was the closest place to get all the essentials, it probably didn't ultimately matter whether or not there was comfortable parking. In and out was good enough.

Tanya parked at the curb in front of Bambino's. "You going in?"

"Sure." I picked up my purse and got out of the car. The hot sun bouncing off the parking lot cooked the familiar smell of tar into my consciousness. They were constantly patching this lot, so tar would forever smell like summer in my hometown to me.

"Hey, Ramie," a girl I absolutely couldn't identify to save my life said as I walked into the carryout side of the restaurant while she was leaving. "Have a good summer!"

"Thanks! You too!" I could swear I'd never seen her before in my life. Wouldn't I have remembered that jutting jaw?

The guy behind the counter, on the other hand, *did* look familiar, though I couldn't remember his name. Jimmy? Johnny? I wasn't sure enough to try either. He was about six-foot-two and skinny as a rock star, with piercing blue eyes and a good strong chin. His skin was marred with the red spots we all battled to some degree at that age, but I could see he was going to be a good-looking man.

"Yo!" he said in greeting, then hesitated with what seemed a slight expectation.

I was stymied. What was expected of me? How could there be someone who knew me well enough to expect a response of some sort when I couldn't recall who he was?

When I didn't answer right away, he added, "The usual?"

"You know it." What was the usual? I remembered getting Budweiser, Cold Duck, Blue Nun, and whatever else my budget would allow here. I decided to take the luck of his draw.

Zima.

He cited a ridiculously low price, and I opened what turned out to be a ridiculously sparse wallet and pulled out just enough to cover it, along with a fifty-cent tip. Big spender.

He didn't appear to notice, though, just put the Zima in a handle-free bag that I'd have to carry the same as the six-pack, and handed it over. I thanked him and went back out to the car.

"What's that guy's name in there?" I asked Tanya when I got in.

"What guy?"

"The guy who works there. Tall, dark hair, blue eyes. Kind of cute except for the breakouts?"

"What, Jer Norton?"

Jer. That was it. "That's right. Man, that was going to drive me nuts."

She was looking at me. "Are you serious?"

"What do you mean?"

"You *forgot* who Jer Norton was? Or you just want me to think you have no idea what happened?"

I looked at her blankly. "I have no idea what happened. What are *you* talking about?"

"The party last weekend?"

Party, party, party. There had been so many graduation parties. And so much beer at those graduation parties. Was it reasonable for me to say I honestly had forgotten, even though it had apparently been less than a week ago?

"Don't worry," she said. "I didn't tell Brendan. *Obviously.*"

"Oh. Good."

"But I think you should."

"I . . ."

"Not about Jer, necessarily, but that you need to see other people, not tie yourself down to your high school boyfriend. If it's meant to be, you'll get back together."

Holy cow, I remembered this conversation. I *remembered* it. I remembered I was thinking the same thing. Which isn't to say I had a clue what this Jer guy had to do with it—he obviously wasn't the reason I broke up with Brendan—but I do remember thinking that I'd never had the kind of dates they showed in chick flicks and TV shows.

In high school, it's not like you lead an extravagant, worldly life. You go to the local joint for pizza, you drink beer from a keg at a field party and make out in the back of the car, you go out to dinners with your parents, then you go off to separate schools and meet older people and have more grown-up dates until you dump *them* and get a job and, in my case, focus all your romantic energy into your career and leave the piece of yourself that blooms in relationship behind.

Not for the first time, I wondered if it had been a mistake to leave Brendan. Especially if I could stay with him, somehow knowing what I know now. Which I did . . . now.

"What happened with Jer?" I asked her again. Then added, "I seriously don't remember."

"You made out with him at Angela MacPherson's party. In her *room*. I found you, lucky for you, and it didn't go too far. All of which I already told you, but I guess you were probably still hammered when you woke up. You had a *lot* to drink."

"Ugh."

"Not just an *ugh* amount, almost an *alcohol-poisoning* amount. You really have to be careful!"

I was now, but at least that gave me a perfect excuse to ask for details. "So we didn't do anything more than make out?"

She shook her head. "Not unless you did it with your clothes on. Or took them off and put them back on, then continued to make out. Which I guess isn't *impossible. . . .*"

"Not my style."

She laughed. "No, you're right."

We drove for a few minutes in companionable silence; then another question occurred to me. "At that party last weekend," I asked, "what was I drinking?"

"That was the worst part of it all," she said, then gave a huge laugh. "*Zima!*"

CHAPTER FOURTEEN

"OH, MY GOD," I SAID, AND HELD UP THE SIX-PACK OF ZIMA from the brown paper bag.

"You asked him for that?" she asked incredulously. "Way to lead him on!"

"No, he asked if I wanted 'the usual' and I said yes because I didn't know what *the usual* was to him, but figured it would be something I *usually* liked, so, whatever, this is what he gave me."

"Yuck."

"I know, but what am I supposed to do? Can you return beer? Or whatever this is?"

"Probably not." She shrugged. "We'll just deal." She turned left onto Falls Road and kept going the usual route to the lake. It didn't really matter what we had to drink, though straight vodka might have been good, as I'd already started the day with that. But the main thing was, no matter how I choked the story out, I just wanted to talk to her about this insane thing that was happening to me.

The radio played one hit after another that would now be featured on a "classics" station, but the DJs kept announcing them as "new hits" rather than "oldies." I sang along with every word to "Wonderwall" even though it was new and obscure, and Tanya looked at me sideways as if to ask what was wrong with me.

There was no way she'd ever really believe what was actually wrong with me.

But I was going to give it a try.

She parked on Alloway Drive in Potomac Falls, and we took the completely conspicuous brown bag of Zima along the path, past the last house on the left, over the large fallen tree I was always afraid to pass on a horse, and across the small creek that was always there, through rain or drought. Then the world opened up before us, the trees receded, and the lake spread out ahead, not as big as those up north, but still big enough to reflect the sky, clouds, and sun with some glory and solitude.

Most important was the solitude.

We stopped where we always did, on an open bank where we used to ride the horses into and out of the lake and always lost horseshoes in the thick mud. But I was grown up now, or close to it—according to the body I was in—so there were no horses, no swimming, no skating, nothing but some shitty alcoholic drinks and a quiet moment to say something thoroughly unbelievable.

We sat, the earth cool beneath us. I kicked a dead branch out of the way and dug my heels into the mushy lakeside mud, and said, "So. You want to hear something weird?"

"If it's less weird than you've been all day, yes," she said. "If you're going to add to the ante, I don't know."

I had to laugh. "I'm going to add to the ante."

"Then I don't know. Or I hope I don't know." She looked me in the eye. "Did you actually do Rusty Schwedan? Because I totally knew you did."

"No!" I objected too hard and too fast, given the lack of importance that accusation held either way. But still—I didn't do it! Rusty was her ex-boyfriend and he'd dumped her before she got the chance to get sick of him, so she'd always felt something there was lost. "You seriously think I could have done that without you knowing?"

She shrugged. "I don't know."

"Yes, you do."

"Well, whatever, it's just something I heard." She met my eyes again. "But I guess I didn't *really* believe it. I mean, Rusty, of all people . . . that would have been shitty of you."

"Tanya." I started out just saying it in the joking manner we'd always had, but then the reality of the situation took me over and I said, "Seriously. Please."

She looked at me, sobriety registering in her eyes. "You're really not pregnant, right? I shouldn't have joked about that earlier. I promise I wouldn't tell anyone if you were or anything, but that's not what this is about, is it?"

How clumsy. If I were pregnant, it would have been hard to admit at this point, but of course my truth was much harder than that.

"No," I said, trying to think of some gentle way to ease into what I needed to say. After all, I was supposed to be the adult here, in some way. I shouldn't be finding it so hard to talk to a teenager.

But I hesitated, because if she was going to be that potentially upset about a pregnancy, which I'd just shot down, how on earth would she react to my unbelievable story about being a time traveler?

"I'm not pregnant and I haven't had sex with your ex."

"Thank God," she said, fanning her face with her hand, completely oblivious to what I really had to tell her. "I could not take one more fucked-up thing this year, believe me."

That gave me pause. I hadn't remembered senior year as being particularly traumatic. "Define *fucked-up*."

She looked at me. "You know what fucked-up means. Pregnancies, police raids at parties, deaths, ex-boyfriends suddenly coming out as transsexual." That was Tuck Surjan, I remembered. Tanya's homecoming date, who had shown up with his six-foot-three frame garbed in a dress nicer than hers. He'd done it as a joke, but she had definitely not found it funny.

No woman wants her date to be prettier than she is.

"I'm not a transsexual," I said, with the only confidence I'd had all day.

"Good."

"But."

"God, no. Is it worse? Not transsexual but gay? Please don't tell me you're in love with me." Honestly, she actually looked serious. "Whatever you do, don't make a pass at me. . . ."

It cracked me up inside. That was so Tanya. Trying to anticipate and evade any and every possible uncomfortable situation that might be heading her way. Much better, and easier, for her to say, *Don't even try to tell me you're in love with me,* than to say, *Don't ever try to kiss me again, ew, I'm not into you!*

"But I'm in love with you," I said to her, my face so straight the corners of my mouth hurt.

"You are not—" She stopped and scrutinized me. "I see those dimples. You can't lie, you suck at it, so I know you're not in love with me. I'll cry about it later. Meanwhile, what the fuck is the deal? Why did we have to get a six-pack of fucking Zima and come here, of all places, on the night before the last day of school? You're freaking me out."

This was not the Tanya of the future, I have to say. I didn't remember that she had so much *shrillness* inside of her. In the future she was as calm and unflappable as could be, always wise, ready with good advice.

That was the Tanya I needed to talk to.

Right now it looked like I'd have to wait twenty years for her. And if I spent the next twenty years like this I'd probably end up in the loony bin.

I thought about that for a moment. What was the worst-case scenario? Never returning to my real *now*? In some ways that would seem like a blessing—financially, certainly, with my foreknowledge of where to invest—but I was already doing extremely well. For me, waiting twenty years would be biding my time. Learning the same lessons again, reliving deaths in horrible detail. All to reach the point where I could finally become thirty-eight, so I could move forward in my life.

To me, that was a nightmare.

"Speak up," Tanya said.

"Well," I began, "it's almost as unbelievable as me being in love with you. *Which I'm not.* So I need you to not totally mock me for this or dismiss it out of hand, even though it seems unbelievable."

She was frowning. If I were to guess, I'd say she was probably close to shaking it out of me. "What are you getting at?"

"You're my best friend," I said, with a whole lot more history under my belt than she could ever believe. "You will be for the rest of my life, as far as I can tell."

"Okay . . . ?"

Wow, this was so much easier in theory than in practice. There was no way she was going to believe me about this, when she already needed convincing about minor sexual escapades that happened—or didn't—a hundred years ago.

"Something really weird is happening to me."

Her shoulders lowered with exasperation. "You're killing me here. Can you just get to the point?"

"Remember when we went to that psychic in Georgetown and she seemed to know all that stuff about us? And we couldn't explain why, but we knew it was real?"

"Vaguely."

We *had* enjoyed a lot of beers that night at Crazy Horse. In fact, it's possible that's why, in memory, I thought the accuracy had been so uncanny.

"Okay, well, my point is that we both know that unexplainable phenomenon can and *does* happen. All the time."

"I guess."

"So what if I told you that I have been to the future? That I'm coming from the future right now?"

She screwed up her face and studied me for a very tense moment before cracking up. "Holy shit, you almost had me. I was trying to imagine telling your mom you'd popped your clutch and had to be taken to St. Elizabeth's. I mean I was right there, mentally, really, to have you committed. Good one, Raim. So now that you've broken the ice, what did you *really* want to talk about?"

Not the response I'd been expecting. I hadn't even gotten my toes wet in the truth and she'd drowned me. This was a very clear sign that I had to shut up about it. Now.

I made a show of sighing, and took a swig of Zima. This stuff was even worse than I remembered. Like flat Sprite. I hated it. "All right, I haven't exactly *been* to the future, but I had a premonitory dream last night. And you were there."

"Yeah? If I was there, I guess that means I wasn't dead. So that's a good sign right there."

"No, Tanya. You were happy. You were married and had two kids and you were happy."

"Really?" Her skeptical face went a little pink with pleasure. Everyone liked to believe good stuff was coming for them. "Did I marry Kenny? I did, right?"

Had I said yes, her skepticism would have dissolved. She would have jumped right on board with believing me. But of course the answer wasn't yes and I didn't want her to spend her life imagining she was supposed to have married some guy who never knew who she was. "No. Totally different guy. You don't even know him yet." It occurred to me that I could give her some valuable hope here. "So next time you're feeling brokenhearted? Forget it. The real guy, the one you love enough to marry, is still out there waiting for you."

Her face fell. She'd been counting on Kenny. She had a

"psychic feeling" that he was *The One*, and for most of high school she'd maneuvered around the halls and keg parties, looking for the opportunity to bring her fate to fruition. I measured my next words very carefully, knowing that, even though she probably shouldn't, she was likely to take them very seriously. "You wouldn't trade that guy or those girls for anything in the world. You'll be so glad you waited. Trust me."

CHAPTER FIFTEEN

SHE LOOKED AT ME WITH A CHALLENGE IN HER EYE. A CHAL-
lenge *and* a question. And I knew her well enough to know the
question was stronger. "What are their names?"

"You'll find out!"

She sighed. "You're just messing with me."

"I'm not."

"Okay, then, what did I do for a living?"

I hesitated. She was a paralegal who ended up marrying her
boss; her husband was a criminal attorney. But I didn't want to
tell her *any* of that because what if, for some reason, in this sur-
reality she was on a different path? I didn't want to influence her
unduly. Set her up for a self-fulfilling prophecy that wasn't really
her own destiny.

"I don't know *all* the details," I ended up saying. "Come on.
It would have been a pretty boring dream if we sat around talking
about our jobs, wouldn't it?"

"Not if my job was movie star."

"If I knew for sure you were going to be a movie star, I'd be a lot nicer to you."

"Hmm. That's probably true."

A few seconds passed, and she tentatively asked, "Was there anything else? In the dream, I mean. About me?"

I could have spent days telling her about her future. "Not really." I shrugged. "We were, like, in our thirties. All I know is that you were really, really happy. The details are kind of foggy now. You know how dreams are. . . ."

She nodded. "But that's good to hear, you know?"

"Oh, definitely. The future's bright!"

Apart from some horrifying historical moments, political scandals, market catastrophes, and, for each of us, our fair share of heartache as well as happiness. But there was no need to point that out. Everyone knows life isn't always great and fair. Sometimes it's enough to just have faith that it's going to get better, that the sun *will* come out again.

We clinked bottles and finished, then put the two empties back into the six-pack.

"I hate that stuff," I said.

"Me too."

"It smells like"—I sniffed it—"antiseptic. The hospital." I felt a gag reflex tighten my throat.

"Huh?" She frowned and sniffed her bottle. "I think it's like 7Up. It's good with a Jolly Rancher in it."

"Ugh. You really *are* eighteen, aren't you?"

"Yeah . . . ? So are you."

My face went hot. "Sorry. Dream joke."

"Ohhh."

"And I don't remember making out with Jer Norton."

"I'm not surprised." She rolled her eyes, like suddenly she was the superior one. "That night I don't think you even remembered your own *name*."

Usually I didn't drink that much. I got full or dizzy before I could ever have enough to black out. But there *had* been some occasions around graduation where the partying was hard. There was no denying it. Apparently the results were as unfortunate as I might have feared.

It just made me feel funny to know I had cheated on Brendan and didn't even remember it. Cheating was something that really bugged me. It always had. I never did it (usually) and, to my knowledge, no one ever did it to me.

In fact, that's why I'd actually broken up with Brendan. There had been moments of jealousy, of course, but the bottom line was that I thought it was too constraining for us to go from being high school sweethearts to being married forever, but I wasn't going to step out on him to experience other people, so there seemed like there was no choice but to end it and move on.

In retrospect, no great shakes had come along. There are a lot of clichés and adages about every relationship and event in our lives somehow enriching us and making us stronger, better, smarter, you name it. But to be perfectly honest, I've had a lot of experiences, and memories, in my life that I could have done very well without.

Most of them had to do with dating.

So, yeah, we'll skip the platitudes here. What I really wanted, and had a renewed determination to do, was to figure out exactly what I needed to have a do-over here, and how it would change my life in the future. Whether it was related to Brendan, my parents, my career, or a stray cat I should have rescued, I needed to figure out what had gone so wrong in my life that evidently I had to come back and fix it.

My gut told me that it was Brendan.

But, on more than one occasion, my gut had been a big fat liar.

"Let's go," Tanya said. "I want to go to the mall and get something awesome to wear tomorrow night. I have got to look hot for Kenny. Tomorrow night," she said knowingly, "is the night. Whether *you* think so or not."

I, on the other hand, knew tomorrow *wasn't* the night. Because *no* night ever ended up being the night. Within two years she would have all but forgotten him, but there was obviously no way to convince her of that right now.

Funny how fickle fate could be for teenage girls.

Oh, well, it was always fun to have a crush, to have someone to dress up for, whom you hoped would notice and appreciate it.

It had been a long time since I'd felt that way.

Come to think of it, I was in the rare position of knowing about *tomorrow* night. Brendan would be picking me up and I had the chance to, for once in my high school life, wear something flattering, and do my hair and makeup in a more subtle, and attractive, way.

"You know *everyone's* going to be there, right?" she questioned. "I mean, even kids from Wootton. This is going to be huge. We might both hook up with our future husbands there!"

Nope.

I was going to get mad at Brendan and eventually break up with him if I didn't get to stay long enough to stop that.

The party was *important*.

The more I thought about it, the more I felt like tomorrow night would be the end of this ordeal. That I could, maybe, undo what might have been the biggest mistake of my life.

"One more thing, Tanya," I said, measuring my words really carefully. "In that dream?" Surely this small detail wouldn't hurt. Especially since I knew she was going to go through some struggles before she got to feel contentment.

"Uh-huh?"

"You had a very happy life. There is a lot of good stuff coming that you can't even believe right now," I said, hoping these words would sink in and comfort her deeply—though perhaps without a remembered source—"you had daughters in particular." Maybe going that specific, without going further, would even knock that jerk Kenny, and the three boys she thought she was going to have with him if he ever noticed her, right on out of her head. "All you have to do to get there is follow your heart."

THE NEXT DAY would be the last—the day we took the rest of our books back and had our teachers sign off on everything—and I was acutely aware that it would be my last chance to experience high school.

Even writing that now it sounds silly. It was well *past* my last chance to experience high school, but somehow I'd ended up in this place of repeats and I didn't know how many days, hours, or minutes I was going to get to relive.

However, when I woke up the next morning in my old room, I knew the dream, or whatever, wasn't over yet.

I decided to walk in to school. It was just a few blocks; I don't know why we had been all about driving it anyway. But since graduating, it was a walk I'd taken many times, with my mom and her dog, and I was eager to take another look at the area as it *was*, rather than as it is now.

Potomac has a reputation for being very posh and wealthy. Even when I was in high school it had held that distinction, but for me it had been a very average suburban place. The set for just about any nineties family sitcom you could name.

There had always been *nicer* areas, of course, but it was undaunting, back then, to live near them. When I'd checked Ted Koppel in for a court at the Potomac Tennis Club, I'd thought of him as a "local anchor," not fully taking in his national reach at the time. There were a handful of other very prominent anchors and actors there, too, though I was always more wowed that the boxer Sugar Ray Leonard lived a mile from me, than by the fact that the actress who played Wonder Woman was also a stone's throw away.

There was even a rumor that the creator of *Beverly Hills, 90210* had gone to my high school and based that show on it, and when you took "Beverly Hills" out of it, I could see how that might be true. Back then.

Now the wealth was much more evident. And, to be honest, I was a bit sad for it. Yards that I could remember playing Ghost in the Graveyard in on summer nights were now expensively manicured and cordoned off. Houses that used to welcome trick-ortreaters with hot cider and candy on brisk Halloween nights now turned off their lights and turned on their alarms.

So it was really nice to be able to walk up the old, familiar road to school one more time, and pass the houses as they once were: garage doors were open, weed whackers and rakes hung on the walls, lawn mowers rested, covered in green specks, with the scent of gasoline rising off of them and mingling with the sweet fresh grass scent, to make that perfect perfume of late spring.

The cars in the driveways were humbler too: dented Chevettes, a couple old muscle cars, and the fanciest of the lot were BMW 320i's and the odd Mercedes here and there.

In short, this was my childhood neighborhood like I'd never see it again. It was beautiful.

The school was different then too. Very ordinary, big flat brick building. There was a marquee-style sign out front with its name and relevant dates, including, right now, LAST DAY OF SCHOOL. Later, the entire thing would be rebuilt, the name emblazoned on the brick, the building carrying off the look of a very fancy theater.

And it was, basically. What was high school, but theater, drama, role-playing?

I was doing it right now. Only I was getting ready to go in and play myself again. Someone I hadn't been in a long, long time.

We had A days and B days back then. Yesterday had been an A day, and that had covered half my classes, though I'd seen virtually everyone there was to see and remember. Now I'd just see them again. And maybe it would be less alarming. I hoped so.

But the minute I walked onto the campus, I knew that wasn't

to be. There, right inside the front door, effectively blocking the hall from anyone who might want to slip past, was Anna Farrior and her group of bitchy, hair-sprayed, made-up (and made up pretty well, I hated to admit) friends. Perfect hair, perfect skin, perfect teeth, tiny waists, narrow shoulders—they were a breed unto themselves and I had never matched them, not even when I was nine.

For some reason, Anna had had it in for me since tenth grade.

"Oh, look, it's *Ramie*," one of her friends said as I walked through the door. I hadn't even had the chance to *notice* them yet, but leave it to one of those bitches to call attention to me.

Anna looked up, the leader called to attention. She raked her gaze across me like she was looking at vomit on the ground outside Nordstrom's automatic doors. "And she still hasn't got that makeup thing down." She shook her head. "What an infant."

I remembered her saying this kind of thing to me. Making fun of me because of my makeup and because I occasionally had a breakout, which she found so repulsive that it was apparently a disservice to the entire school community that I didn't cover it up properly.

Her razzing used to bug me a lot. It was humiliating. I could literally remember hurrying past and fighting tears when this stuff had begun.

But now, of course . . . now it just sounded stupid. It *was* stupid.

Best ignored, as any grown person would say.

Unfortunately, that was what my mother had said, and so Anna was used to counter-striking when I ignored her.

"Oh, don't be *embarrassed*, Ramie," she said, so loudly that it would have been impossible for *anyone* who was the object of her derision to *not* be embarrassed. "No one notices you anyway."

I stopped. Normally I would have scurried along and hoped this kind of crap would be long past when I got to college, but this stopped me cold. I wondered why it never had before.

I turned and took a few steps back toward her.

Predictably, her stupid friends made a small collective *oooh* sound and opened ranks so she was facing me. Honestly, it was just like a movie about high school. I guess clichés really *do* exist for a reason.

"Looks like *you* did," I commented.

Anna raised her chin. "Looks like I did what?"

"Noticed me."

Uncertainty crossed her eyes. "Well—"

"I mean"—I gave a laugh—"you *just* said 'no one notices you anyway' to me, *proving* that you did the very thing you were claiming *no one* does. Which begs the question, Anna, why are you so jealous of me?"

Her face *flamed* red. "Me? Jealous of *you*? Ha!" She made a point of false laughter and looked to her sycophants to back her up, which they did, albeit somewhat limply and with an overall sense of confusion.

"Yeah." I nodded. "It's pretty obvious, don't you think? I can't walk anywhere near you without you making some comment about me. *To* me. Though you pretend it's to all of them." I swept an arm, indicating her friends. "But don't you think they're on to you too? I mean, no one pays so much attention to one person, right down to criticizing their makeup, unless they feel threatened. Obviously." I caught the eye of Dawn Jacowski, who was still something of an outside member of Anna's group and who had been in my psychology class last semester. "Right?" I said to her, urging a nod.

She gave one too. A very vague one, followed by a quick, shamed look back at Anna.

"Anyway," I said, "I'd think you'd be *delighted* I never got 'that makeup thing down,' because that leaves the stores nice and full for *you* to go stock up. Which, from the looks of things, you must do pretty frequently." I could have been meaner. Part of me *longed* to be meaner. But since I really didn't understand what we had against each other, I didn't have it in me to try and *wound* her. Only to try and defend the part of me that had managed to be hurt by her bullshit for two and a half years.

I turned and walked away, fully expecting some sort of retort, but, to my amazement and great relief, she said nothing.

It was funny; Anna Farrior had been a recurring and annoying thorn in my side during those years of high school. Sometimes she was a major character in my memories—to this day I mentally rolled my eyes every time Facebook suggested maybe we knew each other because we had so many common high school connections.

But, for the most part, she was not part of my day-to-day memories of life.

I think the thing that gave her any power at all was the fact that she loomed large in one very important memory: my breakup with Brendan.

CHAPTER SIXTEEN

MY SCIENCE TEACHER, MR. GIULIANI, WAS MY FAVORITE EVER. Of all the people from high school, students *or* teachers, he was probably the one I wondered about the most. He had taught us about the Heisenberg principle of uncertainty *way* before *Breaking Bad* had come along on TV, and he had tried like hell to be engaging and get us enthusiastic about science. And he probably did ratchet up the interest of those who were already inclined. But most of his students didn't get, or care about, his brilliance.

To be honest, my worst grades had been in his class, because I just felt like I couldn't *get it*. It was the only time in my life I'd felt downright *stupid*. But he had been the teacher who I thought cared the most. Proven, perhaps, by the fact that he was my favorite even though I'd barely scraped by in the end with a *D* (and that was thanks to extra-credit work he'd given me).

Eventually, though, what he'd taught had begun to make sense to me. This, after college classes and twenty years of just plain *living*, and I'd often wished I could find him and thank him for his patience. Tell him it hadn't been all for naught.

He had reserved our last day of class for us to ask any lingering questions we had, just for the sake of *learning*, since our grades were already turned in. That's how passionate he was about his subject; he just wanted us to *learn*, to be as enthusiastic about the possibilities as he was.

I remembered that last day and the disappointment on his face when no one had raised a hand to ask anything even remotely interesting. There had been a lot of fidgeting, eagerness to leave for the last time, the quiet scratch of some surreptitious yearbook-signing. But no interest in our topic, or our instructor, now that he no longer had an impact on our futures.

I remember frantically trying to come up with an interesting or relevant question that day, just to make him know that his efforts hadn't been in vain, but I'd done too poorly to have retained anything.

Now, however, that was no longer the case.

I raised my hand.

To his credit, he didn't show any impatience or lack of faith in what I was going to ask, though he was probably ready to bet money I was going to ask for a hall pass to go to the bathroom. "Ramie!" he said, as if he were delighted to entertain anything I might say. "Question?"

"Yes." I cleared my throat. "I've been reading up since finals"— certainly *some* explanation was necessary, and telling him I'd come up with some thoughts after being desperate enough on a long flight to read an article in *Scientific American* probably wasn't going to play—"and I think I've finally figured some things out."

He looked very pleasantly surprised. "Excellent."

"So I've been thinking. Do you think if we all had our stem cells from birth, which is obviously too late for all of *us*, we would be able to reintroduce them into our systems with some regularity and, theoretically, extend our lives and resist disease continuously? You know, kind of like using bio-identical hormones to maintain certain systems?"

To say he looked shocked would be a vast understatement. "What an incredible insight!" His unexpected enthusiasm, and I suppose my unexpected comprehension, got the attention of some other students, who looked up at him with curiosity.

Mr. Giuliani composed himself and said, "I have proposed this as a longevity intervention myself. Yes, if we could figure out how to introduce them so they differentiate correctly into adult stem cells, that could work. They have tried simply injecting stem cells into arms or legs and they produce teratomas, which are cyst pockets of all kinds of mixed-up tissues, including sometimes teeth and bones."

"Gross!" someone said, echoing probably everyone's thoughts, but, at the same time, calling the attention of some other students who had resisted the siren call of Ramie Phillips getting something right in science.

Mr. Giuliani nodded, clearly thrilled. "Really yucky. But there is a whole field called regenerative medicine that is working on using embryonic stem cells to renew several specific kinds of tissues, like regrowing damaged spinal cord tissue. Allowing the paralyzed to walk again."

It was rather amazing that we'd all had access to such a brilliant mind in high school and we'd wasted it by coming into class
high or sharing notes and copying others on tests.

It was Kelvin Lee who spoke next, unsurprisingly. He aced
everything. I don't know what became of him as an adult, but
I'm positive he's at the very top of *whatever* field he entered. "You
said there is a hierarchy of cells, adult stem cells that can differentiate into specific blood, muscle, or other kinds of normal cells.
Does that mean that even during the gestation period those stem
cells go from being essentially anything to having designated
properties? So that by the time the baby is born, and cord blood
can be safely collected, some of the 'universal' qualities are gone?"

Honestly, Mr. Giuliani looked like he had just learned he'd
won the lottery. "The short answer is yes for most of the cells
in the newborn baby itself. The baby has much growing to do,
but by that time all two hundred varieties of cells are already in
existence. But the placenta and the cord both contain a lot of
embryonic-like stem cells, and these are often being used for harvesting stem cells nowadays."

I took a shot at one more question. "Is there some safe method
of harvesting stem cells prior to birth?"

He nodded. "You could probably get them from the amni-
otic fluid, but I would not want to mess with the fetus itself;
that could be dangerous. But just one tiny cell could be repli-
cated to create an infinite number, if needed. It's actually very
old technology."

Kelvin raised his hand, but the bell rang and in the clatter of
everyone eagerly gathering their things to get the heck out of
there—cysts with teeth were one thing, but replicating cells

didn't light a fire under the average student—his question was lost in the chaos.

When I walked past Mr. Giuliani to go out the door, Kelvin was talking with him privately and Mr. Giuliani looked more *alive* than I'd ever seen him before. It gave my heart a little thrill. I'd always wanted to thank him for caring about my education, but I'd never found a way.

Maybe now, in some small way, I had.

EVEN THOUGH IT had been a long, long time, I think I can honestly and confidently say that I had never come home from school as rattled as I did that last day.

When I was little we went to Disney World. I remember going on the Haunted Mansion ride and being terrified, but compelled, by all the "ghosts" there, the stories implied by the setting and decorations there. I'd even gotten a set of View-Master slides, which I played in my room on the ceiling, rewatching, reliving, the ghostly ride and scaring myself to sleep each night.

It was so perfectly rendered as fantasy that I never believed it deep in my soul. I always knew it was pretend, and that's why I had the luxury of spooking myself. I think human beings have a need to *feel* big things, particularly in the safety of home or bed, or a theme park where they can walk off the ride and get an ice cream shaped like a mouse head covered in hard chocolate and forget the fear in ten minutes.

But the experience I had going back to school and interacting with all those ghosts from my actual past—including some kids who were headed toward their doom, whether death or ruin, and had no idea—was seriously disconcerting. I felt completely discombobulated and didn't know what to do with myself.

"Why are you so frickin' quiet?" Tanya asked on the way home. "Hello? Last day of school—you're supposed to be elated."

I looked at her. "Are you?"

"Obviously!"

"Do you realize how much is over?"

She snorted. "Yeah. English, math, typing, notes for being late, notes for being sick, visits to the principal's office. I think I have a pretty good idea how much is over."

I smiled. "True. But, Tanya, this is the end of our childhoods. This is the end of all the things we *had* to do. It's like . . . there really is no Santa Claus."

She feigned a look of shock and horror. "*What?*"

I sighed. "You know what I mean. We've gone from kindergarten to twelfth grade with at least half these people. That's almost like being in the cradle. Now we're finished."

"I could not be happier about this." Her tone was definite. She guided the car carefully down Gainsborough Road, where there were always speed traps around the turnoff for my house. "And neither could you. You've said the exact same thing for the past month. Now, all of a sudden, you're this old woman looking back on our lives like they're over. Get ahold of yourself!"

Was I an old woman? Was thirty-eight so old compared to eighteen? I used to think I had a pretty good grip on things like age. Other teenagers would talk about thirty like it was the other side of midnight, but I knew thirty was still young. Didn't I?

Well, I certainly did now.

"So—tonight," Tanya said, tired of the Vitamin C song I was paraphrasing. "What are you wearing to the party?"

"I don't know, cutoffs, a cute top. Something that looks like I'm not trying."

"Hmm." She nodded, considering this. "Good plan. I got a strapless cotton dress at Express last night, but I think maybe your plan is better. Look like we just came in from walking the dog."

I laughed out loud. That was a perfect description. "Exactly. The walking-the-dog look. We'll start a sensation. Honestly, we should be designers."

She nodded and turned onto my street, slowing down next to my house. "You want me to drive?"

Actually, I had originally gone with Brendan, but when we'd gotten in that fight, Tanya was already gone and I'd walked home. It had been a *long* walk. "Yeah, if you don't mind."

"No problem."

I opened the door. "Call me before you come."

"I'll be here at seven. Make sure your ass is ready."

"*Call* me so I can be!"

She gave an exaggerated sigh. "Fine, fine, fine. Whatever you want, Princess Di. Let me know if there's any other way I can be of service to you."

"I'll give it some thought."

"Great."

I shut the door and turned to go up the freshly cut front lawn. It smelled of grass and earth, with a hint of the wet-penny smell of the neighbors' sprinkler, which was easing back and forth over a small patch they'd reseeded. I had to hand it to them, though, the Connors' lawn always looked fantastic. Even to this day. All their work paid off. Even if it did make the rest of the lawns in the neighborhood look burned out and shabby.

I opened the front door, smiling at the old creak of it, and was about to go upstairs and prepare for my first teenage party in twenty years when I heard my mother's voice from the kitchen.

"Ramie." It was sharp. Angry.

"Yeah?"

"Come in here." This was about the harshest I'd ever heard her. "*Now.*"

CHAPTER SEVENTEEN

THIS WAS A TONE I HADN'T HEARD IN A LONG TIME. ADMIT-
tedly not quite twenty years; I'd continued to get in trouble for
a long time past high school, but still.

"What's wrong?" I asked, walking into the kitchen. My mind
was at ease, but my body responded with a familiar twinge of
apprehension. Guilt. Bracing myself for the worst.

She leaned both hands on the counter, fingertips pointing to
the sides, her weight on her palms. "Do *you* want to tell *me* what's
wrong, Ramie Jane?"

She almost never called me that. Later she'd told me she didn't
even know why she'd given me that middle name, since she hated
it—it was only that it flowed. It certainly did now, when she was
apparently using it to make a point. "I'm . . . not sure?"

"There's nothing you want to tell me?"

"About the last day of school? I didn't get my grades yet, but
as I recall they were—"

"About the missing vodka," she interrupted, just in the nick of time, actually. Snippy, angry, but she stopped me from doing any "mysterious prognosticating" about my grades and graduation.

"What missing vodka?" I asked, for a moment completely forgetting the previous morning.

"I came in here this afternoon to make sauce for my penne alla vodka and took the bottle out to find there was a *considerable* amount missing." She raised an eyebrow in that way that used to be completely intimidating to me. It was a motherly art. "I know because I had it out to make screwdrivers for bridge last week, so I know *exactly* how much was in the bottle."

My first mental response was, *Phew!* followed by a quick, *I thought it was something serious.* "Oh, *that.* I had some yesterday morning before school. I was so nervous you wouldn't believe." I shook my head, and meant it more than she could ever imagine. "It was gross, but better than throwing up my Froot Loops all over because I was so nervy."

She looked at me in disbelief. "So you admit it? You had vodka for breakfast?" Her tone was new. Something between heartbreak and defeat. Like I'd just admitted something that, in the mother-daughter game, I was supposed to deny, and now I'd broken the barrier and she was going to have to *deal* with it.

How did I keep forgetting? Maybe it was because her kitchen hadn't been redecorated in decades, so my subconscious kept finding this environment to be *normal*, in part. And, let's face it, I wasn't used to being eighteen.

"Wait, no." I thought fast. Not well, but at least fast. Vodka

for breakfast sounded bad. I'd never do that under normal circumstances, but it was far worse under *these* circumstances.

"What do you mean, *no?*" she demanded. "The vodka is missing. I think we just established that quite clearly."

Think think think. "No, I didn't *drink* it. I was nervous about
how I *looked*. And I just read in a magazine how rinsing your hair
with vodka makes it really shiny." I touched a lock and pulled it
around as if I were trying to examine it. "But I'm not sure it really
made much of a difference. What do you think?"

"I think that sounds like a lie."

I feigned surprise. "What do you mean?"

"How, pray tell, would rinsing your hair with vodka keep you
from throwing up because of your nerves?"

Good point. Of course. Although the whole rinsing-with-
vodka thing really does make your hair shiny. "You know, because I didn't think I looked good." This was lame. Just like I
was in high school. So, in a way, I was being convincing, even
though my story was idiotic.

My mother was having none of it. "Go to your room."

"God, Mom, you don't seriously think I'd have vodka for
breakfast, do you? How gross!"

"Your room!"

"O . . . kay?" I mean, what could I say? I'd done it. She didn't
know who I was now; she only knew who I was "now," so this
was an infraction of the rules. "Why?"

"You're grounded."

Grounded! I was grounded? I couldn't be grounded! I didn't
know how long I would be here, and I *had* to go to that party

tonight. "But, Mom, it's the last day of school! There's a party tonight! I can't miss that!"

"Oh, you're missing it, all right!"

"Mom!" Suddenly I really felt the urgency to not be in trouble. "It's the last chance for a last-day-of-school party. Come on, please? Don't make me miss out because of one *understandable* mistake!"

"*Understandable?*" She scoffed. Really well, in fact; I realized now where I had learned my best derision skills—from her. "I can't trust you!"

But she could! I'd always been really careful, even in high school. She *could* trust me! Especially now—I was a grown-up! Why, I was more capable of handling any sort of emergency or problem than anyone else who would be at that party! I had to pull out my adult powers of persuasion. "Mom, seriously, do you think I could have *made up* such a crazy story? You know you can trust me."

She looked at me evenly. "You're right."

"I am?"

"Yes, it *is* a crazy story. Go to your room." Her voice was firm. Like, steel-firm.

This wasn't good.

I needed to think, though. And she needed to calm down. This was something I'd learned in the years since high school. If I stood here and argued with her, she was going to continue to say no, if only so that she wasn't teaching me that I could bull-doze her.

"Fine, I'll go upstairs. But will you *think* about it? Please?"

I could see her hesitate, so I jumped on it.

"I mean, seriously, *look* at my hair. Smell it!" Because confidence went a long way toward covering a lie, I moved toward her, but she shot me a look and I stopped. "Anyway, you saw me yesterday morning and I was obviously not drunk. I mean, I'd totally have been drunk if I drank all the stuff I poured over my hair, wouldn't I?"

"Well . . ." She looked wobbly within her determination. And it wasn't because she was weak or ineffectual; it was because she trusted me. I knew that. I always knew that.

But I couldn't *count* on it now until *she* realized it.

"Think about that, Mom. Please." I didn't give her a chance to refuse. Instead I just turned and headed for the stairs. "I'm doing what you asked because I know you hate when I argue, but please let logic prevail here. You know me. I'm not a drinker and you *know* it!"

Yes, it was a semi-lie—I'd had the vodka in the morning, but at the time in question, the age at which I was being accused of this indiscretion, I definitely *didn't* drink much, and since then I'd never had cause to worry that there was a problem. So I didn't feel an iota of guilt for fibbing.

On top of that, I had seen my mom have screwdrivers with brunch many times while I was delicately sipping a mimosa so I could be the designated driver. That was vodka for breakfast! And for another thing—it can't be said too much—I was thirty-eight years old. My teenage self and future were not in jeopardy because I'd calmed my time-traveling nerves a little bit the other morning before school.

I went upstairs, Zuzu following me, her nails clicking solemnly on the wood, and hoped like hell my mother would reconsider.

But given the state she was in—and the state she thought *I* was in—that didn't seem all that likely.

"I'M GROUNDED," I had to announce to Tanya two hours later. It was time to be getting ready for the party and I'd done my hair and picked out a perfect walking-the-dog outfit, but my mother had been unmoved by my argument. I'd already called Brendan and left a message that I was in trouble and things were iffy for tonight.

I didn't know what to do.

"What do you mean, you're grounded?"

"I mean I can't go tonight."

"*What?* That is not possible. You *have* to go!" She sounded like I was the mother and *she* was the one being grounded.

"I know! I'm *trying!*" I knew the truth was I was going to have to go no matter what. I just really hoped I didn't have to sneak out, because I had no idea what the ramifications for that would end up being.

"Well, try *harder!*"

"I will! It's just that I don't know if I can go when you're ready to."

"It's graduation night. We have, like, no parties, no high school fun left. This is the end of everything, and—"

Call waiting beeped in.

"—you will be there."

It didn't take a lot of imagination to realize she was talking yet again about her one perceived last chance at marital bliss with a guy who, as of yet—and as of our adult lives—had still not noticed her.

"Okay, Tanya."

"So, *seriously*, you have *got* to work on your parents because—"

Call waiting beeped again. I wanted to answer it, even though we didn't have caller ID yet.

I knew it was Brendan.

"Tanya, I have to go," I said, knowing there was little time after the second beep. The call would be dismissed—we didn't have voice mail yet—and he would be gone for now. I couldn't afford to lose any time. "I'll do my best and call you back to let you know."

"But—"

I didn't wait for her reply. I knew what it would be. She wanted me to do whatever I had to do to go; it was no different from any other time I'd been in trouble and unable to go out with her on a planned evening. I was always the letdown, the buzz kill who ruined everything because of my *stupid strict parents* (whom I appreciated now more than ever).

But this time, I really did want to get out of my punishment.

I clicked the receiver over.

"Hello?"

"Are you the girl in the iron mask?" Brendan asked, a smile in his voice.

I'd always liked that about him, how he got nearly every reference I could throw at him and how he threw some unexpected ones back. The girl in the iron mask. Trapped in my prison, unable to go out, much as I wanted to. My face . . . not my own.

That was good. Even today, that was pretty good. Better than he could have known.

"So far," I said, thinking about how alien I felt when I looked in the mirror now. "It's not looking good." Except it was. I never would have said I was the prettiest thing on earth, or even in the top 20 percent, but compared to the older, somewhat stressed face I'd left behind, I was definitely looking pretty good.

"This stupid party doesn't matter." Brendan's reaction was a stark contrast to Tanya's. "I can meet you out back later if you want. Or climb the magnolia tree and come in your window."

"I hate that."

"I know."

The stupid scrapy tree against my window was bad enough without a teenage guy climbing up it and making it scream against the siding like a demon. Sometimes at night it was really scary, even if the scraping was because of a regular old summer thunderstorm meandering through the lazy, soft suburbs of Washington, D.C.

"So, no. I mean, I could sneak out back if it came to that, but let me talk to my parents first. Try and do this right." The truth was, everything had to go as close to "normal" as it could. If Brendan skipped the party and came to my house instead—even if I told him not to—it would inevitably shift the sequence of events, and I didn't want that.

"Okay, so you do that." His voice was so nice. Even by my thirty-eight-year-old standards, it was a good voice, low and masculine, with a really subtle hint of rasp. Not enough that an impressionist could make him hilarious, or even mildly funny, but enough to make me tingly. "All right, Raim?"

"I'll let you know," I said, mentally reciting the phone number I'd never forgotten. "Either way, I'll let you know." I paused and then asked, "Brendan?"

"Yeah?"

"I want you to go, even if I can't."

"Mm." I could visualize him shrugging. "We'll see."

"You can always come here tomorrow."

"Whatever you want."

I had no idea what I wanted.

Apart from him, that is. At this moment, I wanted him. And who knew how long I'd be here to *have* him? But back then? I was not in touch with what I'd wanted at all. A beer? To party and dance? To forget? To *remember*? Was this a last hurrah for me or a first blowout? I couldn't say, because it held the potential for so much.

And yet, I knew now, with the advantage of age, it also held the potential for so little.

So little.

Meanwhile, I had to let his life play out the way it was supposed to. It wasn't all about me.

"I'll call you back," I said. "As soon as I know what we're doing. But, Brendan . . ."

"Ramie."

"Be happy, okay? Do what you need to."

He laughed. "I'll give that a try."

We hung up, but while I knew that once I would have felt confident, even with his answer, this time I wondered exactly what he meant.

CHAPTER EIGHTEEN

I DECIDED TO ASK MY FATHER.

When I was growing up, I'd actually felt closer to my mother, but now that I was in this weird vortex of return, and I knew he was actually gone from my time, I think my concentration on his aliveness made him feel more approachable to me.

Which may seem crazy, now that I think about it. I mean, the very fact that he was actually gone presumably could and should have made him *less* approachable to me. Nevertheless, I thought I'd have better luck getting out of my grounding with him.

When I heard him come in the front door at 5:23 (like clockwork, it was always between 5:20 and 5:25, though usually—I had noticed—5:23), I hurried down to meet him and ask if he could come talk to me in my room when he was settled.

Settled usually meant he'd had a bourbon on the rocks. A small one; if I were measuring, I'd say no more than two fingers *with* ice, but he had it every evening. I'd like to say it added to his longevity, since we all want to say alcohol consumption leads to longevity, but his early demise would suggest otherwise, though I'm sure it didn't contribute in any way to his death.

"Have a seat and let's talk now," he said, easy, completely un-self-conscious of my mother's overhearing ears.

"I'm *grounded*," I stage-whispered, half hoping my mom could actually hear, wherever she was. "And it's *totally unfair*."

"Ah." He laughed. *Laughed!* "Then you'd better get back to Elba, huh?"

Another good reference. Napoleon. I had to appreciate it. "Very funny, Dad. Can you just hurry? It's important."

"Ten-four." He saluted me. "I'll come talk to you as soon as I get cleaned up."

"Hurry."

"You can't rush genius." It was his old joke.

Which led to mine. "So I can rush you?"

As always, he tilted his head and looked at me as if I'd just said the most insulting thing imaginable. "Yes." He didn't smile outwardly, but it was in his voice.

I went upstairs, vaguely annoyed and thinking maybe I should have just approached my mother with a Clarence Darrow–worthy argument and skipped Dad altogether, since he clearly was going to take the whole thing lightly—that old act all but assured me of that—and undoubtedly side with Mom.

I waited for what seemed like forever. I spent about ten minutes putting makeup on—this young face was so much easier to do than I had thought at the time!—then tidied my room, went through the cedar chest at the foot of my bed (all linens! nothing interesting at all!), and even organized my cheap mall jewelry. Then I sat on the bed, scratching Zuzu's belly for what seemed like forever, although it was strangely meditative.

Finally Dad came to the door, knocked twice, and came on in.

"I talked to your mother," he said without preamble as he sat next to me on the bed. "She said you drank a great deal of vodka."

"I told her I used it to rinse my hair," I said vehemently. Because, yes, I *had* told her that. Then, with every bit as much sincerity, I added, "I read that it makes your hair shiny."

"It also makes school seem a little easier," he said. "If you have to face a tough day and you're nervous."

I felt my face grow hot. How did he know? Then I remembered: old me had forgotten I was young me and had been very frank with my mom about my need for alcoholic enhancement before going to school.

"Okay," I told my father. "Though it's true, I *did* read that a vodka rinse makes your hair shiny. Beer too. Remember that beer shampoo I used to have?" I probably had it in the shower right now, but he probably hadn't ever noticed it. For some reason I just felt compelled to defend the idea that alcohol=beauty when utilized in a nonconsumptive way.

Which was, we all knew, not the way I'd used it.

And his raised eyebrows made clear that he knew that wasn't the way I'd used it. So rather than fighting the foolish fight, I went on, "So it's not like that *idea* was out of the question; it's just that, yes, yesterday I was particularly nervous about school." I thought about it and, before he could answer, added, "More nervous than I have ever been in my life. For that one day. So, yes, I used a crutch. But that doesn't mean I have a *problem* or that I'm *bad* or anything negative like that. It was just a tough day. And it's going to be a tough night, but I just hope you will agree to let me have the tough night I need, rather than the one you punish me into."

He leaned back, though there was nothing to lean back on, sitting on the soft mattress of my bed, and let out a long sigh. "You know this is hard for me."

"Actually, Dad"—I gave a semi-involuntary but humorless laugh—"I have no idea what this is like for you. None at all. But I know it's hard as hell for me."

He was unfazed by my uncharacteristically harsh language. "We're in similar boats, you and I."

I frowned. "How so?" Mom was no tyrant to him. He had always had the final say in everything. Even though I was nearly twenty years outside of his rule, I was all but begging for his help and he was giving me this nonsense about being in the same boat with me? Like he couldn't help, we both just had to hope Mom would be benevolent?

I was all ready to go off on him, attacking him for that and for his retro-misogynistic comment, when he said, softly, "We don't know how to help each other. We want to do the right thing, but even with an elevated vantage point, neither of us knows what the right thing really is to say or do."

That gave me pause. *Elevated vantage point* seemed a bit grandiose for his parental role—good lord, he had *no idea* what I was really going through (if I didn't myself, how could he?)—yet of course he still had to take the high road to my low.

"I'm sorry," I said, figuring that was the easiest out in a case like this. They had me nailed, as far as they were concerned. I was smart enough, in retrospect, to work from my disadvantage, rather than cover my eyes and ears and pretend something other than the truth. "Okay, yes, I drank some vodka before school because I was so nervous that I figured if I didn't have that, I'd probably end up puking right in the hall in front of everyone. Just imagine that!"

"Vodka can do that too."

Sigh. "Well, yes, but this was a major panic attack. Not a psychological I-don't-think-I-can, but a physiological freak-out. So"—I shrugged, I couldn't even help it—"I did what made the most sense, given that I had two and a half minutes to think."

There was a long pause as he surveyed me. "Alcohol is never the answer. You know that."

"It was yesterday."

"Why? Because you thought you *couldn't* handle it on your own? Of course you can. Why can't you be the mature person you're supposed to be and just take a deep breath and move forward unaided?"

"Maybe because life is a *little* hard to go through unaided?" I answered sarcastically, then realized how bad that sounded. Particularly given the case I was trying to plead. "Though usually I do. It's better than smoking all those cigarettes, right?" It was kind of a low blow, but he didn't know it was as much as I did.

He looked down, though. "Touché."

I'd taken a few pre-law classes in school, when I thought I was going to move into that field, but I'd stopped and switched to finance after my father died; still, I tried to pull out the would-be lawyer in me. "So I was nervous about school ending. It was a big challenge, more than you could ever know or believe, and I had only a few minutes to make the decision that was fastest and easiest and *safest* for me, so I did. I had a couple of shots of vodka. I watched you drink six Irish coffees at Normandie Farm one night, so don't tell me I'm in some kind of danger zone."

He laughed. Heartily. "That was an unusual night for me," he said, more to whatever small, imaginary audience might have been in his lap, where he was looking down and smiling while shaking his head, than to me. Was he trying to explain to my mother? Himself? "A fun night. A sleepless night. But a good one, and definitely unusual."

I tried to remember any salient facts from the night that I could, but nothing came to me. The truth was, at the time it had sounded like "coffees" to me, as I had no idea what the "Irish" added, and even so I didn't know or appreciate the danger of so much caffeine. So all that had remained in my mind, really, was the waitress's amazement, not my father's consumption.

But, of course, *now* I knew what all that Irish coffee meant. It meant a lot of shots of whiskey and a lot of caffeine. No health benefits whatsoever.

"No harm done, I suppose," he said with an offhand shrug.

"I'm not so sure."

He sighed, and I realized, for the first time, this wasn't really all about me. He was entering the last stretch of his life, and quickly. Now that I really looked at him—instead of marveling at my retro surroundings and friends and so on—I could see he was seriously faded. In my memory, which is quite good, his eyes were not such a pale, watery blue as they were now. His skin had never been this white-crayon pale, though despite the pallor, it *did* look better than I had remembered as far as scars and age spots went. Then again, he had less than two years to make himself indelible and unchanging in my memory.

"Listen," he said, very seriously. "Here is a lesson you need to learn, whenever you take it in, because it speaks to your quality of life, now and always. You need to be able to handle your stresses and moods and fears on your own, without artificial aid, or you will never be as happy and confident as you should be."

He was alarming me. It was such a *last speech*. "Dad—" I started to say.

But he held up his hand to stop me. "You need to have the tools *inside of you* to take care of yourself no matter what. Not alcohol, not sedatives—none of that stuff offers anything more than a temporary solution that ricochets back harder later. I spent a good portion of my life dealing with anxiety the wrong way, as you have pointed out. And in the end that resulted in a price I've had no choice but to pay. If you take nothing forward from here, take that: You have everything you need inside you. You are Dorothy from *The Wizard of Oz*, you know? You already have everything you need."

I sighed, not dramatically but with the exhaustion of bundled emotion. I'd lived long enough now to know that was true in theory but not always in practice. I *wanted* to believe it—don't we all? Wouldn't we all want some private stash of harmless and natural Xanax that would flow automatically into our veins the minute life got tough? Of course! But the fact was that life was sometimes far more than any of us bargained for, certainly more than I ever expected it to be and way more than I felt prepared to handle, and on those occasions a crutch was helpful.

What I was going through was tough! Completely confusing, impossible to comprehend, and even harder to walk through without leaning on the conceit that this was some highly imaginative dream I'd concocted in my subconscious in order to teach my conscious a thing or two before moving forward into my middle age.

But the truth was, obviously, I didn't know just what the hell this whole thing was.

Who *wouldn't* want a slug of hard liquor in my place?

Yet that wasn't an argument that was going to hold water with my dad. Why should it? This was some form of reality for him and Mom and everyone I knew and was seeing now.

Including me, I guess.

There was no point in keeping it up. "Dad," I said, "you're right." Because I knew he was and, more importantly, I knew that was what he needed to hear. "I'm a kid"—lie—"and I don't have all the faculties you have to deal with nerves. Today was my last day of school. It's the last time I'm going to see many of these people. *Most* of these people." I thought of the deaths coming, the divorces, the messed-up kids, all the weedy screwups that grew from the fertile ground of youthful hope. I got choked up thinking about it, talking about it. Tears flowed from my eyes and I had no ability to stop them; it was like a magic trick. "Please don't be disappointed in me. Please don't let this be your lingering impression of me."

My father's expression softened. Soft gray, that's how it struck me. Aged, more than it should have been for his forties. I'd *dated* men older than this. Not to be all TMI, but I'd *done* men older than this. To me they'd seemed vibrant, fun, interesting. Not old. Yet Dad seemed like a sad old soul to me.

Was that the visage of impending death?

The tears came faster as he reached over and mussed my hair. "I will always be proud of you, Ramie." I thought I felt his hand tremble for a moment. "To the day I die, and beyond. I know that to be a fact, and you must believe it too."

That was hard to hear. I couldn't speak. And it didn't matter because I wouldn't have known what to say even if I could.

He got up, apparently feeling everything had returned to normal. No one truly has *not a care in the world*, but he was about as close as he could get to that. "Mom and I are going out for dinner tonight. Why don't you go on to that party? I'll talk to her about it."

The party. That didn't feel like it mattered as much after this talk. But, of course, it might. Anything in this weird vortex might matter. Even though I wasn't positive Brendan was the key to the rest of my life, I knew that this night in particular had been a left turn for me and if it wasn't the relationship, maybe something else had changed along with that and *that* was why I was back. To fix something else. Who knew?

I was pretty sure the only thing that *didn't* hold at least a chance of getting me back where I came from was sitting alone in my room. So the party was important.

Then again, nothing I thought mattered or resonated for the future so far, so I wasn't good at identifying the things that mattered versus the things that didn't. As a matter of fact, I wasn't feeling like a super-huge success in any way, given this apparent opportunity and my sheer failure in terms of changing anything, most importantly my dad's smoking habits.

It was beginning to feel an awful lot like I was back here as a witness, nothing more. An observer to my life, for better or worse, without power. Sure, maybe I was supposed to turn this around into something new. Maybe I was supposed to gather all these lemons and make them into lemonade: determinedly suicidal father, weak mother who didn't exert any change through her own actions, a self who couldn't do anything that was actually meaningful.

Speaking of which, I told myself, switching gears into business mode. *It's time to start looking at Costco.*

"Thanks, Dad." I got up and went over to hug him. Who knew if I'd ever get another chance? That's how every moment of this felt. "I love you."

He patted my back. He smelled lightly of Aqua Velva and smoke, a scent I remembered well now but could never replicate, though I did have a small plastic bottle of the aftershave in my bathroom drawer that I sometimes smelled just to try and bring back the memory. "I love you too," he said. "Forever. Remember that. I'm always on your side. Just try to make better choices, eh?"

"Oh, I'm going to make a lot of bad choices," I said with a dry laugh. "I'm certain of it. But I try to get it right."

"I'd never ask more of you than that. I want you to have a happy life, Ramie. Make every moment count."

I smiled. "When in Rome . . ."

"Better to have a bird in the hand than two in the bush." He laughed. "Sometimes clichés become clichés because they're good advice."

I nodded. "I promise you I'll always do my best."

CHAPTER NINETEEN

I DIDN'T RIDE WITH TANYA TO THE PARTY AFTER ALL. SHE WAS eager to get there as soon as it began, and I had to take some time to calm down and get myself together. Besides, I still had all the time I wanted with grown-up Tanya, assuming I got back where I'd come from, but there was very little time left with Brendan at all.

I touched up my makeup and hair, and spritzed on the Obsession cologne I hadn't thought about in years but found on the bathroom shelf and remembered had been a favorite of Brendan's. Tonight I felt compelled to wow him. I still felt vaguely weird about it, but I reminded myself he wasn't some kid I'd just encountered and was inappropriately older than. This Brendan was the only Brendan I'd ever known and he'd never left my memory, so in that sense he'd kind of "grown" with me over the years.

If nothing else, I wanted to have a little more time with this sweet memory of mine.

Actually, that's a bit disingenuous. I didn't just want to enjoy living in the live photo album this had become—the part of me that wondered how things would be different if Brendan and I had never broken up was getting louder and more insistent. I needed to know, one way or the other, if my life would have gone in a different direction if we hadn't ended our relationship.

So was this my chance to undo that ending? Or even to mix it up so we had at least a little more time together? It wasn't something I'd thought much about over the years; I was so determined in my career that I couldn't afford to look back. But that day on the yacht had certainly made me question my ever-diminishing choices, and that had clearly taken me back to the beginning of my adult life's path: the end of high school.

Was that why I was back here again? To take the other road at the fork?

He picked me up at eight. It was still light out and I saw his old station wagon—oh! the embarrassment I'd felt riding around in that back in the day!—pull up in front of my house.

Truth be told, station wagons are some of the best cars out there to drive. Even more unvarnished truth be told, they are just about the *best* vehicle to have sex in, if you're going to have sex in a vehicle. I've done it on more occasions than I care to admit, and nothing beat the ol' station wagon for roominess and semi-privacy out in the open.

I shouted good-bye to my parents, and bounded out the door, feeling, for just a moment, *exactly* as I had at eighteen. There was a lightness to my life. I was young and fit and strong, the world was still somewhat innocent, as I didn't care about politics and 9/11 was still many years in the future, and I was bounding down the freshly cut green front yard of my childhood home at dusk, going to a party with the only boyfriend who'd ever really made me feel safe and coddled.

The reason for that, of course, was that I grew up and realized that I shouldn't aspire to have someone else make me feel safe and coddled; I was supposed to take care of myself.

Nevertheless, in these halcyon days when I could still pretend, it felt pretty damn good.

So I was going to let it feel good now too.

"Hey there!" I slid across the seat and kissed him on the cheek.

"Hey, don't be stingy." He pulled me toward him and kissed me on the mouth. For a good, long, tantalizing time. If no one had been home, I'd have been sorely tempted to take him back inside and satisfy the longing that was suddenly raging in me.

I guess what they say about women reaching their sexual prime later in life is true. That, combined with a teenage body teeming with hormones, was lethal. Every time I'd seen or talked to or even thought of Brendan in the past couple of days, I'd felt a flush run hot right down my core. That body. That face. That passion.

"So why were you so determined to go to this thing tonight?" he asked me.

I couldn't tell him the truth—that I thought it was the one chance to change the way things had gone downhill for us—so

I just shrugged and parroted Tanya. "It's the end of school, the last chance . . ."

"So let's go someplace more private instead," he suggested, and gave me a knowing look.

I smiled. It was so tempting. "Let's just go for a little while at least. Tanya's expecting me. She'll be pissed if I bail."

"Right." A muscle twitched in his jaw and he put the car in gear and began to drive.

"What's wrong?"

"Nothing's wrong." He cast a quick glance my way. "I just feel like we do a lot of things because of what Tanya will do if we don't."

"Really?" Was that true? I didn't remember that. Certainly she'd been a huge part of my teen years. There was almost no event I could think of that hadn't included her. But that was because we were friends. It had never occurred to me that for some reason Brendan might not have liked that, or might not have liked *her*.

"It doesn't matter." He drove on and changed the subject to the fate of next year's varsity football team, now that he and his pals were going to be gone. It was funny to hear him speculating about such small pieces of the future as if they mattered, when what I really wanted to know about was how his life *had* gone. . . .

Questions I'd never be able to ask him right now.

When he turned into the driveway off Persimmon Tree Road, I recognized it. I remembered the mailbox with cardinals on it and recalled wondering if cardinals were lucky or if that was just bluebirds. Not a significant memory by any means, but it had

happened. And when we came to the house, a tall white structure with a long porch, sort of like *The Waltons* house on steroids,
I remembered that too. A pretty place. Probably a very peaceful
retreat on a summer's evening when there weren't two hundred
recently graduated teenagers blasting the Black Crowes and
throwing back beers. The pungent, earthy scent of weed also
hung in the air, of course. Hell, I'd smelled that outside the
school itself, though it wasn't something I was into.

We followed the cacophony to a huge crowd of people in the
backyard, covering a patio and extending into a stretch of grass
and dark woods, occasionally lit by random fireflies flickering on
and off, making me think of high piano notes with every flash.

As I had in the halls of the school, I recognized many of the
faces and knew the sad fates of more than one. But also as I had
in school, I felt tight and anxious, like I didn't belong here—
which I didn't—and like I couldn't breathe.

"You okay?" Brendan asked, clearly seeing the change of expression on my face.

"It's hot," I said. My skin was tingling. I felt flushed. Nause-
ated. "Is it hot?"

"Hot?"

"Stuffy."

"We're outside."

"Ugh. It feels stuffy to me." As I said this, though, the feeling began to ebb. As it receded, I recognized it as a premonition.
Whether that was significant or not, I couldn't say. I'd never
been a huge fan of crowds, so this might have been the reaction
I'd had the first time around as well. Whatever had happened

originally, not only had I survived it but it hadn't mattered
enough to register in my memory, so I had to just let this play
out the way it needed to.

"Do you want a drink?"

I considered. "Yeah, could you see if there's a Coke or Pepsi
or something?"

"Sure." He eyed me questioningly for a moment, then headed
into the crowd.

For my part, I backed off a little and sat down on a stone gar-
den wall, hoping to recede from the crowd and observe. Maybe
pretend I was home, comfortable, watching all of this on TV,
rather than standing right here where it was happening, trying
to make sense of something that couldn't be logical.

And all the while, I kept having flashes of recognition. Only
brief seconds—probably not even seconds, just fractions of a
second—where it felt like déjà vu. But with all of the moments
being so small and insignificant, it was hard to hold on to them
and examine then. Why would my mind have held on to the
fleeting image of Janet Brooks huffing past, looking pale and
angry, with her hapless boyfriend, Tom . . . something . . . following? I'd seen it before, my subconscious told me that, but that
was all. It didn't matter. It was gone quickly, and left little trace.

Naturally Anna Farrior was here, and, naturally, she was the
first to approach me. "Um, I don't think *you* were invited to this
party."

"Better call the police."

She acted as if she didn't hear me. "Where's your invitation?"

"My *invitation*?" I repeated automatically. What a stupid notion, that a teenage keg party would have invites.

She took my question the wrong way, though, and found it tremendously funny. "See? You were so totally *not* invited that you don't even realize there are no invitations!"

I looked at her evenly. Had I not realized how very *stupid* she was back then? I knew she was a nasty bitch, but how could I have let such unimaginative insults bother me, ever? "Why do you feel so bad about yourself?" I asked her.

That threw her. "W-what? I don't! Why do *you?*"

"It's pretty basic psychology. If you'd paid attention in Mrs. Breen's class, you'd know it, but you were too busy unconsciously demonstrating it to understand and learn about it."

"Is that supposed to be an insult? That I didn't pay attention in class?" She looked around to where her entourage would normally be, but she didn't have them at the moment.

Not that it would have mattered to me if she had. This was a principle all of them should learn. It would serve every one of them later.

"You try to make yourself feel bigger," I said, "by making others feel smaller. But it doesn't really work, does it?"

"You're crazy." She cranked her finger by her temple. Classic third-grade behavior.

"Everything you attack me for is something that you envy or because you envy me on the whole. It's really obvious. Like, the makeup thing."

She unconsciously raised a hand to her cheek. "What *makeup thing?* The fact that you can't put it on?"

"The fact that I don't feel like I need it as much as you do. Because really"—I shrugged—"is that such a biting insult? That I don't wear as much makeup as you? Ouch?"

"You're being weird." She was visibly disconcerted. "What are you on now? Brendan should see this."

"Brendan brought me here."

She winced. And there it was. The main, if not the only, thing about me she really hated. I had Brendan. "You're a pretty girl, Anna," I gave her, perhaps too generously. "Just because Brendan's taken doesn't mean you can't find another boyfriend."

She had nothing to say to that. She just looked at me, fuming, then turned on her heel and stalked away.

I watched her go and for the first time in my life I actually felt sorry for her. Not hugely. She'd been a real jerk to me, over and over, and I resented the unpleasantness she'd brought to my teenage years, but what would have been the point of telling her that I was sure she'd spent an hour covering the one zit she had that would have been far less noticeable with no makeup? That might have given Teenage Me a satisfying moment, and Teenage Me was definitely still inside, but it would have been cruel. One thing I'd learned with age was that *an eye for an eye* never left anyone at peace.

"*Ramie!*" I felt, as well as heard, Tanya's voice as she came toward me from the dark to my left. "*There* you are! Where the hell have you been all night?"

Clearly she'd been drinking beer. A lot of it. It sloshed over the sides of the red Solo cup she was holding so tightly that it crunched slightly under her grip.

"He's not here!" she wailed.

No sense in asking who. Kenny Singer. "Looks like you're having fun anyway." I nodded at her cup and held out my hand. "Give me your keys."

"I'm *fine!*" She laughed and handed over the keys. "I'm so not fine. Either you or Brendan had better be, because I'm pretty sure I'm gonna need a ride home."

"We'll give you a ride and you and I can come get your car tomorrow."

She took another gulp of beer. "Thank god. Because I need to find a boyfriend tonight. This is ridiculous. Do you *know* how *long* it's been since I had a boyfriend?"

"Like, a month?"

"A boyfriend I *loved?*" She gave an anguished moan. "I've never had what stupid you and stupid Brendan have."

I had to laugh. "Yeah, stupid us." But I knew she was going to find something even better than what Brendan and I had because she was going to find something warm and happy and lasting and she was going to have two beautiful children to show for it. I couldn't reassure her any more specifically than I already had; she'd think I was crazy, and maybe that "prediction" would even interrupt her path, I couldn't know. Everything I knew about this situation came from movies like *Back to the Future*. Not exactly a clear blueprint.

"You guys are gonna get married," she said, then took another glug of beer and sniffed, as if the prospect of Brendan and me getting married caused her great distress. "You're gonna get married and I'm going to be an old maid forever."

"I'm pretty sure neither of those things are going to happen," I told her. "In fact, I'm *really* sure."

She looked at me, surprised. Suddenly more sober than I thought she was, and latching on to the one thing I didn't want to have to dive into. "You don't think you and Brendan are going to get married? Since when?"

And I remembered that back in those days I *did* think I'd be with him forever. For a while, anyway. Once upon a time, I had been sure—deep-in-my-soul sure—that Brendan was *The One* for me. Was that based on something real, or was it just the lies of hormones and teenage attraction?

It made me wish I could have a little sit-down with Teenage Me, instead of Teenage Tanya. Tanya wasn't the one who turned out to need good advice, once all was said and done. Tanya found her way all by herself into a happily-ever-after anyone could envy.

But Teenage Me, on the other hand—the *real* teenage me, not this spooky thirty-eight-year-old who was inhabiting my teenage body—that girl could have used some good advice. It was all really excellent to go to school and start a successful career, and there was a whole lot to be said for never being financially dependent on a man.

Yet, at the same time, there was a lot to be said for having a good, solid companion, someone to traverse the difficulties of life with. For better or worse, as they said.

I'd never really had that.

Honestly, I don't think I ever really believed I'd had that with anyone, though there had been a moment, when I was thirty-six and still saw hope for a family, that I thought maybe I could have it with Jeffrey. I certainly knew now that he hadn't been solid, but he made sense in more ways than not. Dating him was the correct move at approximately the right time. It was a math calculation, not a warm heart decision.

We'd met at a conference in Reno. At first the one thing we

had in common was that we both disliked Reno. As things to bond over go, that wasn't really all that stellar.

But then we'd learned that we lived in towns that were only about forty-five minutes apart, so I guess that fact and a mutual physical attraction was enough to get us together. But it never drew us closer; we'd stayed forty-five minutes apart.

The sex was pretty good. Not great. Not earth-shattering. But satisfying. I'd been out there dating post-Brendan for eighteen years by the time we met, so I'd had plenty of disappointing encounters, believe me. And sex is *important*. I told myself for a long time that it wasn't, but it is. So that part of our relationship was okay.

But not good enough.

And that was the last relationship I'd had. The closest I'd come, so far, to *forever*.

"Can you get me another beer?" Tanya's voice interrupted my thoughts, and I was back in the past.

Teenage Me probably would have done it.

Real Me knew she didn't need more beer and so Real Me wasn't going to contribute to that.

"How about I get you some water?" I suggested, sounding noticeably parental.

"Not quite what I asked for."

I put a finger to my chin and pretended to think. "Yet exactly what you need."

She got it. She smiled. "Fine, fine." She waved an airy hand at me, and sat heavily on the stone wall. "I'll be here."

"Okay." I headed into the house to find the kitchen and hoped she wouldn't start puking before she started to sober up.

"Ramie."

I stopped and turned back to her. "You're not going to puke, are you?"

No me wanted to deal with that.

She shook her head. Then stopped and looked as if she were reconsidering.

My nerves strung tight.

"No," she said finally. "I'm think I'm okay. But can you try and find, like, a cracker or a piece of bread or something? A graham cracker would be perfect."

"I'll look but don't count on it." I left her and went into the house, which was far, far bigger than my own. Where mine was just a foyer and three rooms, including kitchen, on the first floor, this one seemed to have dens, parlors, family rooms, living rooms, everything but a bowling alley. I took a few wrong turns on what I had thought would be a simple mission. And one of those wrong turns took me to the entrance to a small, dark room where a girl was crying, hanging on some guy, her arms draped over his shoulders.

I froze.

I'd been here before.

I knew how this night had ended, obviously. But the truth was, at the time I'd been a bit more tipsy than I was now—I hadn't had the close call with my parents because of the vodka so I'd arrived earlier—and also I hadn't registered all of the things leading up to The Event. After all, it was only The Event that ended up mattering, and the only things that had been left to my memory were a blur of tears, betrayal, and anger. And more betrayal. It was the betrayal that had ended it for us.

"Why can't you just tell her it's over?" the girl whined, followed by a dramatic sob as she buried her face in his shoulder.

A shoulder I knew well, by the way. A shoulder I had just been clinging to, naked, in the backseat of a car a few nights earlier. Past me and present me both felt the sting of jealousy. Anger rose in one of us, and I had to stop myself from lunging at both of them and ripping them away from each other.

It was clear that I wasn't just inhabiting my old (young) body; I was commingling with all of those old emotions. And even though I knew where this would lead, and I'd intended to go into it with a more adult head on my shoulders, the rage took over and all but obliterated every other thought I had.

CHAPTER TWENTY

"ANNA." BRENDAN'S VOICE. THOUGH OF COURSE I HADN'T needed to wait to hear it because I knew it was him. I'd have known it was him even if I didn't recognize the light blue T-shirt he was wearing, or the belt he always wore that I'd unbuckled countless times, or the hair I'd run my fingers through a million times.

And *of course* I knew it was her. I'd been expecting this.

Still, my stomach clenched.

A rage that felt like it was not my own built in me like some sped-up version of Tetris, anger on top of anger on top of anger.

This was not my reaction. Or, rather, this was not my present self's reaction. How could it be? I'd been building up to this all night. My intention had been to let it float on past and see what was on the other side of it.

Wrong.

This was bleed-through of the old me; I was feeling some of what I'd felt before, when this had originally happened. Just as I'd been getting nudges of the old me's emotions for days, I was feeling the impulses of my genuine eighteen-year-old self popping up against my better judgment, and those impulses included screaming, running in and ripping the hair off that girl's head, and running away.

The part of me that was *me* felt detached, interested in where this was going, in finding out what it was. He'd always said it was nothing, that I was wrong to take it so hard. But the part of me that was emotional, the part of me that was eighteen, suddenly won my whole psyche, for the first time since I'd been in this predicament.

I turned on my heel in fury and left the room, forgetting all about my mission to find bread and water for Tanya.

Fuck him! rang clear in my head.

Fuck him! Asshole!

Of all the "old" feelings I'd experienced hints of since I'd been here, these were by far the strongest. Earlier feelings I might have just characterized as memory, but this reaction was clearly outside of my present self's realm. I could almost view my emotions objectively except that I was *feeling* them all too, which was seriously disconcerting.

Why was I so mad? I hadn't even stayed long enough to find out the truth, when that had been my whole plan! I hadn't heard his response to her obvious overture. I just ran away, while part of my intellect was a child, dragging behind, saying, *But wait . . .*

My body was retreating rapidly, ready to go out and take

Tanya's keys, and car, and of course Tanya herself, and just go home. Let him wonder what had become of me. Let him wonder if I'd seen his little tryst with Anna.

But that was stupid. I was leaping—with great energy, it seemed—to conclusions. And that could only hurt me. Hurt him. Hurt anyone who wasn't getting a fair shake.

So I forced myself to slow down and think. My old mind receded faster than I expected, the pounding rage of jealousy dimming into the light beep of my heartbeat, like that damn alarm clock that clawed me out of bed in the mornings.

I recognized this. Not only the immature hormonal rush of jealousy, and the almost insane hotheadedness, but this situation in particular. I remembered this happening. I remembered this being a real cog in the wheel of our eventual breakup.

But I also remembered wondering later, as I suffered in his absence, if I'd done the wrong thing. If I should have listened, and given him another chance. If I'd be happier if I had.

This was my main question since I'd gotten here.

I had to fight my old impulses, fight the *reaction* of the eighteen-year-old hothead inside of me, and go back to undo the past.

Maybe create a whole new future.

Or, rather, present.

And future.

Maybe.

It was my only chance to try. This was the first shot at Fort Sumter, a thing that could have been resolved but wasn't, and it was leading to the civil war that was going to be our end if I didn't stop it.

So, I asked myself now, what if I reversed my reaction? What if I went back and just asked him, right to his face, in the moment, what was going on, why this was happening?

"Hi, Ramie."

I'd been so lost in thought that I hadn't watched where I was going and I nearly ran into Jer Norton, the guy from the pizza joint who sold me the Zima.

"Hey, Jer." I couldn't force cheer into my voice, so it sounded hostile. My mind was racing. "How are you doing?" I added, hoping he'd missed my previous tone.

He hadn't. "Whoa, what's the matter with you?"

"Nothing."

He put his hands up, the universal sign for surrender. "Okay, okay, whatever you say. Don't bite."

I gave a small laugh that fooled no one. "Sorry, I'm just . . . dealing with something."

"Something you want to talk about?"

"No. Thanks." I started to walk away, but he stopped me, catching my arm.

"Wait, there's something I've been meaning to ask you."

The last thing I needed right now. "What?"

He hesitated, then said, "Ramie, I know there was nothing really behind . . . that night. You and me. Whatever. But I really like you, so if you'd ever like to hang out . . ."

Ugh. It was excruciating watching him struggle. Especially since I was feeling such unkindness toward him for picking now to do it. "Oh, thanks, Jer. Seriously. But I have a boyfriend."

His face colored. "Oh, yeah, right, I know. I just meant, you know, as friends."

"I know, it's just, he can be jealous, so . . . I don't know." I needed to get off this hook. "But, yeah, maybe sometime. That would be nice." *Just let me go!*

Some of the shame left his expression and his face brightened ever so slightly. "Cool."

Now I felt bad. It hadn't been necessary to hurt his feelings. "I'll look for you at Bambino's, right?" I asked, avoiding the awkward next step of exchanging phone numbers when I had so much else on my mind.

"Sure, yeah. Almost every day."

I smiled, but I was desperate to get back to Brendan. "Cool. Thanks!" I turned to go back.

"Weren't you going this way?" he asked, puzzled.

"I left something behind." I looked at him. He really did have a nice face. I felt just awful for having been short with him.

So, a nice little lift for the ego, on the heels of what had begun as a big blow.

It was interesting how easy it was to fall back into the rhythms of my former life. I could even talk like I used to, though the laziness of teen-speak sometimes made me cringe. But it was fun, like playing a game or being in a play. A play I still didn't know the end of.

I made my way back through the rooms, thinking how annoyed I'd be today if a bunch of teenagers were wandering around my house like this, uninvited, unwelcome. I wasn't going to steal any of the tchotchkes I saw and knew to be valuable, but I wasn't sure the same could be said for every drunk kid there.

Nerves thrummed inside of me as I got closer to Brendan. I recognized, once again, old me coexisting inside with my own consciousness. I really had to fight off her anger. It was crazy. How could one spirit and one set of memories be divided so distinctly and travel the same trajectory at the same time? There was probably some "easy" quantum mechanical explanation for it—something Mr. Giuliani would have been happy to talk about with me—but all I knew was that it felt really odd.

I walked, half wishing I'd left a trail of bread crumbs so I could find my way back to the room in the maze of Potomac extravagance.

With another few wrong turns, I did find my way back to it.

They were still there. But this time they were sitting on a sofa, their silhouettes clear from my vantage point, and they were facing each other from a decent distance. Not a huge one, within an arm's reach, but at least not an intimate one.

"I know you feel the same like I do," Anna was saying. Slurring, rather. I hadn't noticed that the first time, though it wasn't really a surprise. But still—had I realized that Once Upon a Time? Had I known she was drunk? Or had I been so concentrated on the fact that she was a bitch that I didn't care?

The show wasn't for me, so it wasn't like she was ever going to come and offer apologies or explanations, but context would have been helpful for me.

"I'm sorry," said Brendan.

I could see in her eyes the same confusion I felt myself. Sorry he hadn't axed me long ago, or sorry he'd led her on?

Looked like neither of us knew, though it was clear which she was hoping for.

I couldn't remember exactly when he and I had broken up. The date hadn't stuck with me, but I did know it was sometime before the end of summer, because I remembered thinking I needed to get used to being unattached while I was still in the safety of my home and family. I was ambitious and determined, but not without heart by any means, so when I'd broken up with Brendan, I'd forced myself to stay away by reminding myself that this would be a lot harder the longer I waited.

Though, honestly, even that was in doubt. Would we have gone to opposite sides of the country? *Had* we? I wasn't even sure I could remember what his college plans had been. Maybe we would have been close enough to stay together and maybe we would have done exactly that. Until . . . what?

There was a long silence in the room before me, and I was nervous that my own pounding heart would call their attention to where I stood watching them.

"Don't be sorry," she wailed, and reached for him, clumsily taking a fistful of his shirt and trying to pull him toward her. "Do it. Please. Just *fix* it."

He didn't budge. "Anna," Brendan said. "There's nothing to fix. I'm not the guy for you."

"You are!" She moved toward him and pressed her open mouth against his.

And for a moment, just a moment, I saw him respond. Saw the telltale movement of his jaw and tightening of his throat that came from the movement of his tongue into her mouth.

The rage resurged in me, a new one, because eighteen-year-old me had not stuck around long enough to see this and it was new. Yet thirty-eight-year-old me found it a fascinating study in sociology, if nothing else. He'd just been with me, we'd had steaming hot sex in his car two days ago, and I knew—I *knew*—

young Brendan had believed himself to be truly in love with me. One thing I had felt all my life was that no one else had ever loved me as much as Brendan had.

So what was he doing, making out with this other girl, when he was at this party with me? I'd been right all along—he'd told me I'd run off before I could see nothing had happened, but that wasn't true.

My heart sank, not because an eighteen-year-old was cheating on me, but because there didn't seem to be any consistency in men at all. Was it really so hard to just stay loyal and honest with your *one person*? Even if it was one person *at a time*, as it almost inevitably was in high school? Could he really be tempted by this drunken slop-tart, even while he knew—he had to have known—that I could have walked in on him at any moment and seen all of this (and did!)?

I started to turn and walk away, calm but resigned, when he pushed her away. Not hard, not ungentlemanly, but he pushed her away. He didn't know I could see him, but he did the right thing.

I froze, riveted.

"Anna, no," he said firmly. "I'm not doing this."

"But you want me." She leaned back into him, hoping, clearly, to repeat the moment they'd just had.

"No"—his voice was getting firmer—"I don't. I love Ramie, and you know that. How many fucking times do I have to tell you?"

"But you just kissed *me!*" Her words echoed my own thoughts. "I know you want me, I could feel it in your kiss."

"What, this?" He pulled her in and kissed her, hard, seemingly passionately. Then he released her. "That's easy. That doesn't mean anything, apart from the guilt it's made me feel about Ramie."

I was stunned by the gesture. It seemed so . . . adult. So on point. Yet also, so damn harsh.

She looked hurt, and for a moment I shared that with her, on her behalf. It seemed mean of him to do that, even though it would have satisfied my immature self tremendously to have seen it back when it first happened.

But no, I'd taken the small piece I'd seen and run with it, fiercely holding it against him and including it in a long tally of undoubtedly petty offenses that had led to my excuse for breaking up.

I watched as his expression softened toward her. "Anna, look, we've known each other since we were kids. Our parents are great friends. *Obviously* I don't want to hurt you. But you need to get that guys will use you and throw you aside afterwards if you come on to them the way you came on to me tonight. I don't want you to get hurt. I don't want to hurt you. But, man, you have to get this. You're drunk, we've known each other a long time but you know we are never going to be more than friends. You're just lonely and reaching out. If this had happened with someone else, who knows how far he would have taken it?"

She shrank back, suddenly looking like a wounded child, where I had only seen a stupid slut a moment before. There was no more look of seduction on her face, only the timid expression of a kid who had been caught being naughty in some way, shape, or form. "I'm not lonely," she said in a small voice, as if that were the most salient point.

"Okay." I knew Brendan well enough to recognize that he was humoring her. She was desperate for a boyfriend. "Whatever's going on, just take care of yourself. Don't give yourself away just because you're impatient. You're better than that."

She was crying then, and I almost was myself.

How had this eighteen-year-old boy gained so much wisdom? How did he have the control to check his physical impulses and back up, then say something so nice, and so *wise*, on top of that?

"I didn't mean to throw myself at you." This girl I had thought was such a bitch a moment ago now just looked pitiful. How on earth had I imagined I was so much more mature and worldly than Brendan was? I'd been too blind to see his truth. At least some of it.

"Hey, you didn't. Forget it." He put a hand on her shoulder in a pointedly platonic way. He leaned in and gave her a kiss on the cheek, then stood up before she could get her clutches on him again, which I thought I could see she was gearing up to do. "I've got to go find Ramie."

"Go." She pushed a wobbly arm against the air, I guess to dismiss him. "Ramie Ramie Ramie. What*ever*."

I saw a smile tug at his mouth. "Yeah," he said quietly. "Ramie Ramie Ramie."

And at that moment, I realized I'd learned something huge by going back and seeing the scene through, rather than just following my angry impulse to take what I thought I'd seen and run.

I'd learned that maybe no one was exactly who I'd decided they were. Including me.

CHAPTER TWENTY-ONE

AS SOON AS I'D SEEN BRENDAN IN RETREAT MODE, I'D RETRACED
my steps to get out of the house so he could find me outside.
Unfortunately I hadn't managed to find water or bread for Tanya,
who was looking a bit worse for the wear when I got back out to
her, so we all decided to leave, with me driving Tanya in her car.
Brendan was going to go home and wait for my call to meet me
later.

She was hammered. "I can't believe he didn't show up," she
kept saying, over and over.

"Maybe it's for the best," I suggested, knowing full well that
it was. "I mean, no offense, girlfriend, but you are not exactly at
your best right now. Would you really want your first encounter
with him to be something you literally couldn't remember
tomorrow?"

"I'm going to remember *everything* tomorrow!"

"Oh, please. I could tell you I'm a Russian spy right now, and insist you call me *Natasha* all the way home, and tomorrow you would have no recollection of it whatsoever."

"Wait, what? You're a Russian spy? As if. You don't even speak . . . Russian. *Nyet.*"

"I rest my case," I said, more to myself than to her. I was having my own little monologue here; she was just a heckler sitting nearby. Might as well use her as a sounding board for what was really on my mind. "So I'm thinking maybe I shouldn't break up with Brendan this time around." I glanced at his headlights in the rearview mirror. It was comforting knowing he was back there.

"Yeah, no way." Tanya was really slurring now, and her head lolled like a water balloon with a slow leak.

"For him, this is just another night. He doesn't even know how close we came to the end."

Tanya made a noise, but I don't think it meant anything in response to what I was saying. She was just drifting off.

I went on, to myself. "So that's one major change I've made. One hugely life-impacting change."

She made another sort of grunt of agreement. I was losing her to sleep fast. Just as well.

"I'd like to save my dad too," I ventured. "Because"—I glanced at her and she was sound asleep, her head tilted at an angle that was going to make her neck hurt tomorrow—"he's going to die in a couple of years." I hated to say the words out loud. I had avoided them. Not just the words but the very thought. Even while it was with me all the time.

Tanya's breath was loud and even.

In less than two years she would be right there for me, during the funeral, after the funeral, long after the funeral. She wasn't one of those people who thought it was enough to be there for the first shocking week, not that I didn't appreciate everyone who showed up, but she understood that the grief hadn't even begun until long after the funeral.

Though I'd always worried about my dad's smoking, he seemed, to others, like he was in good shape. He played tennis, racquetball; when it eventually happened, it was just a week or so after he'd cleaned out the garage.

So right now, at this time in my life, I had been blissfully unaware of what was to come, confident that I would have a sitcom life with a sitcom dad who would come over to my overly elaborate single-girl apartment and fix the stove, or replace the doorknob, or whatever else a sitcom single gal would have needed from her dad.

Now here I was, in the twilight of his life and the homestretch of my innocence, and there was nothing I could do except look at him in wonder and wish that I could think of something profound to say or heroic to do. But it was too late. Even when I'd told him to stop, he'd acknowledged it was too late.

I drove in silence for a while, breathing in the familiar scent of Tanya's car, with its Bath & Body Works air freshener—linen, always linen—and viewing a world I hadn't seen for two decades through its windshield.

As I got close to my house, I found I didn't want to stop. Since I was always conscious of the fact that I didn't know when this oddity was going to end, part of me wanted to soak up every bit of nostalgia that I could. I definitely wasn't tired now, and Tanya was down for the count, and way too drunk to take to her house yet, so instead of turning onto my street, I drove straight down to the local strip mall.

There was the Giant grocery store I'd been going to since I was a toddler shopping with my mom for Cap'n Crunch. Actually, I rarely got Cap'n Crunch; the closest she'd come to junk food was Life cereal, and that was because there was an illustration of an egg and two slices of bacon with an equals sign pointing at a bowl of Life. How a bowl of cereal equaled an egg and two slices of bacon I still don't know, but I did love the stuff. Even though I'd been to that grocery store a million times over the years, I still thought of shopping with my mom when I saw it.

Then there was the Szechuan restaurant with the gas torches out front. They were there! I hadn't seen them for so long. It was a great restaurant; I don't know why it failed. But if it had been open that night as I drove past, I would have gone right in and ordered fried dumplings and five-flavor shrimp.

Next to that was the long, narrow two-screen movie theater that would shortly be replaced by a bank and a series of unsuccessful delis. I saw *Tootsie* there. And a rerelease of *Jaws* long after it seemed realistically scary. But at this time in history, Daniel Hanover was working there as an usher and sometimes he'd let me in for free. Later—twenty years later—many of us would wonder what ever happened to Daniel. He seemed to have dropped out of everyone's spheres, and there were rumors that he'd died, but no one seemed to have any details to back that up.

He'd been a nice kid, with white-blond hair and vivid blue eyes. Always smiling. The idea that something might have happened to him bothered me, and I'd done a pretty thorough job of trying to stalk him online to see if he'd just moved far away and was living a happy life in Idaho or something, but there was no sign of him.

If I stopped this car in the parking lot right now and slept for sixteen hours, though, I'd probably see him walking in to work.

It was eerie. Sad. I felt like I was looking at a very dark watercolor painting.

Next door, however, was the stationery shop filled with colorful, cheerful things. The window displays were lit up all night, and I could see *Garfield* stuffed animals, and *Cathy* coffee mugs, and a huge display of *Far Side* cards.

Driving on, I passed the Peoples Drug store, which was going to be changed to a CVS soon. It's funny, I grew up with Peoples Drug and, deeper in Potomac, Drug Fair, and I'd never thought of those names as being weird, but with today's mentality they might as well have been called Meth "R" Us or something.

I exited the parking lot, past the Roy Rogers where I'd worked for two miserable weeks, and headed back toward my neighborhood, meandering through the back roads rather than taking the main strip. I wanted to see the houses of people I'd known, houses those people were currently in, sleeping, most likely, their familiar cars parked out front. It was all just so strange. Even if this was a dream, I had to be tapping into some tremendously deep memory storage, because the details I was seeing were greater than anything anyone could possibly just *remember* over the years. While the three cars in the

Brummers' driveway were familiar when I saw them, they sure weren't worthy of memory, so I wouldn't have committed them there.

I drove past our old elementary school and turned right onto Tanya's street, careful to park a little ways down in front of her house, so that the car wouldn't wake her parents up. Somehow I had to get her drunk butt up to bed without anyone being the wiser.

"Tanya." I poked her.

She slapped back at me. "Tired," she mumbled.

"I know, but you're home."

"He ate the quarter."

"What?"

"Over there. Behind the cactus."

"*What?*"

"Wha . . . ?"

She was totally out of it. This was going to be a huge pain in the ass. "Okay," I said, and got out to get some air. I wanted to meet Brendan so badly, but I couldn't just leave Tanya here, passed out in her car, to wake up alone and confused at some point and . . . well, do god knows what. Clearly I wasn't going to be able to meet with Brendan tonight and that was disappointing. But I couldn't leave Tanya like this. I had to be responsible for my friend, or else this night could change from one life-altering mistake to another.

So I went to the passenger door and opened it. She almost spilled right out onto the street.

"Ow. *Shit!*" She stumbled into a standing position and looked at me accusingly. "What was that?"

"That was your drunk ass falling out of the car."

"Ugh." She rubbed her eyes with the heels of her palms. "I feel horrible."

"No doubt." I was smug, even though the first time around I was probably just as drunk as she was.

And I'd gotten mad at Brendan that night, so I probably wouldn't have allowed him the chance to help me home. I probably hadn't let him get one word in edgewise. I'd probably just slurred some obscenities at him and stomped drunkenly away.

That was why I didn't remember that night, or the significance of going to the party or anything. Originally I'd probably been matching Tanya beer for beer and getting just as shitfaced as she was. Who knows how far that scene with Anna and Brendan had gone the first time? Had I interrupted the moment I saw them, never even giving him a chance to do the right thing or me the chance to see it?

I guess I'd never know. All I knew was that I'd done things differently this time, and I was glad.

Especially looking at Tanya. I was *really* glad I didn't feel the way she did right now, or the way she was bound to feel when she woke up in the morning.

"Come on," I said, hooking my arm across her back, supporting what felt like most of her weight. "Let's see if we can sober you up enough to go in without waking up your parents."

"I jus' wanna go to bed."

"I know. Me too, believe me. But I can't carry your ass up the stairs by myself and I'm pretty sure the sound of you tumbling down them would wake your parents, and you don't want that."

"No. . . ."

"So let's go for a little walk." I half dragged her several yards down the quiet street, the only sound the wind whispering through the leaves on the Bradford pear trees that lined the lane. Tanya's motor skills came back, slowly, as we went.

"What's the name of the people in this house?" I asked, trying to remember. They never seemed to leave the place, but the rumor was the husband had a prosthetic leg, thanks to the Vietnam War, and they had a pool out back that he could swim in for exercise. No one else in the neighborhood would have had a pool, so that prospect seemed very exotic back in the day.

"Jalenskis."

I wasn't sure if she was right, but I needed her thinking. "And next door?"

"Dooleys."

"Good. Take a deep breath."

She did. She wasn't normally so acquiescent.

Gradually her steps became a little more solid and her answers became a bit more coherent. She wasn't going to miraculously sober up, but I figured I could at least get her upstairs without problems.

I was wrong.

The moment we walked in the front door, we were met by the glares of her parents.

"It's two A.M.," her mother said. "We have been worried sick."

"Sorry," I said, adjusting my hold on Tanya so that I was just subtly holding her elbow. "The time got away."

Even though I knew they wanted and expected more of an

answer than that, I tried to maneuver us toward the stairs so we could get in trouble for being rude and late tomorrow and not for being drunk tonight.

Unfortunately, Tanya said, "Oh, hey, Mom! Dad! How're you guys doing this fine night?"

I could have strangled her.

From the looks of it, so could her dad. And her mom.

Poor Tanya. She had no idea.

"Have you been *drinking?*" her father demanded.

"Or smoking those weed cigarettes?" her mother added, casting a knowing look at her husband.

"No!" I said. "Of course not! It's just been a long night and Tanya's just, you know, *really* tired."

"Sooooo trrrd," she slurred.

Shut up! I thought.

But that was it, the jig was up. They knew she was hosed. They'd have had to be blind to miss it.

"We thought you girls had better sense than this," her dad said. "Did you *drive* drunk?"

"I drove," I said. "I haven't had anything to drink at all. Honest, you can test me." They couldn't, of course. Home Breathalyzers were still a few years away, but at least I had been sincere.

"He wasn't there," Tanya said. "I was supposed to finally hook up with him and we were going to start dating and get married and my whole life depended on it, and he *wasn't even there!*"

I met her mom's eyes. "So she had a few beers because she was upset."

Understanding lightened her expression so slightly it was

almost imperceptible. But Tanya and her mom were close— they still were to this day—so she probably knew exactly what I was talking about.

"You're okay to drive?" she asked me. "You really didn't drink? Or do anything else?"

I shook my head. "I really didn't."

"Then go ahead and take her car home." She flashed a surreptitious glance at her husband. "I don't think she'll be needing it for a while. We'll coordinate picking it up later."

"Okay." I nodded. "And I'm sorry. But she'll be fine in the morning. She was just, you know. Upset."

She gave a nod. "Good night, Ramie. Thank you for being responsible."

That was me. That was me in a nutshell, actually, if you looked at how my life had gone afterward. Responsible. Mature. Serious.

Unfulfilled.

CHAPTER TWENTY-TWO

WHEN I GOT HOME I WAS EXHAUSTED, BUT MY FATHER WAS STILL up, night owl that he always was, sitting in the living room, reading James Michener's *Space* and smoking those damn cigarettes. There was an assortment of snacks on the coffee table in front of him, including those red-candy-coated peanuts and a brick of baklava, which I could not—and cannot—stand.

"Hi there, chicken," my dad said, a stark contrast to the uneasy "welcome" Tanya got from her parents. "I thought you were staying the night at Tanya's."

"Little change of plans."

"Well, did you have a good time?"

Good question. It had been an *interesting* time. Illuminating, certainly. Possibly life-altering. But when all was said and done, could I really say I'd had a *good* time at a teenage beer blowout? "Not particularly." I laughed. "Since you ask."

"No?" He didn't really look surprised. "You're an old soul,

Ramie Phillips. You don't really fit in with your crowd so much
anymore, do you?"

I gave a short spike of laughter. "You have no idea."

He gave a small shrug and took a drag off his cigarette. A
light sulfur scent still lingered in the air; he must have lit it right
before I walked in. The Pall Mall smoke encompassed that scent
and joined the faint whiff of the coffee they'd had when they
got home from dinner. I hate to admit that the smoky smell was
slightly comforting to me, even while it was damning in every
way that mattered.

"Have a seat, kiddo. Let's talk." He moved and patted the sofa
next to him.

I dropped my purse on the floor and went to sit heavily on
the cushion. It squeaked the same now as it had back then. "I'm
scared," I heard myself say.

"What do you have to be scared of? All of life is ahead of
you. The world is your oyster. If you'll pardon the cliché." He
chuckled. We both hated when people threw clichés at a real
situation.

"When in Rome," I said.

"An ounce of prevention is worth a pound of cure."

"Make no bones about it."

"Absence makes the heart grow fonder."

Well, wasn't that the truth?

Things were starting to get fuzzier and I had this strange sensation of thinking of my eighteen-year-old self as *her*, a separate
person who was trying to get in and commandeer my thoughts.
But, really, wasn't it the other way around? I tried to remember
if I'd ever gone through a period of constant disconcertion at

this point in my life, but I couldn't recall anything beyond the usual teenage thoughts and angsts.

This wasn't real. I wasn't "haunting" myself; there was no way that made sense. It was a dream. A long, drawn-out nightmare of a dream. Or dream of a nightmare. I guess I didn't know yet.

"What do you want to do with your life, now that you've graduated high school?" my father asked me. "Where do you see yourself in five years?"

I could have answered that exactly, but he reworded his question before I felt tempted to.

"How would you like to *feel* in five years?"

That was an interesting question. I'd always planned my life in terms of what I thought I needed to accomplish, never thought about how I wanted to feel; that just happened, for better or worse.

"I want to feel *relaxed*," I said, recalling how *stressed* I had been in grad school, looking for an internship—along with a million other equally qualified and equally ambitious students—that would propel me into the next stressful segment of my life.

I liked the success I'd had. Or the *idea* of success, at least—certainly that beats feeling like a failure, but had the cost been worth it?

My thoughts were racing far ahead of the conversation, of course. "Then you must feel your way along your life's path," he said, looking me kindly but steadily in the eyes. "Reevaluate now and then to see where you are and how you feel about it." He paused, then shrugged. "Quite simply, ask yourself if you're happy."

"I never ask myself that."

"Time to start, eh? Life doesn't go on forever. You don't know when the dice will come up snake eyes. I know it's not practical to live *each* day as if it were your last—"

"When in Rome."

We laughed.

"But it absolutely makes sense to check in and make sure that at *most* times you're more happy than sad."

I had never done such a thing. Never evaluated my emotional state at all. I had always done what needed to be done, whatever it was. It had worked for me, for the most part, but *was* I happy? Not entertained now and then, not just tipsy on good champagne now and then, but did I smile like a Disney princess when I woke in the morning, and have a nice big stretch, smiling at the world for the chance to do another day?

No, I woke up too late every day, charged around getting ready, chastised myself for never taking the time to put on more than a little mascara and lipstick, and hurried off to work, mentally building a to-do list every step there, to go with the to-do list I had left over from the evening before.

"Are you happy?" I asked him.

He smiled so genuinely that I couldn't help but believe his answer. "I am *so* happy. Every single day. You and your mother mean the world to me, and that is what I live for."

There was an awkward moment, when I imagined us both thinking of his impending death, but I knew it was just my thoughts coming in so strongly that I was afraid they might penetrate into *his* consciousness somehow.

So I cast the thought from my mind. "I'm glad," I told him.

"You are an inspiration. I will never forget that. I will never forget this conversation." And I wouldn't.

Emotion took hold of my throat and suddenly I was having trouble swallowing the lump there. It was so damn unfair that he was going to go. It was so damn unfair that he was going to leave my mother right as their child went off on her own and they could finally start living their golden years together.

Maybe it was fate, maybe there would be some big answer when I got to the Great Beyond, and I'd understand that everything needed to be the way it was, but I sure didn't get it now. And it didn't look promising that I ever would.

"Dad."

"Mm?"

"Would you see the doctor and get a thorough checkup? Just, you know, to make sure everything's all right?"

He stubbed out his cigarette and blew the last of the smoke into the air, watched it for a moment, probably aware of the irony, then looked at me. "What makes you say that?"

"Nothing in particular," I said quickly. The last thing I wanted to do was intimate that he *looked* sick or that he needed to spend his endgame worrying. "I'm just thinking that because my friend . . ." I tried to think of a name. "Debbie Soldour, remember her?"

He shook his head, of course, because I'd just made her up.

"Anyway, her dad is, like, a tennis pro and a runner and never smoked or anything"—my eyes traveled to the full ashtray—"and he just had a heart attack. He's fine, thank goodness, but he had a heart attack and no one saw it coming. It just made me feel worried."

"Well, I'm sorry to hear that. But there's nothing for you to worry about, I have been checked thoroughly. There is nothing going on in me that the doctors don't know about." He met my eyes for a second, and in that instant I knew—I just *knew*—that he *did* know the state of his health. And he knew it was too late.

Grief so huge came over me that I couldn't stop the rush of tears that fell from my eyes.

"Hey there." He put his hand on my shoulder and pulled me in for a hug. I cried against the crisp cotton of his J.C. Penney button-down shirt and wondered if this was the last time I would feel and hear his reassurances. Even though they were empty, I didn't want this comfort and feeling of safety to end.

"Sorry," I snuffled against his shirt. "I don't want to wake Mom up with my crying."

"It's all right," he said, and gave me an extra squeeze. "Neither of us is ever going to feel put out if you need us. You know that."

"Thanks, Dad."

Then, of all times, that stupid alarm started going off up-stairs. The shrill *beep beep beep* seemingly getting louder and faster. "I better go shut that thing off," I said, and drew away from him.

He looked puzzled.

I gestured vaguely toward the stairs. "Stupid clock-radio thing. It keeps going off at weird times and I can't figure out how to turn it off. Anyway, thanks, Dad. I really appreciate . . . well, everything. I love you, Daddy."

"I love you too, chicken."

I gave him one more hug and said, "Good night."

This was how I had to remember him.

I went upstairs into my room, but the beeping had stopped. Aggravating. For some reason it smelled funny in my room. Like Vicks VapoRub or something. Maybe some kind of new anti-bacterial cleaning fluid. I don't know, but it was so strong that I went to open the window before brushing my teeth and climbing into bed.

Once there in the soft cotton cloud, I thought about the clock again. If it went off and woke me up in the middle of the night, I was going to go insane. I needed some sleep. All of this was taking a huge toll on me. So I forced myself to haul my butt out of bed, feel my way to the little red numbers that provided the only light in the room, then I reached for the wall behind it, where I knew the outlet to be, and yanked the electrical cord.

The lights went out, mercifully.

I got back into bed and drifted into a deep, dreamless sleep almost immediately.

Because I'd unplugged the clock, I don't know what time it was when I heard the noise. At first my mind registered it *as* the clock, which didn't make sense, and I lost all sense of where I was for a moment. That was a seriously disconcerting feeling. Nothing about my situation currently made logical or scientific sense, but at least it was a scenario that was familiar and one that I could maneuver, strange as it was. But to wake up with no sense of time or place was like waking up insane, and it was scary.

I blinked hard against the blackness and willed my eyes to adjust to the light.

"Ramie!" I heard the loud whisper somewhere close by. Under the bed? Outside the door? I couldn't tell.

My heart pounded with strange anxiety and I almost imagined I could hear that damn alarm beeping along to the frantic tempo.

"*Ramie!*"

Wait. I knew that voice. And it wasn't floating disembodied from somewhere in my room; it was . . . outside. I strained to see the outline of the window, the narrow gap between the shade and the sill where the meager light of night shone through. I got out of bed and headed toward it, stubbing my toe on the bedpost and swallowing a curse.

When I got to the window, I touched the shade and felt my way down to the bottom, I gave it a tug, and the spring released, so it rolled up fast and loud, scaring me half to death. It had been a long time since I'd had window shades like this.

"About time!" I heard out there.

I touched my forehead to the screen and looked out. There, on the grass beneath the window, next to the magnolia tree, was the outline of Brendan. "What are you doing?" I rasped.

"I had to see you."

"*Why?*" But my heart did a little flip. He wanted to see me. He was making a romantic gesture, however lame. Man, it had been a long time since anything like this had happened.

I saw him shrug. "I missed you."

"What time is it?"

"Late."

"Hang on," I said. Surely dad would have gone to sleep by now. "I'll be right down."

I was wearing only a long T-shirt, but I knew no one in the neighborhood would be up at this hour. They never were. It was a sleepy little enclave, reliably so.

I hurried down the stairs and carefully opened the front door. It creaked—it always creaked—but I stopped it and stood still, listening for any sound of movement upstairs. There was none, so I slipped through and out the screen door.

Brendan was standing just outside the light on the front lawn and I ran to him and jumped into his arms and wrapped my legs around him, holding on for dear life. "I'm so glad to see you!" I said. And I was. Good lord, my heart was positively pounding. Teenage hormones really *were* a whole different thing.

"Good thing I came over," he said, between kisses.

"No kidding."

We kept kissing and he eased me back down onto my feet and around the corner of the house into the dark privacy by the magnolia. Even someone inside the house couldn't have seen us from the windows and there were no houses facing us.

We were completely free.

And I was going half crazy on him. I mean, I was on fire. Once again I was reminded how long it had been since I'd had an impulse like this and been able to follow it through.

We did.

I leaned against the brick siding and pulled him against me. He was young and instantly hard and hungry. I felt like he was devouring me. Every touch of his tongue, his fingers, everywhere his skin touched mine sent shock waves of pleasure and urgency through me.

It went quickly; the need was too great to take our time. And I didn't want to. I wanted it hard and rough. I needed to feel the brick against my back and him thrusting so hard it was almost painful. I needed that like I needed air.

When it was over, we slipped our clothes back into place and sank to the ground to lie in the grass on our backs, side by side, looking up at the stars and the silver linen clouds drifting past them and in front of the full moon.

"What made you come over tonight?" I asked, reaching for his hand in the darkness.

"I just thought we didn't get enough time together tonight. Something's been feeling different. Distant."

That was undeniable. I didn't know what to say.

"I was sure you were going to break up with me."

"Brendan..." What? I did. Once upon a time, I did. Had that fact bled through to him the way my eighteen-year-old thoughts were bleeding through to me? Did we have paths in our lives that were so firm that even deviating from them didn't erase their shadows?

I resisted that idea. We had free will. At any given time we could change our path. I refused to believe that every change, every act of spontaneity we thought we had engaged in, had actually been planned out for us before we were ever born. What would be the point of life, then? To show we could ride on a roller coaster on its set path? There was no doubt where you'd be at the end of your two minutes on Space Mountain, but I had to believe that life was more fluid than that.

"I didn't" was all I could say. "Did you want to?" The thought came to me, sudden and unwelcome, that maybe we were so destined to part ways that if one didn't do it, the other would.

But he said, "No. It's going to be hard enough with us going to different schools next year."

I nodded, though he didn't see me.

We lay there for a long time in the darkness.

"Brendan?"

"Ramie."

I loved the way he said my name. Wow. Sometimes it really was the simple things. "How do you want to feel in five years?"

He turned to face me. "Huh?"

"You know, kind of where do you think you'll be, but more *how do you want to feel?*"

"Happy? Happy, I guess."

His answer fell a little short. Somehow in the haze of sexual bliss and the beautiful night, I had hoped he'd understand the question and have some great answer that told me, definitively, that I had fixed whatever was wrong in my life and could make it back to reality now.

"You guess?"

"Well, yeah. That's a weird question. I want to feel warm if it's cold outside, and cool if it's hot outside, and satisfied if it's time to eat, and, whatever. Happy."

I sighed.

He gave a dry laugh. "What was the answer?"

"What?"

"I obviously got it wrong. What was the right answer?"

"There is no right answer." I felt a little snappish and hoped I'd hidden that in my voice. "Your answer was fine."

"All right." His tone was long-suffering.

A few more minutes passed and I began to feel cold. And the grass was making me itch. And I kind of wanted to break up with Brendan. Something inside of me told me that we hadn't broken up all those years ago just because of a little misunderstanding that could have been avoided by a hair more patience from me, and five more minutes' time. It was a convenient excuse to hang my hat on, but it wasn't really *the* issue.

The issue, it felt at this moment, was that something here just wasn't right.

I recalled what my father had said just a little while earlier.

It absolutely makes sense to check in and make sure that at most *times you're more happy than sad.*

At this moment, I wasn't. But what had I felt like over the past few months? I couldn't really remember. I had to rely on that voice inside of me, the one I'd been thinking of as *her*. She was me, and she knew best.

I needed to think about this, because at the moment I wasn't sure which, if any, of these feelings to take the most seriously, so instead I just sat up, brushed myself off, and said, "I need to go in. My parents are going to be up soon."

He stood up, and reached a hand down for me, to help me up. As soon as I was standing, we both let go.

"Good night," I said, and leaned in to give him a kiss on the cheek.

He touched my shoulder. "Night."

"I'm glad you came," I added, hoping to obscure, if not erase, the weird turn our mood had taken.

"Me too." He laughed, and I didn't know whether he was talking about the sex or making the trip over.

Didn't matter. Either way, I was glad he came.

I just didn't know if it was going to happen again.

CHAPTER TWENTY-THREE

THE NIGHT MY FATHER DIED I WAS HOME VISITING FROM college. My mom had taken a trip with her sister to visit an elderly aunt who seemed on the edge.

Nothing unique happened that week, nothing to give me the sense of foreboding I later realized I'd had. Dad had gone about his business as usual: he went to work on time, came home on time, cleaned out the garage, and fixed the long-broken porch door as a surprise for my mom.

But a couple of times I'd heard him up in the wee hours of the morning, walking around. I'd call and ask if he was okay and he would say yes. Another time he took a late shower. I still don't know why he did; it didn't seem like something I should ask about later, but it was a detail that afterward wouldn't fall into place.

One that almost did fall into place was a toothache he had

that wouldn't go away. Dad was not a fan of going to the doctor or dentist, so the fact that his tooth hurt enough to go was telling. Perhaps it was even more telling that they didn't find anything wrong. No cavity, no abscess, none of the usual suspects. The dentist just told him to get some Sensodyne and not to worry about it.

I'd like to get mad about that, but he couldn't have known what was going to happen.

So on the night in question, I went down River Road with Tanya to a party at someone's parents' giant house. We got bored early on, no one interesting there at all, and decided to go down to one of the old locks and have some wine. We took the remains of a bottle she was able to grab from the kitchen, and drove down one of the side roads to its dirt ending along the Potomac River. It was cold outside, but we had warm coats and the sky and stars and water were all so beautiful they were irresistible.

I think that, up to that point, it was one of the most beautiful nights of my life. We had a really good talk. We laughed about the antics we'd shared since meeting at thirteen, and cried about a few heartbreaks along the way (Brendan being one of them), and we talked about our futures and what we wanted. What we *really* wanted. We even went so far as to write our intentions down on a slip of paper—actually a duplicate check from my wallet—then crumpled them up, say a prayer, and toss them in the water to be carried off to their fruition.

Which, now that I think about it, they did. For the most part.

On the way back, I suggested she come to my house and we

sleep over. I had a copy of *Grease* on VHS and we could go down to the rec room and watch it, singing along as loud as we wanted to because my dad, I told her, slept like the dead.

I said that.

We went to her house so she could pick up a few things, and I used the phone to try and call my dad. It was about eleven-thirty P.M. and I figured he'd be up watching reruns of *M*A*S*H*, as usual. He didn't answer, and that was the last time in my life that I would get no answer on the phone from someone who should have been there and not feel a stab of worry. Or full-on dread.

Instead, Tanya and I ate a few Oreos and joked about the old pictures on her fridge, and then I tried him again.

This time when he didn't answer, I was . . . not *worried*, but curious. "That's weird," I said, wondering uneasily if he was having another late-night shower and what that could possibly mean. Fever? He felt cold so he needed to warm up? I didn't know.

"I'm sure everything's fine," Tanya said. "Look, why don't I meet you there so I can take my car home in the morning and you won't have to drive me? I'll be like twenty minutes or so."

"Perfect." I went back out to my car, excited about the fun ahead. I wondered if we had Jiffy Pop. My mind really stuck on that. Jiffy Pop. An absolute necessity for a sleepover.

When I pulled into the driveway, I noticed that the light was flickering weirdly in the window, the way it did in the days before cable when the networks signed off for the night and the screen got fuzzy. Someone I knew used to call that "the ant races." But why would the ant races be on in this day and age?

I went inside, and the minute I was in the front door, I saw it *was* the ant races. Everything seemed to go quiet. I knew something was wrong. I couldn't have guessed what, and if pressed to try I wouldn't have gotten it right, but I crept into the room and saw him.

He'd been on the sofa, sitting up, so he'd fallen over face forward. Later, I'd remember that and realize that it meant he'd had no pain. He hadn't tried to stand up, it seemed, or go to the phone to call for help. He'd just been watching TV, a movie on the VCR (which had since ended, thus explaining the fuzz), and at some point something had happened and he'd just— gone.

But that wasn't possible. In my mind, it wasn't possible. I went behind him, as scared as a kid in a graveyard on Halloween night, and touched his back. "Daddy? Are you all right?"

But no one just fell asleep that way. No one dropped forward like that into a peaceful sleep. I knew it was too late, that he was gone.

I didn't know what to do.

Anyone, even a five-year-old, would know to go to the phone and call 911, but I dithered for a moment. It felt like an hour. I was afraid to stay in the room with him. My father, whom I loved so much and who had always been the daddy teaching me to ride a bike or slipping me some cash when I was going out, my father, who had been the greatest dad there ever was, was terrifying to me.

I went upstairs to the phone in my room and dialed the three digits, 9-1-1, with trembling fingers. It felt like the phone rang forever, and then they actually put me on hold. What if I'd been reporting an intruder in the house? Would those moments, or minutes, or hours, or whatever they actually were, have meant the difference between life and death for me as well?

That's what it felt like. Crazy as it sounds, knowing there was a dead body downstairs—no longer my father but "a dead body"—made me feel like a girl in a horror film, vainly trying to hide from the inevitable.

When I was finally able to report the emergency, in an inexplicably hushed voice, I went back downstairs but didn't go back into that room. One glance told me what I already knew: that his position hadn't changed. It wasn't going to. Not under his own power.

So I went out front and sat on the cold cement front step and waited.

It was Tanya who showed up before the emergency crews. In the confusion, I'd forgotten she was coming, but I was so glad to see her. As she came toward the door, her gait slowed, and she asked, "What are you doing out here?"

That's when I lost it. That's when the numbness loosened and I burst into tears. "My f-f-father." I gestured helplessly toward the door, but when she started to go, thinking I was ushering her in, I grabbed her arm. "He's gone."

She frowned. "What do you mean, he's gone? His car is right there! What are you *talking* about?"

I sniffed. The tears felt icy on my face in the cold. "Dead," I managed. "He's dead. He's . . . in there, but he's dead. Oh, my god, I have to call my mother!"

Even in the dark I could see Tanya went pale. "Dead?"

I nodded, and then, as if timed perfectly in a play, the fire truck and ambulance and two police cars came screaming onto the street. We both stood there, watching, paralyzed, as they pulled up to the house and men in uniforms got out and came to the door.

The rest of the night is just flashes for me. The impression that the firemen in their boots and gear looked *huge* inside the house, like they were dolls from a different play set from us. The police asking the questions they must ask when a person dies alone: "Do you know when he was last alive?" "Do you know if anyone called or came by?" "Was he having any problems outside the home?"

No. No. No.

No.

We followed the ambulance to the hospital. It went slowly. Lights on, no siren. That's when I learned that that means the person inside is deceased. There was paperwork to sign, questions unanswered, sadness insurmountable.

I called my mother from the hospital pay phone. Her aunt didn't have caller ID, so I guess when the phone rang so late at night, she thought it was more than likely a nuisance call, maybe a wrong number. So I had the additional difficulty of making her understand it was me, as I broke into her fog of sleep, before going on to tell her that her husband was dead.

"Are you okay?" I asked idiotically.

"No." Of course not. Of *course* not. But I just needed her to be Mommy and fix everything.

I needed her to be Mommy and him to be Daddy and I needed to go back to bed and forget this nightmare. If I was quick, if

I could wake up quickly and then go back to sleep, I'd forget it all by morning.

But I couldn't, because it wasn't a dream, it was my new life. It shot me out of the cannon of childhood, straight into adulthood.

When it was all done and it was time to go, I hesitated, trapped by a strange feeling that I couldn't leave him behind. Was he already in a drawer somewhere? Were those chilled? They must be. I hated the questions, I hated thinking about that stuff, but I couldn't stop myself. There was so much that felt unfinished here. No, that felt *wrong*. Like a mistake. But it wasn't a mistake. Even though I could feel that I was in shock, I could feel there was a shield up in me and that a lot of things were going to hit me later, I didn't know what to do, except keep breathing and putting one foot in front of the other, and doing what I'd always done. I didn't know anything else.

This me with no father was someone I'd never been before.

When Tanya and I pulled up to the house, she said, "Do you want to wait here while I go make sure everything's locked up?"

"Wait here?" I echoed dumbly. "Then what?"

"We'll go to my house. You can't sleep here."

"But, we had plans. I think there's Jiffy Pop in the cupboard." Even to my own ears I sounded like a lunatic, but some part of me was still trying to push through and make this horrible thing go away. Be so determined to go about things as planned that I could make it all *un*happen.

"Ramie," Tanya said quietly. "You can come back tomorrow

after we get your mom from the airport, okay? Tonight you need to just come to my house and be away from this."

I nodded. The house probably still smelled like firemen, whatever they smelled like. Or death. Both. But wait—was he there? Had he left his body and gotten confused? He wouldn't have left me; shouldn't I stay here for him?

But I pictured the reality of that; I would be afraid to go any farther in than the foyer. I didn't want to clean up the French peanuts and baklava right now. I didn't want to see what movie he'd been watching. I didn't want to think about his last meal from the dishes in the sink. I didn't want to go in and dive into a life interrupted here in the middle of the night when I was exhausted and grieving and unable to think clearly. I had the strangest sensation of being an actress in a bad play, completely unprepared to recite my lines.

I do my thinking in the morning.

And I did. By morning, I had suddenly bloomed into the completely capable, cold businesswoman I became for the next two decades. I cleaned all the mess that was left behind. I turned the heat up so it wouldn't feel cold when my mom came in, and took down the anniversary card from him to her that had been on the mantel since their anniversary a week and a half before.

From then on I was changed. I never thought about how I wanted to *feel* because I no longer believed there was any choice in that matter. Instead I was completely focused on what needed to be done.

CHAPTER TWENTY-FOUR

WHAT WAS THE POINT OF ALL OF THIS?

What was the point of *any* of it?

Was this just what going insane felt like? Had I lost my grip on sanity somehow, suddenly and without warning? Was this the result?

It was all well and good for me to imagine or pretend this was some sort of actual time-travel experience, but that wasn't possible. Yet neither could it be a dream, because who ever had a dream that went on and on like this, with times of sleeping and waking within it? On top of that, I couldn't ever remember having a dream that included all the boring parts of life. The sitting around, waiting for something; turning over and going back to sleep, or waiting on the front stoop for a ride to pick me up. I'd had so many "down moments" that I couldn't imagine this was a dream.

If it was a real phenomenon somehow, then why wasn't the point of it obvious?

So it had to be insanity.

With that in mind, I decided to push it a little.

In the morning, I went out with my mom for her morning walk. Two miles around the neighborhood. She did it every morning, even twenty years later. I think it is the secret to her vibrant longevity.

Under present-day circumstances, I'm not sure I could keep up that well, but eighteen-year-old me had no problem.

"Something weird is happening," I said as we turned left out of our driveway.

"Already?"

"I mean in my life."

She glanced at me. "Tell me you're not pregnant." That was such a recurring theme in our lives back then. Not Being Pregnant. Back then, that seemed to be the worst thing that could possibly happen. I didn't blame her for fearing that.

I laughed. "I'm not! Good lord. I'm not sure I'll ever be, but I can *promise* it won't happen for a long, *long* time."

It was her turn to laugh. "Goodness, that's strongly worded. I didn't mean to imply *never*. Don't wait *too* long or your dad and I will never get to be grandparents."

If this was a dream, it was so tempting to just blurt it out, to say, *Dad's never going to know it no matter what.* But even in a dream I couldn't be so final.

So how could I put this?

"So, like I said, something weird is happening. And I don't

know exactly how to explain it. Do things feel . . . *normal* to you lately? Like, over the past week or so?"

She looked at me, surprised. "You feel it too? Yes." She sighed. "I don't know what's gotten into him. Ever since that accident . . ."

"Wait, what?"

"Weren't you talking about your father?"

"What about him?"

"His behavior seems a little off since he had that accident. I can't put my finger on it, but he seems detached. Don't you think?"

Well, of course the fact that he was walking and talking at all was strange to me, so I didn't know how to gauge whether he was suddenly different than he'd been the day before I had returned.

"I wondered if he was having an affair," she went on, as if speculating on a football team's chances of making the playoffs. "But that's completely out of character for him."

She didn't ask for confirmation, but I agreed. I knew he wouldn't have done that. "Absolutely. In fact, he just told me the other day, you mean the whole world to him."

I think I actually saw a pink flush light her cheeks. After all this time! That's the way it should be. Maybe it was even worth the loss just to have had something that meant so much to both of them. "You and he mean the world to me too." She frowned. "Still. Something's changed. I hope he's not ill. And that nothing happened in that accident that we don't know about yet. Sometimes you hear stories of people who have very slow internal bleeds and you don't know about them until it's too late."

I hesitated. "Well, it's not like Dad has the healthiest habits in the world."

"That's true."

"But this is kind of what I was saying. Ever since that day I've been in a sort of déjà vu. Like, I feel like I've come back in time and I'm reliving this time for some reason."

She stopped and turned to me. "What do you mean?"

"I was . . ." It felt wrong to get too specific right now. "I was older; I was having these experiences later in life, like I'd already finished college and gone into the job market, and suddenly I was back in high school, here, now. I know it sounds crazy, but it's like *something's* a dream and I don't know which part."

"Maybe *I'm* the one going crazy," she said, half to herself. But she seemed shaken. As I guess you would be if you were just talking to your daughter about your husband acting strangely and she told you she was a time traveler.

"Definitely not," I assured her, and we started walking again. "Maybe it's the moon or sunspot activity or something. Or maybe we're just all overtired from the end of school and the weather getting warmer, or *something*." I don't know why, but I felt like we shouldn't continue the conversation. Dream or not, I felt like it was upsetting her too much. Damaging something. "Anyway, Mom, just know that Dad loves you more than anything else in this world. No matter what happens, ever, you have something very few people ever get."

She put an arm around me. "You'll have it too, baby. Don't you worry. It might not be with Brendan," she cautioned—she obviously thought there was no way a high school relationship was going to become the real thing—"but it will be with the *right* man."

I snorted. "Whoever *that* is."

"He'll show up."

"What if he doesn't?"

"He *will*. Maybe not in your time frame—we're all always so impatient for the good stuff—but when the time is right, he will come to you."

I was going to have to hold on to that hope for a *long* time.

When we got back home, my dad was in the garage, tinkering with something at the worktable, Zuzu lying at his feet. "Ahoy!" he called, and raised a hand to us. "I dropped a quarter by the couch and reached down, and look what I found under there." He held something up and we went closer. "It's the missing handle from the rolltop desk. Looks like the Halls' dog might have gotten ahold of it when they were here visiting, though." He held it at eye level and, indeed, it did seem to be covered in tiny tooth marks. "So I thought I'd sand it out a bit and stain it."

My mom was thrilled. "I hate to admit it, but that's been bothering me inordinately," she said with a laugh. "Every time I see that piece it seems lopsided because of the missing handle."

"Worry no more, milady. I have it solved."

"But, no," I said, thinking about the handle more than about what I was saying. "We never found that. It's still missing."

"Not now!" my mom said, smiling but with a slight crease in her brow. "That's what your father is saying, he found it."

I looked at him, then at the handle. He had indeed. But when

I was thirty-eight, it was still missing. And far from hating to admit it, my mother had told me countless times that it drove her nuts that it was missing, but she was never able to find anything close enough, even though it had become something of a life quest to look for one at every thrift shop, antique store, and flea market she happened upon.

I didn't remember this event, but maybe it had happened and the damn thing got lost again. It's not like it could have that much significance; we never used the drawer because we couldn't open it, so it wasn't going to suddenly have a lost copy of the Declaration of Independence in it or anything.

"You're my hero!" my mother said to Dad, and gave him a peck on the cheek and squeezed his shoulder.

"All in a day's work," he replied.

She went in through the garage door and closed it behind her, sending everything pegged on the wall there—tennis rackets, jumper cables, and so on—into a jangle.

"Dad," I said when she was gone. It hadn't worked with Mom. Maybe it would work with him. For some reason, this new wrench in the works compelled me more. "I feel like I've been here before." Bad intro, I know.

And, obviously, he didn't pick right up on my meaning. "It sure wasn't to clean up!" He laughed and looked around.

I smiled. "No, I mean, in this place and time. I know this sounds crazy, believe me, you don't have to call the guys in the white jackets or send me to Chestnut Lodge or anything; it's just . . . to me, all of this feels like a dream."

"As the great Lewis Carroll said, *Life, what is it but a dream?*"

"Okay." I sighed. "Maybe in the greater sense, but I'm talking about *right now*. In my head, and maybe in reality—I believe it is in reality—I have lived way past this time. I'm thirty-eight, or I was about to be, but suddenly I've been thrust back into my eighteen-year-old body. My eighteen-year-old *life*."

He stopped what he was doing, and rested his hand on the workbench, still holding the drawer pull I did not yet know the final fate of. "So that's what it feels like for you."

"What do you mean?"

"I've noticed a certain difference in you, of course. It's been an odd few days, though I guess graduating from high school forever does that to a person. You're old and you're young. Every time I thought you'd become very serious and very *mature*, for lack of a better word, you'd come up with something that sounded just like the Ramie I knew, and I thought it was all in my imagination."

"I don't understand."

"No, you can't. I'm not making much sense, I suppose. All I mean is that I sensed something was troubling you but I didn't want to push, because the worst thing in the world you can do with someone who is struggling to regain their balance is to push them."

I nodded. *That* I understood. "And how's your balance?"

"A little off, kiddo. I'm a little off myself. Different situation from yours, though. We're all on different paths, even though love keeps us together. What is it that's troubling you the most about the way that you feel?"

"I don't know what to do. I don't know how to act. I feel like a fool acting like . . ." I struggled for words, then just pointed at myself. "Like *this*. I'm thirty-eight, not eighteen, so how can I show up here and act like a young girl? Talk like a young girl? Every time I say *cool* I feel like a complete poser."

He laughed heartily. Which was better than looking alarmed and asking my mom to call 911, but not quite as good as taking me seriously. "Then consider it a fun game! Playacting! That's the best we can do. If you fight it, you're not going to learn anything."

"So you think I'm here to learn something?"

"We're *all* here to learn something." He looked at me seriously then. "Sometimes we learn it in the worst possible way. Sometimes we have to face something we don't think we can live through in order to show ourselves that we can live through hell and still come out on the other side. Do you know what I mean?"

He could have been describing his own death. "Yes. I know what you mean."

"I want you to remember that."

"I don't think I'll ever forget."

He touched my wrist, drawing my attention to his face. He was looking at me intently. His eyes were bluer than I'd ever realized. I felt like I was seeing him for the first time. "Everything happens for a reason. *Everything.* Don't spend your life regretting one thing, no matter how big it is."

I took his hand in mine. "I don't think you fully know what you're saying."

"I do. You're stronger than you think. And your instincts are better than you believe. Always. That will serve you well in all areas of your life."

I nodded.

"Whatever your circumstances, whether it's normal everyday discomfort or something that feels really bizarre, just go with it and do what feels most appropriate. You know what they say."

"No, what?"

He smiled, waited a beat, then said, "When in Rome..." Then he returned to his work.

"You can catch more flies with honey than vinegar." I looked down toward the street and clenched my jaw, trying to quell the tears of frustration. The sun bouncing off the car that was so emblematic of my youth was both comforting and sinister at the same time.

If I could dive into this and stay, knowing that time would go forward from here, would I? What would I do differently? I didn't know. I didn't know from moment to moment what to do differently, and every change I made felt like a misstep, so maybe it was really a curse being thrust back in time.

Maybe I'd seen enough of this car back when we had it. Maybe now it was time to see the sun bouncing off another windshield. Maybe soon there would be yet another one. Maybe someday, if *The Jetsons* were to be believed (which I feared they weren't), I'd be looking at the sun on my spaceship. I mean, come on: George Jetson and Mr. Spacely Skyped, which a few years ago we thought was impossible, so why not?

In other words, maybe I had to stop looking for answers in my past. Maybe I needed to stop trying to *fix* my past.

Yet, given how empty my present felt, I didn't know where else to look.

I turned my attention back to my father and watched him carefully sand the handle.

"I don't think I can get all the tooth marks out without making this half the size of the others," he said with a chuckle. But he was right, some of the cuts were deep.

"No one will notice," I said. "I don't think anyone noticed for years that it was gone." I focused on the handle, trying to recall whether or not it had been returned, chewed, to its original spot. I looked up to ask my father when the dog had been in the house, but he wasn't there.

He wasn't there.

What the hell?

"Dad?" I looked around. Had I gotten so lost in thought that he'd stepped away and I hadn't even noticed? "Dad?" I called again, louder this time.

But there was no answer.

I was alone in the garage.

The handle wasn't there. In fact, the sandpaper was gone, all the tools that a moment ago had been strewn all over the table were gone. It was tidy and clean, the way my mom kept it.

I glanced at the driveway, half expecting to see her BMW or my Lexus there, back in the future, but there was nothing there. No easy answer. When I looked at the back wall of the garage, the tennis rackets and cables and old jump ropes and everything else that had been there for thirty-plus years were still there. No clue struck me.

"Dad?" I called again, but a little softer this time. I was self-conscious that maybe I was back in my thirty-eighth year and someone would hear me and grow concerned that I was calling for a man who'd been dead for eighteen years.

I went into the house, via the garage door and the laundry

room, where my mom had just gone in. "Dad?" I called again. Then, louder, "Mom?"

No one answered.

"Zuzu?" That was when the panic grew. Zuzu always came running when I called, no matter where she was. Even she was gone. "Zuzu!" I tried again, but nothing. There wasn't even a sign of her around. No water bowl in the laundry room, no treat box on the counter.

The eeriness was overwhelming.

I looked for clues of the year, but on the main floor there really weren't any. It had never changed much. Which wasn't to say my mother was stuck in the past, but only that the décor was kind of timeless and she had never been compelled to change it.

I looked in the kitchen, hoping a newspaper might be lying around, even the small community one, but she was so fastidious about not letting junk sit around that of course there was nothing there.

My head hurt.

And I was scared. Honestly, I was really scared. Nothing was predictable right now; nothing was making sense; the universe had lost all the order I had believed it to have. So I was as vulnerable as I'd ever been in my life.

I went and sat down on the couch. Right in the same spot where my father either had died eighteen years ago or was going to soon. I sat and put my aching head in my hands and cried. What if this was some weird new permutation of this disturbing event? What if now I was here, alone, trapped in time—or the lack thereof—possibly forever? It felt like a *Twilight Zone* episode. Maybe that one where the bank teller is in the vault reading when the end of the world comes, and when he comes out he steps on his glasses and has to spend eternity alone in a fog.

That was my idea of hell.

Had I done something to deserve hell, and was I in it now?

I started to cry. Then the tears came faster and hotter and I cried and cried and cried, sinking down onto the sofa where my father had fallen, and wishing, like him, I could just be gone.

CHAPTER TWENTY-FIVE

I WOKE UP. COMPLETELY DISORIENTED, STILL QUAKING WITH confusion and grief, but I woke up.

So I wasn't dead. Probably. I don't believe death has as many aches and pains as I was feeling. Mostly my head. Always my head. What the hell had happened to my head? Some sort of traumatic brain injury that caused brain damage and shooting pains, and thus all this supposed "time travel"? Or was it just a hangover? Last I could recall, before my strange interlude of twenty years ago, there had been an awful lot of champagne on that yacht before I decided to go off the board.

Had I drowned? They said that was a very pleasant experience. Likely due to the cold water and slow oxygen deprivation to the brain. Anyway, that's how I understood it, and I took that to mean that one might go back to an easier time and place, or a more pleasant time—real or imagined—or, I suppose, the more complicated and self-torturing among us might go back to our most angsty time and imagine we could change it, fix it, heal everything.

But I didn't feel that way.

If anything, I felt the opposite. I felt *less* powerful than I'd felt the first time I was a teenager. I just wanted to roll over and go to sleep. Again and again. Actually, I could envision that going on forever. There was no reason to get out of bed ever again.

So I rolled over, and pulled the sheet with me. The bed wasn't well made, so the sheet pulled free from my feet, which was aggravating. I know if I'd been a caveman, many thousands of years ago, any of these soft coverings would undoubtedly have been welcome luxuries. But I wasn't a caveman, I was a lost investment banker trying to find her way back to some logical coordinate. And the sheet coming untucked from under the mattress and cutting off at my calf and leaving my foot free and cold was uncomfortable. And it called attention to the fact that my foot was hanging slightly off the end of the bed.

I opened my eyes and looked at the room, expecting to see . . . well, actually, I don't know what I was *expecting* to see. I'd stopped expecting the expected. I just hoped for, I don't know . . . something familiar, surely. Something that made some sort of sense. My office, my hotel in Florida, my room at my parents' house, my room at my own apartment, the Hot Shoppes Cafeteria on the corner of Wisconsin and Old Georgetown Road. Something, anything, that would peg me in the time I'd reached and allowed me at least some insight into just how crazy I was . . . or, hopefully, wasn't.

Yet . . . all that said . . . boy, I would have liked to have rolled over and gone back to sleep. Again and again.

Instead, I looked at the red LED clock on the bedside table and saw it was 6:56 A.M.

But, wait. That wasn't a clock I recognized. It wasn't a table I recognized. With instant and resounding reluctance, I took in my surroundings. And I had no idea where I was.

It was a room of perhaps twenty square feet, with two large windows that revealed the green leaves of a very big oak and let the sun in to slant down across the hardwood floor. Gleaming, clean, and utterly unknown to me.

I was in a four-poster bed, queen-sized, with what seemed like a million pillows at the head, hence my position squished down with my feet hanging off the end of the bed. The sheets had a small flower print that looked like Target's version of Laura Ashley, and there was a pale lavender chenille bedspread. I hated chenille. It never felt like it got really clean. And don't let the dog up on it; that's a mess.

That thought came from left field, but I paused to be grateful that, with my ninety-nine—and counting—problems, a dog with muddy paws wasn't one of them.

My head ached so much that it felt like my thoughts were squeezing painfully through cracked cement. I wanted to go back to sleep, to some sort of oblivion that allowed me to not have to puzzle out all these mysteries of time and place while I was feeling so crummy.

So I closed my eyes and tried to will it all away. Even while I lay there, like a child determined to will the monsters away, I could tell that nothing was changing. All I could do was play chicken with no one until I got so bored of lying here with my eyes closed that I got up and tried to make sense of whatever world I was in now.

I took a deep, deep breath, threw the covers back with a confidence I did not have, and stood up from bed.

If it was time for me to handle something in this insane journey, then I was going to handle it, damn it.

So I took a step forward.

Okay, yes, I know that's anticlimactic. Yet so far all I had been able to achieve was that which happened when I believed I was asleep or was knocked straight out. I couldn't just cross my arms in front of me like Barbara Eden in *I Dream of Jeannie* (another rerun favorite of mine), blink my eyes, and make time jump to wherever I wanted it to. Or, rather, make *myself* jump to whatever place in time I wanted to get to.

Instead I had to work with what I had.

Who knows? Maybe this was all a crazy dream that would never amount to anything more than the nightmare about talking strawberries in your salad accusing you of stealing kittens, the sort of dream that lingers with a question mark for a few minutes, then disappears into the ether of the day and *reality*.

I walked around the room, taking inventory of what felt like a very ordinary place. Actually it's disingenuous for me to say it wasn't familiar, because in a way it was. In a way it was completely predictable. It was an extension of the house I'd grown up in. A watered-down version of shabby chic, some dark wood antiques (the dresser and two bedside tables), and some things that looked like they were from IKEA (a lighter wood armoire and mission-style bed frame).

When I went to the window, I saw a picnic table, a coiled hose hanging on the brick wall of another part of the house, and a lot of green grass that I just knew was hell to mow in the summer and a bitch to rake in the fall. Particularly with this huge oak tree. There were probably a hundred thousand leaves on it right now.

The idea of those chores made me weary. I could imagine them all too well.

I peeked in the bathroom. Ordinary. A tub/shower combo (I hate those—they feel dangerous, and I never want to sit in water where people have been standing and peeing), medicine cabinet slightly open and reflecting the American Standard toilet, and a double sink with a pressed wood console. One side of the counter had man stuff: a toothbrush, a stainless steel razor, Old Spice deodorant (I confess I've always loved that; Brendan used to use it), and a few splatters of toothpaste on the mirror. I almost laughed at that. My ex-boyfriend Jeffrey was fastidious about that—it drove him nuts—so he kept one of those pop-up containers of glass-cleaning wipes under the sink in case any slight sign of use left its mark on the mirror or sink.

The other side of the counter was clearly a woman's domain: there were Victoria's Secret lotions and body spray, an electric toothbrush with Sensodyne toothpaste (I felt for her—I have sensitive teeth too and it's really a pain), a neatly folded pink washcloth with a bottle of Phisoderm cleanser on it, and a red bottle of Olay. I used to use Phisoderm before I started making more money and could afford my favorite Alchimie Forever line, so I could have slipped into this woman's bathroom life and not necessarily have felt that displaced.

I squirted the Victoria's Secret body spray into the air and sniffed. It was nice. Wild at Heart. It reminded me of something. Love's Baby Soft, maybe. It was sweet. Innocent.

I tried to imagine the life that was being lived in this house. At least in the bedroom and bathroom. There was only one way to find out. I needed to venture out of the room and find out who had brought me here and why. At this point, I figured if I was still eighteen, a friend or neighbor had probably come by and found me upset and taken me to their place until my parents got home.

If I was thirty-eight, I had to assume I had had *way* too much to drink on my birthday and this headache was indeed a hangover and now I was, embarrassingly, in the home of someone I didn't know well enough to be passed out in.

If that were the case, where the hell was Sammy? Why would he do this to me?

I made my way through the bedroom, stopping to snoop briefly in the closet, where there were a *lot* of jeans and surf-brand tops, and more different-colored flip-flops than I'd ever seen in my life. So I was either in Florida again or in the home of someone who was so completely devoted to summer that they could stuff a closet full just for the one season.

Assuming it was Florida, that was a huge relief. I was back where I belonged. I'd overdone it, likely made a fool of myself, and now had to go face the music . . . and figure out who the musicians even were.

Honestly, I thought, walking through the hall and nearly tripping over a pink stuffed elephant, Sammy should have been right here by my side the whole time so I wouldn't have this awkward moment of trying to figure out where I was and who I was with.

After all, five years ago, I'd been there to take his dumb, drunk ass away from his ex's wedding just as he was about to take the mic and start to sing "their song" to all the confused guests. I had stayed with him all night, stopped him—forcibly—from sending some ill-advised texts, and reassured him in the morning that people *probably* hadn't really noticed his tears or that terribly awkward moment when he'd tried to wrench the ring off Curtis's newlywed finger. He hadn't remembered much, but he recalled enough to feel humiliation boil up in him within thirty seconds of waking up in the morning.

"Oh, god," he'd moaned, upon realizing what he'd done.

"Yup." I'd patted his hand. "Hell of a night."

"I didn't . . . *do* anything, did I?"

"You mean like call Curtis's new husband a selfish bitch and accuse him of stealing your man?"

He'd winced, and I couldn't blame him. "I said that, didn't I? I remember saying that."

I nodded. "But *fortunately* you only said it to me."

"But I remember—"

"You were practicing your speech on me. You never made it over to him."

I saw the relief relax all the muscles in his face, and I sympathized. I knew the feeling. Don't we all?

"And the spastic dancing to Kelly Clarkson?"

"You did that."

He'd sighed, heavy and ragged. "Of course I did. With the hand motions?"

I'd just shrugged. "Of course."

I needed Sammy. I needed my sidekick, my confidant. Where the hell was he now?

Okay, okay, I didn't *really* blame him for not being here holding my hand. He'd been drinking with me; maybe he felt every bit as crappy as I did. And even if he didn't, I'd clearly gotten myself into this mess, and it wasn't up to him or anyone else to get me out of it. I just had to thank whoever I needed to thank, write a check for whatever kind of damage I might have done, and get myself home and into a hot bath with a mug of coffee and the latest *Financial Times*.

I needed to feel normal again.

The bottom step spilled onto a slate foyer, and I heard a male voice talking in the kitchen. I assumed it was the kitchen anyway. These houses were all alike in some way—they all felt like home for some reason—and I was easily able to follow the voices into what did, indeed, turn out to be a decent-sized eat-in suburban kitchen.

I pushed the swinging saloon-style door open with great trepidation, having no idea who I was going to see there. Lisa and Larry, maybe? In their pregnant suburban life?

But no. They lived much higher on the hog than this. I'd seen their apartment on Key Biscayne; it was gorgeous. And, anyway, she was pregnant for the first time now. There wouldn't have been a stuffed animal lying around Lisa and Larry's house. No way.

I could be facing anyone.

I mean, I actually had that thought. *I could be facing anyone.* I couldn't have imagined who that would be.

"Sit!" he commanded. "Stay. Stay . . . stay . . . Don't look at

Mommy—stay. *Stay.*" He wasn't talking to me, but to a golden retriever self-consciously sitting before him, eyes darting toward me and back to the man in front of him, with a Milk-Bone on his nose.

Unsurprising scene, in a way.

Brendan had always loved teaching his dogs tricks.

CHAPTER TWENTY-SIX

"YOU FINALLY GOT UP!" HE SAID TO ME, THEN GLANCED AT THE dog and quickly said, "*Okay!*" whereupon the dog shook his snout and caught the bone, crunching eagerly in case another one was coming.

"I ... yes. I guess. ..." I squinted at him a little, trying to make sense of him. Where were we? Why did he look different? I couldn't put my finger on it.

His hair, I thought. It was shorter. Parted to the side, rather than the haphazard storm of brown waves it had always been when I knew him. But his face was the same. Maybe a little ... I don't know ... older? No lines, really, but something about the set of his expression was more serious. Less goofy than the guy I'd known.

Then again, what had I known? A boy. In high school. Two years seemed like infinity then, but ten times that had passed and

I'd grown enough to know that no one's eighteen-year-old self tells you who they really are.

"Man, that baby's really taking it out of you, huh? I haven't heard a coherent sentence come out of your mouth in a month." He laughed. "Even Barnaby makes more sense than you." He nodded at the dog.

"I'm sorry," I said. "I'm just . . . confused." I glanced around. Baby? Did we have a baby in this new old life? "What baby?"

He didn't laugh this time. He tipped his head to the left and frowned. "What baby?"

"Well, you know . . ." Of course he didn't know. *I* didn't know. Whatever he was talking about, it sure wasn't the kind of thing a person just completely forgets and has to ask about, outside of a Lifetime movie. *Do I have children? Are you my mother?* This was, to him, insane. "I'm so foggy. I just woke up and had so many weird dreams."

He came over to me then and cupped my face in his hands. "You need to take it really easy. You know the doctor told you that. I don't think you should go to work today. I'll call the school and tell them you can't."

"The school?" I was echoing everything dumbly. I know it made no sense to him. "I work at a school?" Then an idea came to me that might just work. I smiled, sleepily, like I was just teasing him. I was hoping he'd play along.

And he did. "Yes, Mrs. Riley, you teach seventh-grade math at the local middle school, you're twenty-six years old, I made you an honest woman five years ago, and now you're pregnant with your first child"—he gestured at what I now realized was a slightly puffed-out and definitely queasy stomach; I wasn't hung over, I was *pregnant*—"and Barnaby is going to be very jealous as soon as he is born."

"He?" *Barnaby?*

"Okay, or *she*." It was clear we had no idea but that he was hoping for a boy and I was hoping for a girl. This was obviously a conversation we'd had more than once. "But Barnaby is going to be jealous, so can you please say hello to him? He's been eyeing you pretty desperately since you walked in here."

"Oh." I looked at the dog with a sense of recognition, but I'd had golden retrievers growing up, and in my experience they all looked very similar. I'd seen L.L.Bean dogs who looked so similar to my beloved lost Bailey that I did a double- and triple-take.

So while Barnaby was looking at me with expectant familiarity, I wasn't sure if I knew him or just knew dogs.

In either case, I found myself saying, "Hey, Barnaby. Hey, Barn." He galumphed over to me, and I reached out and scritched him behind the ears. He smiled and turned his face up, leaning into my touch. Dogs. They were so easy. "Good boy," I cooed.

"So what do you say?" Brendan asked me. "Want me to call the school? I think you should rest."

Well, hell, whatever job I had wasn't real to me now, so I didn't see any point in going out of my way to protect it. Feeling like I could step back into my teenage "do-over" was one thing, but there was no way I could step into a twentysomething life I'd never lived. A life I had no feel for whatsoever. "Please," I said to Brendan. "I really want to stay in today. Tell them I don't know when I'll be back." Truer words were never spoken. At least not by me.

He nodded. "If you want to add anything to the grocery list, give me a call."

He did the grocery shopping? How sweet he was. I guess I'd really lucked out in this incarnation.

"You know where to get me," he said, and gave me a peck on the cheek. "Make sure you keep drinking water. We don't want to go back to the hospital."

"Right." Better not to push my luck asking too many obvious questions. "I'll do that. And . . . you know where to find me too."

He gave me the thumbs-up sign and went out the front door. I stood there for a long moment, watching the nonexistent jet stream that followed his path. Then I turned to the dog.

"Well, Barnaby. What the fuck do I do now?"

WHAT I DID was spend the next three hours rooting through every drawer, examining every picture on the fridge, every note on the desk in the den, and looking for every other clue to my state of mind in this life. I read a lot of inspirational books. Not religious, but encouraging, self-help with your self-esteem books. Titles like *Prayers for a Simple Life, The Path to Happiness, Three Easy Steps to Meditation,* and *What to Do When You Can't Do Anything.*

There were also a few titles on getting pregnant, like *Getting Pregnant Naturally* and *Old Wives' Remedies for Young Wives.* Actually I thought that was a pretty insulting title and I couldn't imagine myself buying it, but when I opened it up and leafed through I saw an inscription:

*Chin up, young wife! You'll be a tired old wife
with a brood of brats before you know it! I know
you will hate this title but I think there might
actually be some good tips in here. Let's meet
for some raspberry leaf tea soon! XO, Bonnie*

So I had friends. I didn't know them, of course, but at least I had friends. That was good. Disconcerting, too—a whole life, including histories with strangers, that I didn't know anything at all about—but it was good.

It was also good that I knew myself well enough, and was consistent enough, to know I would have bristled at that title no matter what life path I had chosen. I felt a private pride. I might not be living my own life, the life I knew, but at least I was still me.

With that in mind, I went back to the bedroom and looked on my closet shelf. I had always kept a box of keepsakes—letters, ticket stubs, whatever—on my closet shelf at home, and it was something I'd continued doing even though the pieces of my life had changed significantly. So when I went to this Ramie's bedroom closet and looked, sure enough I found an elaborate hatbox, with a T.J.Maxx sticker still on the bottom.

It was heavy and my body was a little awkward. Carefully, I carried it over to the bed and sat down with it. Barnaby clicked into the room and jumped handily onto the mattress beside me. I automatically reached over and ruffled his fur. "You probably understand more about what's going on than I do, right, buddy?"

He sighed and rolled onto his side. There was not an ounce

of fear that I was going to chastise him for being up here, so I guess he was a furniture dog. My mom would have hated that. I know that because I allowed *all* of our dogs to be furniture dogs.

"Okay. You do that and I'll do this." I had a vague sense of sneakiness about this, like I was trespassing on someone else's life, rather than my own. But the fact that it *was* my own meant that, if this life didn't happen or if I made another choice, this was *no one's* life, so, basically, I could do whatever I wanted. If I could somehow be sure I'd get out of here, I might have felt free to make every stupid mistake I'd ever imagined. In fact, if I *really* knew there would be no consequences, or memories, I could even come up with a few more.

But life is uncertain, even—or especially—in the midst of great uncertainty. Even the most ridiculous and cartoonish of dreams seem real while you're in them. Yes, that's Sammy Davis, Jr., riding a camel sidesaddle and holding a sign for that Chinese restaurant that closed four years ago, what of it? If Napoleon and Erma Bombeck can sit and chat with him about sewing dog coats, it must be fine, right?

So here I was, in a life I'd never had, able to predict myself by how I'd always been, but unable to see my present beyond the scope of my past. What could I do, but hope that there was some reason for this, other than some wacky *Dr. Who* time-space continuum mix-up that would thrust me, permanently, into confusion?

I took the top off the box, which was so full that a few things spilled onto the bed. A car key—VW of some sort—and a heavy birthday card with one of those musical buttons in it, as well as a couple of coins I didn't know the significance of, though it probably had something to do with the dates on them or the places I'd found them or the people who'd given them to me. I was like that. I'd pick coins up and read significance into them every time, so sometimes when I had some extra coins lying around, I'd just throw them onto the street or sidewalk for someone else to find and feel lucky for having.

I opened the birthday card on top of the pile. It was from Brendan. And Barnaby. I felt an impatient little sigh inflate inside of me but didn't want to let it complain its way out. This was nice. It was a nice card. It had a recording of Elvis singing "You Ain't Nothin' but a Hound Dog"—another Barnaby reference, I gathered. I closed the card, but the tinny music kept playing. I frowned. Pressed it together harder. It still played. I felt an irritation I couldn't quite name, but felt I knew well, surge inside of me, and I pinched the music button hard. It stopped. I set it aside for fear of starting it up again.

I hadn't realized I hated those cards, but I do. I hate those cards.

Next there was a birthday card from my mom. Nice but totally unremarkable. Bless her, she was one who would just put *Ramie*—above the prewritten message, then, *Love, Mom,* beneath it. There was never anything more specific, more personal than that. It was always just basically, *This message is close enough to the mark for me to give it to you from me,* and I have always accepted it as just that.

Recently she's gotten into sending e-cards instead, which drives me absolutely insane. They always go straight to the junk file, and if I don't find them, they remind her I haven't read them,

which she always takes personally. And I feel guilty. It's this dance
we do.

So in that way, it was kind of fun to see her handwritten im-
personal card to a twenty-sixish me.

But I wasn't sure why I'd saved it.

The more I dug into the box, the more evidence I unearthed
of a life that was very different from the one I'd created. A life
in which I valued things like preprinted movie stubs and imper-
sonal cards and a D.C. Metro ticket from a date that had no great
significance that I could tell, but that was, for some reason, worth
saving. Barnaby's first collar and tag were in there—I gathered
they were his first from the collar's size and the fact that the tag
had a different address from the one more recent correspondence
told me I was in now; in Maryland, it turned out—as were his
bill of sale and a computer printout of a picture of his litter from
the *Washington Post* online.

Fertility books, self-help books, daily affirmations, cards and
keepsakes from a small circle of friends, a house that could have
been glued right onto the one I'd grown up in and not had any
style differences . . . all told a story I didn't quite know. I couldn't
relate to it. Yet clearly my psychology was written all over the
place here.

Nature versus nurture was ceasing to be a question for me.

But there was, of course, one thing I'd been ignoring. One
factor that gave this "movie" a heavier implication: the baby I
was apparently carrying.

I put my hand to my belly and waited. I don't know what I
was waiting for. I've never been pregnant, but I'm not a moron
and I know you can't feel the baby moving around at such an early

stage. What I didn't expect, though, was how hard my middle felt. Almost distended. Tendons were stretching and I felt heavy in a way I never had before. I had to pee constantly. While I'd gone through the keepsakes, I'd had to get up no fewer than three times, and it might have been four. It was uncomfortable, alien, but when I sat and tried to meditate on it, there was no accompanying sense of reality. I had no sense of a child, no sense of the person that child would be. No sense, even, of where my body was headed. It was like I was in a play and this was my costume.

There was no way to answer the metaphysical questions that this situation raised: Did we have many paths out there, lives being lived in accordance with every choice we could possibly make? Or could our own life shift suddenly into another, as mine appeared to have done, and did that happen all the time without our noticing it? If time wasn't linear, did that mean we were as capable of changing the past as we were of changing the future?

All of these questions were moot as far as I was concerned because I hadn't been able to change a damn thing in my experience. In fact, I couldn't even figure out if my environment, or my self, was real. Presumably one of us was, but damned if I knew which.

I put the box back into the closet and searched for another, perhaps the one that contained the really interesting or juicy stuff, but I couldn't find anything. So I went back downstairs and looked around, trying to find some sort of . . . I don't know, clue? Reason I was here?

There were framed pictures of Brendan and me scattered about the house, taken over the years. I recognized one from our graduation / my birthday dinner at the Kona Kai. Others were hard to pin down. We didn't look very different in them and I had no way to know when I had what hairstyle, so it was just a collage of a life we'd somehow had together. A trip someplace tropical—the kind of flash-front, palm-trees-in-the-back shot you might see on 90 percent of Facebook profiles. Skiing, though I'm pretty sure that was local, at Ski Liberty forty miles north. They'll never hold the Olympic ski competitions in Maryland.

There was an office down a hallway off the kitchen, and I went in there hoping to find some paperwork from my job, some clue to what teaching was like and if it was enjoyable. I dug through the drawers and saw folders marked TAXES, UTILITIES, HOME REPAIR, MEDICAL, and so on, very neatly organized.

I had to have a valise or something somewhere. I started to poke around for it when the doorbell rang.

For a moment I froze. My impulse was to hide. To avoid interaction with anyone. But then I reminded myself that if I wanted to figure out what I was supposed to be doing and getting from this, then I needed to dive into it.

As I went back into the hallway, the bell rang again. I quickened my pace and opened the door to the worried face of a brunette woman, about thirty years old, wearing khaki shorts and a pink camp shirt, with a Coach bag slung over her shoulder.

"Oh, my god, Ramie!" She held a hand to her chest in visible relief. "I went by your classroom and they said you called in sick, and I was just so afraid that, you know, after last week . . . Is everything all right?"

What was I supposed to do? Was everything all right how? As far as I was concerned, everything was *not* all right, but I didn't think the subtext of her question was, *Are you time-traveling?* or *Is anything seriously fucked-up happening to you?*

The problem was I had no idea who she was or what her relationship to me was.

"Oh, no, it's not, is it? Something's wrong, I can just tell. What's going on?"

"N-n-nothing's going on," I stammered. "Everything's fine. I'm just not sure what you're referring to. After *what* happened last week?"

"The cramps!" She bustled in, closing the door behind her with a quick glance over her shoulder, as if someone were out there who might hear this secret information. "I was afraid you were having another miscarriage!"

CHAPTER TWENTY-SEVEN

"YOU'RE NOT, RIGHT?" SHE WENT ON. "YOU CAN TELL ME THE truth. We can go to the doctor right now if you have *any* doubts at all. When I heard you weren't at work, I was afraid you'd be here alone, too worried to tell Brendan something was wrong."

"Why wouldn't I want Brendan to know?"

"Oh, come *on.*" She half rolled her eyes. "He'd be all over you; you wouldn't get a moment's peace, and you know it. I thought we agreed that if you had any problems you'd call and say, *I saw Mr. McCormick in the hall today.* Hello? Did you seriously forget that?"

For a moment, I was completely baffled. Who *was* this woman and what the hell was she talking about? But then I smiled. Mr. McCormick. My seventh-grade math teacher. He was *such* an asshole. If I saw Mr. McCormick coming, it would mean I was in trouble.

I guess I'd come up with that as a code to let her, whoever she was, know I was in trouble.

"Mr. McCormick is nowhere near here," I said, though actually I couldn't literally be sure of that. Maybe, in this world, he was my next-door neighbor.

"Thank goodness. Do you have any of that vodka left, honey? I could use a slug. Sorry you can't join me."

"Um . . . yeah. Sure. Help yourself." Because god knew I couldn't help her. Given some time I could probably search out where we kept the liquor, but it might be a little suspect to do that while she was here watching.

I followed her into the kitchen, and she went straight to the freezer. Of course. Vodka was in the freezer.

"You sit down, girl," she said, gesturing impatiently at me to sit at the table. "You shouldn't be standing around, stressing those stomach muscles. Sit down and let me bring you something. Are you hungry?"

"No, I'm good."

"Well, I'm at least bringing you a glass of milk. You need the protein and calcium."

"Okay." Whoever she was, she obviously had kids of her own, because she was very, very good at issuing orders in a kind and caring, yet very firm, way. And I was glad to take them, actually, because I was really tired. Stomach muscles or not, it was fatiguing standing on the hard floor. I wasn't used to this body. It was really uncomfortable.

"Any symptoms today?" she asked.

"I'm just peeing a lot." How was I going to get a name out of her when we apparently knew each other so well?

She laughed. "I remember that. Bad enough that you have to drink gobs of water, but then you have a baby sitting on your bladder. It's murder. Absolute murder." She opened a cabinet and took out a glass, took it to the fridge, and poured in milk.

"And my lower back is kind of sore."

She kicked the fridge door closed and came over to me, glass of milk in one hand, bottle of vodka in the other. Was she just going to sit down and drink it right out of the bottle?

"Hurts steadily or is it coming and going like cramps?" she asked. "If it's coming and going that could be cause for concern."

"No, it just feels like I had a hard workout."

Her shoulders relaxed. "That's typical." She took a shot glass off a shelf full of different ones that I hadn't noticed before, and set it on the table. "My back hurt the entire time. For some of us just a few extra pounds starts the body aches coming." She un-screwed the bottle, poured, then put the top back on and sat down. "That brood of brats has no appreciation for what I went through to have them." She tapped her glass on the table, then lifted it and threw it back.

The gesture was familiar. It was a *thing*. A thing of ours? Or a thing I'd just seen somewhere before? Maybe it was a thing a lot of people did. But something else was ringing a bell in my mind. *Brood of brats.* Where had I heard that before?

"What's the matter?" she asked. I must have been looking at her funny, because she raised a hand to her chin. "Did I spill?"

"No, I was just thinking about having a brood of brats. I'm not sure I can even handle one."

"Well, as you know, I didn't set out to have a brood. Who the hell knew you could have identical twins if they didn't run in the family?"

I knew. It was just mathematical odds. Fraternal twins were hereditary. I knew this because my cousins were identical twins and the random possibility of it both fascinated and scared me as I had once fantasized about my future family life. Had this woman and I really never talked about this before?

"Oh, wait. It's fraternal twins that run in the family." She poured another shot, then screwed the top on the bottle tightly. "You told me that. Honestly, I am so rattled today. Scott and I had counseling this morning and he was just completely uncommunicative."

For some reason, that's when it hit me. The note referring to a *brood of brats*. "Bonnie!" I cried.

She looked at me, alarmed. "What?"

Oops. "Counseling is supposed to make you feel *better*," I improvised.

"Maybe, if you're not married to the most selfish man on earth. Though"—she shrugged—"it's driving you crazy being married to the most self*less* man on earth, isn't it? Why couldn't they just reach some nice point in between, eh?" I could tell she was loosening up. I wanted to encourage her to have another shot, so she'd be less likely to notice if I slipped up, but it wasn't very responsible to try and manipulate someone into getting hammered.

The front door opened.

We both froze.

"Who is that?" I asked her.

"How the hell should I know?" she rasped back. "It's your house, for god's sake!"

"Hello?" a male voice called.

It wasn't Brendan. Who was it? Wouldn't any intruder, upon sensing people inside, do the same? What was the best response?

"Hello?" I called back strongly.

"Hey there." A man walked into the kitchen. Good-looking guy. *Really* good-looking. About six feet tall, with dark hair and blue eyes. Tanned skin, though I had the impression that he always looked like that, not that he had an early season tan. I couldn't guess at his ethnicity, but only because I was bad at that under the best of circumstances.

"Ramie," he said, with a nod to me. Then he looked at Bonnie. "How are you?"

"Very well!" She didn't add *now*, but I sensed it, though I still couldn't tell whether that was because she knew this guy or not. "I'm Bonnie. Ramie's pal."

"Joe. Nice to meet you." He registered her only briefly before his eyes flicked back to me. "You're okay, then?" The words were casual, and to many the tone might have been as well, but there were just enough deeper notes there to give me pause.

I didn't know what to say. "Good as ever," I hedged.

It looked like it meant more to him than I'd meant to convey, but he ended with a nod and said, "I'll just go on out and work in the garage, then. You know where to find me." He didn't wait for an answer but gave that tip-of-the-imaginary-hat gesture to both of us and turned right into the hall off the kitchen.

"He's as cute as you said," Bonnie breathed as soon as he was gone.

"Did I?"

"Did you?" She snorted. "You haven't been able to shut up about him for months. I'm glad I finally saw him up close."

"What did you think?" I couldn't help asking.

"So gorgeous," she said. "Even better than you described. What I don't understand is why you're not doing him."

I had to laugh. Even while normal me would have been intrigued by the idea of "doing" him, it was an absurd question under these circumstances. "Might be something to do with my husband? Or maybe, just possibly, my pregnancy?"

She laughed but accompanied it with a dismissive hand gesture. "I'm not even sure that guy's not the father!"

"What?"

I was startled; my voice had to be hard, maybe even the kind of tone I should apologize for, but she just looked at me, slowly and impassively. Apparently she thought I was the sort of person who might have a child with someone other than my husband, and then pass it off as his.

Dear god, *was* I?

"*Is* he?" she asked. "Is he the father? You know I won't say a word to anyone." She did that cross-my-heart gesture across the front of her Marc Jacobs top. "Honest."

How much had I told her? Whatever it was, it was more than I knew now. So I had only to figure out whether she actually knew something or was goosing me about something she thought was common knowledge but was, in fact, a rumor.

"Bonnie, how many men have you known me to sleep with?" I made it sound like a foregone conclusion, but actually it was a question. A very sincere question.

"Fine," she said, resolute. "I get it, there haven't been that many that I know of. But you know how it's been. . . . No offense, but I wouldn't be surprised if you'd ventured out."

Of course, I didn't know how it had been. At all. And the idea of "venturing out" so casually on my marriage, particularly when I was pregnant, was a little alarming to me. Not because *anyone* might have done that. I didn't have moral judgments for what anyone else might do. But the fact was, my apparent *friend* didn't find the idea of *my* doing it surprising.

So what did that mean about me?

"Bonnie," I said evenly, as if I knew her and I might know this was a joke. "Come on. Have you ever known me to *venture out* on Brendan?" I waited with bated breath. "Ever?"

"No!"

She didn't even hesitate, or look at me strangely, she just rolled her eyes and said, "Okay, right, but there's a first time for everything. And you seemed so struck by Joe—"

"Joe?"

"*Joe!* And with your hormones raging and your husband sleeping . . . well, who could blame you?"

"Did I actually *say* I wanted to sleep with Joe?" I asked, trying to sound like I knew the answer was *no* but secretly unsure of what on earth I might have said to this woman—or why.

Her mouth quirked into a smile. "Okay, okay, if that's the game we're playing, *no.* You didn't *say* you wanted to sleep with him."

My relief was palpable. "There. See?"

But it was short-lived. "I think your terminology has, pretty consistently, been that you'd *do him.*" She didn't even look smug. She didn't look like she knew she'd been put on the spot. It looked for all the world like we'd been playing a tennis game that she

was really good at. There was no way to hit at her backhand unexpectedly because she was already ready.

Maybe even left-handed.

"So?" she queried.

"So, what?" That question applied to so many things, very
few of which it was feeling like Bonnie could answer.

"So, are you going for it?" She gestured down the hall Joe had
taken, out into the garage. "You know this neighborhood is dead
right now. You could go out and bang him with the garage door
open and no one would ever be the wiser. Except me." She gig-
gled. "And obviously I'd hold that over your head forever."

"Of course."

"Along with all the other stuff." She smiled. "So you see? You
know I can keep a secret. Because you'd sure as hell have known
a long time ago if I couldn't!"

In a way this was disappointing news. Obviously I wanted to
know what she knew about me. I wanted all the stories, alarming as they might be. I wanted to trust her, like I'd trust a friend,
but I didn't know her at all. I had no reason at all to dive into
that relationship.

"You know my friend Tanya?" I asked, thinking I'd have
to follow up with a clever and seemingly relevant story if she
said yes.

"Obviously."

What did I do now? "What I mean is," I stalled, trying to
think what on earth I could mean about my best friend, whom
this woman in front of me probably knew better than I did at the
moment, "you know how she always says to take a chance where
passion is involved."

Bonnie laughed. "*Tanya* said that?"

"Well—"

"That explains the kids and the stuck-like-glue devotion to her husband."

Now I got it. Tanya was not only married and mothering, but really devoted. It wasn't that I would have expected anything less from her in any incarnation, only that I thought at this point—in our midtwenties—she would have remained single a bit longer, as she had in my time.

How much had changed?

My thoughts were dizzying. All the questions I couldn't possibly get answers to. It was one thing when my dad was there to impart wisdom, whether he actually knew the odd situation he was addressing or not, but right now I felt well and truly alone.

"They're pretty happily married," I agreed tentatively.

Bonnie shrugged. "That boy of theirs is a hellion."

"Boy?"

"Her son." Bonnie looked at me funny. "The one you were babysitting last Sunday. You don't know two Tanyas, do you? *This is my best friend Tanya, and this is my other best friend Tanya.*" She smiled, but she looked concerned at the same time. "You're not quite yourself today, Ramie."

"No," I agreed. So maybe nothing I thought I knew had turned out the way I'd believed. "I think I should go back to bed and get some rest. Everything is . . ." What? What could I possibly say that would make sense to this outsider? None of it made sense to me at all, and I'd been living the madness for some time. Though it occurred to me now that I didn't even know how much time. "I'm just exhausted. You know how it is." I gestured at my pregnant belly, as if that were the answer.

Apparently it was. "I sure do." She stood up. "Listen, honey, if you need anything at all, you give me a ding, okay? No matter what time. I'm always there."

"Thanks." I made a show of stretching and yawning and walking pointedly in the direction of the front door.

She came along. "Do you want me to call Brendan for you? Tell him to pick anything up on his way home?"

"No, no, I'm fine. I'm sure I have everything I need here."

She gave a bawdy laugh and jerked her thumb toward the back of the house. "With Mr. Hancy Pants out there in the garage, I'm sure you *do*, Ramie. I'm sure you do."

"Stop."

She put her hands up in false surrender. "Okay, okay. But don't blame me for your raging hormones."

I gave a smile, though I was privately finding her extremely tedious. "Talk to you later."

She kissed the air next to my cheek. "See ya! Don't forget to call me if you need anything!"

Even after I closed the door, I imagined I could hear her echo bouncing around the halls.

CHAPTER TWENTY-EIGHT

I WENT BACK TO THE KITCHEN AND SAT DOWN AT THE TABLE and just cried.

There were undoubtedly more comfortable places in the house to go, but this wasn't my house and it wasn't my life and it wasn't my reality and I didn't know what to do anymore. I just wanted to go home.

But I no longer knew what or where that was.

This wasn't the life for me. This was the obvious conclusion for the life I'd worked toward. The very things that had made Brendan such a good high school boyfriend—his calm demeanor, his practicality, the way he took things as they came and dealt with them—were the very things that would keep him from moving in any sort of unexpected direction or territory, ever. At least for me. I'd known him too long.

Brendan was the perfect husband for someone who'd lived a wild life, had sown all of her wild oats, and was ready to settle down and truly appreciate the tranquillity he offered. Maybe someone who liked to stay in and watch movies, eat popcorn; in short, someone who no longer wanted adventure and newness and independence.

As bad as these few hours had told me I felt about being married for all time to Brendan, I could only imagine how unfair it was to burden *him* with a wife who didn't appreciate all the truly wonderful character traits he had, and the companionship he had to offer.

I had been *so selfish* all this time, thinking about what *I* wanted, whether or not Brendan was good for *me*. Did I want him? Did I want to discard him? Had he kissed someone else? How dare he! How dare an eighteen-year-old boy, even for a moment, kiss someone else and see if maybe he was more compatible with someone other than the one girl he'd dated since tenth grade!

How on earth had I thought that that—my fate *and* his—was entirely up to me to decide?

God, I was *such* a jerk!

As nice as things had been between us when I'd left my last high school scene, as sweet and lovable as he was, and even as much as I loved him, it was unconscionable for me to think that the decision for *both* of our futures was entirely up to me.

If I couldn't get out of this present, now, I might well continue ruining *both* of our lives.

I don't know how long I sat there weeping, but it was some time before I felt a hand on my shoulder. I turned and looked up and it was Joe, his face etched with concern. Blue eyes sharp, the white of smile lines showing, as he was not smiling now.

"What's the matter, Ramie?"

I shook my head.

"Hey." He knelt in front of me and took both my hands in his. "Hey, it's going to be okay."

"Is it?"

"Of course it is."

"*How?*" Obviously there was no way the two of us were even having the same conversation, but something about his voice was comforting to me. I wanted him to keep talking.

But he didn't. Instead, he leaned in and kissed me on the lips. Tenderly, but deliciously. Skilled.

It felt so good. So safe. And he smelled wonderful. Some familiar combination of woodsy, smoky, and clean. I closed my eyes and inhaled his scent, and relished the feel of his arms around me. But just for one illicit moment.

I pulled back. "I can't."

"I know."

"Bonnie thinks the baby is yours."

He laughed outright. "Now, *that* would be quite a feat." He shook his head.

"What do you mean?"

"I mean, given the fact that you were pregnant when I met you, unless I managed some sort of time travel, I don't think I'm the father. Didn't you tell her that?"

No, I didn't know that. "Of course."

"Drama." He smoothed my hair back. "Just like you said. Drama drama drama. No wonder it's driving you crazy."

"I think everything's driving me crazy." It was hard to breathe. Everything I'd so far concluded from the day I'd been here, I'd apparently admitted to this stranger.

This stranger I'd apparently told my friend I'd like to *do*.

Pregnant with Brendan's baby, and I was saying I wanted another man.

"I definitely don't feel sane at all," I said.

"You are the most sane person I've met." He looked earnestly into my eyes. "You're in a tough situation and you're handling it like a champ. Give yourself some credit."

"But—" I touched my lips with my fingertips, then looked at him. "We..." I didn't know the end of that sentence, so I just looked at him with a question in my eyes.

"We met a little too late," he supplied. "And we've been nothing short of heroic in containing our impulses. Ramie, I admire your will to show your child responsibility and loyalty. But when was the last time you were truly happy?"

"I honestly don't know." It was devastating to hear that things were so bad in this now that he could say that to me.

"You told me you couldn't even remember what real happiness felt like."

"I said that?"

"You know you did."

"That seems like such a betrayal to Brendan." I hesitated. *Was* it? He was my husband. Why was I so unhappy?

"You said that too," he said, a small smile touching his lips. "He's lucky to have you."

"And you?"

He gave a dry laugh. "Sometimes I feel pretty damn unlucky to have met you," he said. "A month earlier, and we might have had a different story."

My hand went to my abdomen.

He put his on top of mine. "You're going to do great no matter what. It's inevitable." He kissed me on the forehead, then stood up. "Your husband and your child are the luckiest two people on earth."

"God help the rest of you, then."

He laughed. "We'll survive." He rumpled my hair, then cupped his hand to my cheek. "I'm here, Ramie. No matter what you need, you know I'm here."

"Thanks."

I didn't even know his last name.

I WENT UPSTAIRS to the bedroom I'd awoken in a few hours earlier. I wasn't sure what to do with myself there, but it had to be more comfortable than the kitchen.

Besides, I didn't want to run into Joe again. Our conversation, as comforting as he might ostensibly have been, had made me distinctly *un*comfortable.

Had I fallen in love with this Joe? How heinous. Ridiculous. This me didn't have a history I knew of or could remember, so she didn't feel real. I didn't believe I was feeling her feelings or thinking her thoughts the way I'd felt with eighteen-year-old me, because she didn't truly exist to me.

Once in the bedroom, I started searching through the bedside table for some clues about my life. I had always kept a diary, I even had one still, although it was pretty abbreviated, so there was every reason to expect that this Ramie had one too, but it wasn't in the usual place.

I tried the closet, looking up at the top shelf, behind my folded jeans. Jeans I supposed I was probably looking forward to fitting in again. Everything was very neat and tidy, I kept meticulous order, just as I did today. But the diary, if it existed, simply wasn't where I expected.

I even checked under the mattress. The most clichéd of diary hiding places. Honestly, I half expected to find it there, but there was nothing.

I sat down on the bed heavily and looked at the room around me, feeling hopeless. What if this was where I stuck? What if, now that I'd landed here in this apparently unlived life, I could never get out? Was this my new existence, like some experiment I had to make better?

I lay back against the pillows and cried again. I just didn't know what to do with myself. I was lost, far more lost than I'd been a few days ago.

There had to be a clue somewhere.

I no sooner had the thought than something told me to open the bedside table drawer again and feel behind it. Sure enough, there it was. A small leather diary.

I opened it randomly and started to read:

...to his office Christmas party. It was the same as last year. And the year before. And the year before that. And everyone wanted my recipe for grape jelly and chili meatballs, which I took this year, and last year, and the year before, and all in all it felt as if I had been written by Charles Dickens, only instead of getting the ghosts at midnight, all I got was heartburn from Millie Krantz's deviled eggs. Which she also brought last year and the year before, but which I'd remembered as much more delicious than they actually were.

My life is in a rut.

Not a great Christmas, I gathered. I flipped through the pages and read some more:

I was watching *Oprah* today and people were talking about how they "only" had sex once a week. Some were once a month. Not one of them said they literally couldn't remember the last time, but if I'd been on I could have said it.

I'm tired of feeling like such an undesirable loser. What twenty-six-year-old man doesn't want to have sex? We used to have the hottest sex life in the world and now I can't even get him to kiss me. Even if I really throw myself at him, half the time he can't even finish. He doesn't even want to. He's always polite. Brendan is always The Nice Guy. But I think he's bored with me, and why wouldn't he be? I'm bored out of my mind with myself.

I don't know what to do.

My heart ached for this poor woman who was, apparently, me. This woman who must have thought she'd dodged the necessary heartbreak of growing up by defying the odds and marrying her high school sweetheart. Just like in a storybook.

But it didn't turn out that way.

I wouldn't have seen this coming and I'm sure the woman who married him didn't anticipate it either. No one sets out to have an empty and unfulfilling life. Somehow I'd become empty.

All in an effort to stay fulfilled.

I wondered how this had happened. Had Brendan wanted the marriage, or was it just me? Or, for that matter, was it just Brendan? How had this happened and, more to the point, how had it gone downhill so quickly?

I was only twenty-six, but I was pregnant and writing in my diary about how uninterested my husband was in me. That was a pretty dismal state of affairs.

The reality of my twenties was that I'd gotten my own apartment in New York—well, *apartment* is generous, it was a room with a hot plate, but it was my own, and I had worked on Wall Street and built a name for myself, and a place in the world I wanted to practice business.

I'd had friends, and boyfriends, and parties and brunches and a *lot* of good memories. I'd not only completed several levels of education, but I'd built *myself* out of some great experiences. Not because of a man, but because of the whole of my life, all the elements put together to create one whole person.

I'd done it right. At least right for me. After all the dithering and wondering if I'd done the right thing or the wrong thing, based on other people's lives and decisions, it was finally clear to me that I'd done what was best for me. I'd grown a life that was my own and that I was, usually, very happy with.

I lacked intimate love, that was pretty clear in all of my incarnations. That was something I really wanted—I wasn't too cool to admit I wanted it still—but a bad relationship was so much worse than no relationship at all. How many times, and how many ways, did I need to learn that before I was finally able to move on to the next level of the game?

I leafed through the pages of the diary and the words *it was positive* caught my eye:

Took the leftover pregnancy test from last month's two-pack today, thinking it was going to be the same old story as ever, but imagine my surprise when it was positive!

I haven't told Brendan yet. I know he didn't want to keep trying, because it was stressing us both out and, honestly, I don't think he wants kids. At least not now. Maybe not with me. It's so hard to tell with him because he's always so nice about everything. He'd never want to hurt me, any more than I'd want to hurt him, but I feel like we ran out of gas a couple of years ago and now we're just running on fumes.

Should it really feel like this when you've only been married for five years?

I hate to say it but I'm just so bored. I never wanted to be the housewife in a housecoat, waving good-bye at the front door with a cup of coffee in hand, then greeting him in the evening with a pot roast and a Saran Wrap dress, but maybe that is the life he wants and what I should be trying harder to do. After all, I'm obviously going to have to take maternity leave and take care of the baby at home for some time. I can't imagine not working, but I guess that's what I'll have to do, at least for the first few months.

I know you're not supposed to hope that a baby fixes everything but I can't help it. I hope this baby brings us back together.

I just have a terrible feeling that it won't.

Of course it wouldn't. Everyone knew that. It was a futile hope. A mistake made by many, many women over the centuries.

No wonder I—now, sitting on this bed, heavy and pregnant and without any sense of the life inside of me—was so depressed. I knew the truth: that I was bringing a new person into an empty life. What would become of this family?

I couldn't stand to read any more. It was just too depressing. Yet how does one look away when she is able to see right down the sights of her future? I turned to the last entry. It was dated March, so judging from the sweltering heat outside it must have been a couple of months ago:

All of my life, I have had a recurring dream of being in love with a man whose face I could not distinguish. They weren't "sex dreams" really, though sometimes there was sex in them. Mostly kissing. Passionate kissing.

And in these dreams there was always a feeling of, "Where have you been? What took you so long to find me?" It's hard to describe but there is always an intensity of feeling, like I love him so much, and have loved him for so many lifetimes, that I just cannot get close enough to him. I want to climb into his soul. I want to drink every bit of him in, and hold on for dear life, and never, ever let go. There can never be enough time for all of the catching up and connecting we need to do.

When I'd wake up from these dreams, I could never identify one thing about the man. Not his height, hair color, eye color, nothing. Only the way he made me feel. The way I felt in his presence.

Does he really exist?

And, worse, if he does, does it even matter? I could never do that to Brendan. I could never hurt him like that. So I must go the rest of my life knowing he's there, whoever he is, but that I can't be with him, ever.

Once upon a time, I thought I'd gotten to skip so much heartache by finding the love of my life—Brendan—so early.

Now I know that all I did was close my eyes tightly to the rest of the world and deprive myself of what might have been real happiness.

I've made a huge mistake.

The entry ended there. Nothing followed.

This me must really be depressed, because I couldn't think of a time in my life when I'd gone more than a few days without *some* sort of entry in my diary, if only to check in and say what was keeping me away.

My heart felt heavy. My chest was tight.

I knew those dreams. Because of course I'd had them too. I knew the feeling of waking up in love with a phantom and wondering if I'd ever be able to find him. And now that I read the words of this still-romantic twenty-six-year-old me, they struck me as true; the thing I felt when I met Joe was that familiarity.

But not even thirty-eight-year-old me, in this pregnant body, knew what to do about it. Because I was stuck. We were all stuck now. At the moment, the baby felt like a medical condition, not a life inside of me, but soon enough that life would burst forth and become a person in his or her own right.

And I knew that Brendan and I would both doggedly do the right thing. Maybe forever.

What had I done?

How had my life become such a mess, when all I'd wanted was something as simple as love and security?

A wave of nausea came over me and I lay down. Sick, tired, depressed, hopeless.

I fell into a dreamless sleep.

CHAPTER TWENTY-NINE

THAT DAMN ALARM *AGAIN*!

This was torture. Always beeping, but I could never stop it. I could never find it. It had to be part of the dream. A nightmarish element to keep things surreal.

I tried to open my eyes, but they felt like they were sewn shut. The effort of trying to open them was overwhelming. The vague thought that I might be in a morgue crossed my mind. I must have seen that on *The Twilight Zone* at some point. Like the guy who's about to be autopsied but they notice a tear coming out of his eye.

Did they sew eyes shut anymore? Had they ever?

There were voices in the room.

"... it would be a miracle, that's for sure. But I've seen a lot of miracles in my time, so I fully expect one." I knew that voice. I had heard him say it a million times.

Sammy.

Who was Sammy?

Something inside assured me he was my friend. I knew him. I trusted him.

I could hear him whispering in my ear. "You can get through this and you will. You *can* and you *will*."

What? What was I supposed to be doing?

I felt like I'd asked myself that question a million times lately. I was always *supposed* to be figuring something out, but I was just so damn tired. All I wanted was to sleep. And forget.

Then my mother's voice cut through the darkness. There was no confusion there. "Jonathan is waiting downstairs. I'll just pop down and check on him. He doesn't like to be alone for long." The big fat baby. Jonathan was always complaining that Mom wasn't doing enough for him. I had the reaction before any clear thoughts could come to mind.

But, wait. Jonathan? *Sammy?* Those names felt so far away. Like another lifetime. Slowly their places in my life took form. But how long had it been since I'd seen, or even thought about, either one of them? They didn't even seem real.

The thought was quickly obscured by my father's voice.

"We're *all* here to learn something. Sometimes we learn it in the worst possible way. Sometimes we have to face something we don't think we can live through in order to show ourselves that we can live through hell and still come out on the other side."

When had he said that to me? I felt like we were talking about his death, but how could I possibly have been talking about his death with him? The words had given me some comfort, I knew that. Meaning in a time when I had lost all sense of purpose. So he was right and he had helped, but how could he have known?

"Sleep is good for her." I couldn't say who that was, but the female voice wasn't entirely unfamiliar.

The thoughts were too much. Too mixed up. It was like trying to untangle a bunch of thin necklaces with frozen fingers. Exhaustion took over me. I was too tired to think. Too tired to figure out puzzles that had no answers. My head hurt. The beeping sound was driving me nuts. Why wasn't anyone stopping that?

Maybe a vodka *would* be good right now.

I was so tired.

Just so tired.

"I could have sworn I just saw her eyes flicker." That was Sammy again. His voice was high, excited. "Maybe we should call someone. Quick."

"It happens," the other voice said. It was a woman. "I'm sorry, but it doesn't necessarily mean a thing."

"Not *necessarily*, but what if . . ."

The rest was lost in a dense fog of sleep. I welcomed it. I was so tired I would have taken death.

And, truthfully, that was what this felt like, because I hadn't dreamed normal dreams—the disjointed, fragmented ones filled with nonsense and resolution—in what seemed like forever. My brain was so cramped with confusion that even the mental recycling of sleep seemed like a blessed relief.

WHEN I ROUSED again, it was the same story. Beeping. Heavy lids. And, I was aware this time, the distinct smell of antiseptic.

"Turn off . . . the alarm . . ." I labored to say.

"Whoa! She's moving her mouth!" It was Sammy again. "I don't give a damn what that stupid nurse says; she's coming back. I've gotta go. I'll call you back." I heard the beep of ending a phone call, then something clattered right by my head. It sounded like metal.

"Hello?" A clicking noise by my ear. "How does this fucking thing work?"

Where was I? I couldn't move. Even with my worst hangover— and my head was telling me this was a whopper—I'd never had to work so hard to open my eyes.

Then a crack of light shone through. Misty. Blurry. Overhead lights blazed, but I couldn't see what they looked like.

"Nurse! Nurse!" Sammy had moved; his voice was a few feet away now. "She's waking up. Get the doctor!"

I COULD NOT begin to say how much longer it was, but after I'd finally gotten my eyes open and realized I was in a hospital room—Sammy's frantic eyes looking at me from behind the doctor's shoulder—things came into decent focus.

The beeping continued, but it wasn't an alarm clock. It was the heart monitor that had been hooked up to me for what Sammy told me had been nearly three weeks. Good thing it *hadn't* stopped when I'd kept wishing it would.

It was disconcerting how that had pierced through my sleep now and again, before I slipped back in.

Sleep, they called it.

But it was a coma. I'd been in a coma, suspended between life and death, and so my mind had taken me back to high school.

Or, more specifically, to those precious moments before my father died.

And he'd given me the gift of understanding that, even if I'd never accept his death as "for the best," I didn't need to carry the memory of how I found him as this heavy warning that life can suck. Had it made me stronger? Unquestionably. I never would have dreamed I could have gone through that and survived.

But had I also taken his death as permission, or even an order, not to get too close to someone else? Maybe.

"Apparently people don't usually come back when they've been out as long as you were," Sammy was saying, continuing his list of things that had happened while I was sleeping. "There was talk of pulling the plug. Can you imagine?"

I drew in a breath, though it was still difficult. My mouth felt dry and tight. Cotton. "Who wanted to pull the plug?"

"No one *wanted* to," he said, then corrected, "Well, I don't know, maybe Jonathan wanted to. Apparently he's sick of being in Florida. The bugs, you know. We heard *all about* the bugs."

"Jonathan wanted to kill me so he didn't have to stay in Florida?" Oddly, this seemed consistent with Jonathan.

"Sweetie, it wasn't exactly like he wanted to kill you *himself*." That was comforting. "Your mom never let him up here, not once. She said if you sensed him in the room, you'd never open your eyes."

I had to laugh. "True."

"And none of us trusted him with all these pillows around," he added sagely.

"Thanks for that."

"To be honest with you," he began, which was how he always

started juicy gossip, "I'm not sure your mom is really all that into him. Like, at all. She talked an awful lot about a guy named Robert. I gather that was your dad?"

A twinge of sadness pierced through my chest. "Yes."

Sammy nodded. "She kept saying she felt like he was here. At one point she even swore she smelled Aqua Velva."

"Seriously?"

He crossed his heart.

"Did you? Smell anything, I mean."

He shook his head and looked disappointed "You know I'm into the woo-woo. But I couldn't smell a thing except whatever it is they use to scrub down the floors with. Bleachy sort of Pine-Sol stuff."

"I've been smelling that myself. In my dream or whatever it was. Now and then I'd smell this antiseptic scent that wasn't consistent with where I was supposed to be."

I had told him about my experience, my dream or whatever it was, and after a few *Wizard of Oz* jokes, he'd finally taken me seriously and grown interested in the meaning of it all.

"That's kind of cool, actually. Your mind was in a completely different time and place, but your senses were still here."

"But they were there too. I could smell, taste, feel—it was all so completely real."

"The sex was satisfying?"

"Sammy!"

"Well?"

I gave a laugh. "You know there's nothing like teenage sex. Nothing better."

"I don't know," he admitted. "I never had that particular experience." He shrugged. "Woe is me."

"No kidding."

"Back to you, back to you. What else do you remember? Anything else discordant?"

"There were voices," I recalled. "Sometimes I heard voices that didn't quite make sense. But I was so tired so much of the time that a lot of it had a dreamlike quality."

Sammy looked interested. "Wow. I guess that was a clue that you were here. A little bleed-through between your two realities. Did you do anything to, you know, try and change the future?"

"It wasn't a movie, Sammy."

"I know, but we don't know exactly what it *was*, so it's not a stupid question."

"It was a dream."

"Maybe."

"What else could it have been?"

"An actual alternate reality. A road not taken. A preview of what could have been. Or even, if you buy the business of time being all over the place, maybe even an alternate *future*." He widened his eyes dramatically and did flouncy things with his hands. "You never know, it might have been some sort of fortune-telling."

"Okay, or a dream." But I didn't like that explanation either. A mere *dream* was so simple, and this had felt so much more profound than that. This *had* shown me the road not taken. My questions had been answered. Was that a trick of my mind or something greater?

Maybe it didn't matter.

So I answered Sammy the best I could. "It didn't seem like anything was all that delicate a thread," I said. "It wasn't like the movies where you turn right instead of left and half the population disappears. I don't know about the butterfly effect in general, but it sure didn't seem to be at play in this case."

He looked disappointed. "I guess that's not really all that surprising. If you're going to believe in fate, you have to believe it's not so delicate that an extra beer is going to blow it."

And yet for how many people had that exact thing made the difference? The extra beer, the extra five minutes in one place before hitting the road and either knocking down a pedestrian or missing a runaway train. Sometimes those small things *did* make a difference.

Didn't they?

"I hate to think the whole thing is meaningless," Sammy concluded. "Here we were, scared out of our minds that you weren't going to come back, and you did." He sighed and shook his head. "After the odds said you wouldn't, you did. I wish you had something to show for it, other than a head wound."

CHAPTER THIRTY

ABOUT A YEAR BEFORE THE ACCIDENT, I'D BEGUN HAVING PANIC attacks. Not the wimpy, imagined, oh-my-god-I-was-so-scared-I-was-totally-having-a panic-attack variety, but the real deal: The adrenaline surge in the middle of an otherwise relaxing time, or even in the midst of a deep sleep. The kind that paralyzes you and eventually makes you change the route you drive to work, or the time you go to the grocery store, or your willingness to sit in a crowded movie theater.

The kind, in short, that can really interfere with your life if you let it.

My job was a stressful one, but I'd handled it well for years. But in my mid-thirties, out of the blue, I started having panic attacks and the doctor told me to stop drinking coffee. That was the upshot. I didn't want to take medication, and meditation was just so boring that I made the one sacrifice that seemed the most obvious for someone who was having trouble with heart palpitations. I stopped drinking coffee.

And in so doing, I'd stopped going to one of my favorite haunts, Brewed Awakening, downtown. A nice little café with a great, colorful, lively space both inside and out. The owner, Miguel, made the best damn cup of coffee you can imagine. Everything you ever wished coffee could be, but which it always fell short of in real life, Miguel brought to beautiful, delicious life. A toasty, roasted savory drink, smoothed by cream and enlivened with just a hint of sweetness.

Brewed Awakening had legions of followers, and it was always crowded. I'm sure no one noticed when I stopped going, but I sure missed it. Admittedly I could have gone in for the decaf, but something was lacking without the caffeine, and I hadn't wanted to go back and put myself in the way of all that temptation. It was like an alcoholic hanging out in a bar; it would have made my resolution a whole lot harder.

But the day after I got out of the hospital, I decided to defy panic and had Sammy meet me there for a cuppa. Just for old times' sake. I was not only craving the coffee; I was craving some sense of normality. My sense of identity had been seriously shaken, so I wanted to return to some places where I knew I'd felt happy and sane.

The coffee shop was a small thing, but it felt important.

"I can't believe you never told me about this place before," Sammy said, starting on his second cup. We were sitting outside on the sidewalk, the small shade of a palm tree skittering across us as the wind nudged it back and forth.

"I told you about this place a thousand times. I came here

every single day for more than a year and begged you to meet me sometimes so I didn't have to sit here like a loser."

He waved that away, as if I were missing the point. "You didn't tell me I *had* to try it."

"I believe I did."

He took another sip, then closed his eyes for a moment to relish it. "You should have forced me."

I laughed at the very idea. "Because it's *so* easy to force you to do things."

He gave a conciliatory nod, and took another sip of coffee. "So there's something I need to talk to you about."

Did any conversation ever start that way and end with laughter and happiness?

Not usually.

"Tell me you're not terminally ill." Because that's how my mind works. If I could burn calories leaping to the worst possible conclusion, I'd be thin as a rail.

"What? *No!*"

"Good." My relief was genuine. All that angst over him saying he wanted to talk to me about something. This was the kind of thinking that had led me to the anxiety problem in the first place. "Now tell me *I'm* not terminally ill." I was kidding, but for just a moment it occurred to me that maybe he'd learned of some test result at the hospital that I didn't know about.

"You're crazy," he said, twirling his finger at his temple. "Does that count?"

"Not as news, no." I took a gulp myself. God, it was good. Almost chocolate, but not quite. A hint of coconut, but that wasn't quite it. A creamy mouthful that beat the heck out of any hot chocolate I'd ever had, even at Shake Shack in New York City, which tasted like warm, melted ice cream. This was heaven.

I couldn't believe I'd managed to go a year without it.

Forget it, I'd take up meditation or something so I could return to my daily habit. Ironically, sitting here drinking the familiar beverage was actually *relaxing*.

"Not everything is about you, missy," Sammy went on. "As it happens, this is news about Tod and me. Good news," he hastened to add. He knew me well.

"Okay. Renewing your vows?"

He rolled his eyes. "Oh, please. It was hard enough to choke them out the first time! For him, not for me. If I offer him the chance to renew them, he might just decide to revoke them instead."

"You're not fooling me," I said. "Not a chance." Tod and Sammy were completely devoted to each other. Sammy could afford to joke like that because in his heart he could be absolutely certain it would never, ever happen.

Tod was no scumbag.

No danger of that.

"Okay, okay, I guess he's going to stick around a little bit longer. But no, we don't have plans to renew our vows. You know how Tod hates parties."

It was true. Lucky for me. That was why I'd been able to have Sammy be my plus-one for so many events. Tod was always working and Sammy was bored, so it worked out for all of us.

"All right, I'm listening," I said. "What's really up?"

"Do you remember what we talked about on the boat . . . that day?" Sammy asked carefully.

No question *which day*, obviously. "We talked about a lot of things. Lisa being pregnant?"

"Yes, and . . . Tod and I adopting."

"That's right! I remember that."

"Well, what I didn't tell you then was that after talking about it for ages, we started the official process last year."

"You *did*? Sammy, why didn't you tell me?" I felt awful. I was such a shitty, self-centered friend that he hadn't even felt like he could tell me the biggest thing in his life. "I think it's wonderful!"

"You do?"

To be honest, inside I felt a twinge. In my head, I'd recently been pregnant. Admittedly I'd had mixed feelings about it, but not all negative. It had reinforced the necessity of the right life partner. I could only imagine the joy Lisa was feeling, but right here, right now, I could *see* the joy Sammy was feeling.

It was written all over his face. His eyes were alight; his face was flushed; he couldn't stop smiling. Part of that might have been Miguel's coffee, of course, but, all joking aside, this was the look that any prospective parent *should* have.

Lucky kid.

"Of *course* I do!" I assured him immediately, enthusiastically. "Just because Lisa's uterus made me question my own doesn't mean I'm not thrilled for her, and for you, and for *anyone* who gets to take that step when they really want it."

"But your thing with Brendan—"

"Was a dream! Or a warning. Or something completely un-related to this." I was jealous. He was right; my miserly little heart was finding a way, deep inside, to make this about me. "Please.

Tell me all about you. You said you started this a year ago, so I guess that means there's been some movement?"

"Yes. We are traveling to Ethiopia in a couple of weeks with a group of other new parents to pick up our son, Abera." His eyes filled with tears. "That means *he shines*."

He had my full attention now, and soon I was crying too. The way he felt, the way he was expressing himself, was the way a person *should* feel about marriage and family. This was his whole life. These people were everything to him. Work was just a means to support the happy home he was building.

"Tod's work schedule isn't letting up very soon, so I'm not going to, you know, be able to hang out and play so much anymore. Probably won't be any more champagne on yachts for a while."

"Of course! You're going to be Mr. Mom. I'll go over to your place and we'll drink champagne from sippy cups."

"Or coffee." He raised his cup to me. "You've created a monster here. I may never be the same."

"It's good stuff."

He smiled, then leaned over and gave me a hug across the table. "I love you, sista. Soon you're going to have it all too." He kissed my cheek. "I know it. I have a feeling."

I was glad he was hugging me, because the tears began to flow freely. "Don't worry about me," I said, with what I hoped was convincing bravado. "I'm so happy for you, I don't know what to do with myself."

He drew back and looked at me. "Thank you, my friend."

I sniffed quickly and hoped he didn't notice. "So when are we going shopping for baby things?"

"As soon as we have Abera. I haven't wanted to put the cart before the horse, you understand. Bad luck. That's why we didn't tell anyone about this until we had a pickup date."

I nodded. "Everything will go smoothly, I know it."

He touched my lips and pointed at the sky. *From your lips to God's ear.*

"Gotta fly," he said. "Talk soon!"

I blew him a kiss and watched him very nearly float down the sidewalk to his car.

It wasn't the coffee. It was happiness. I wondered what that brand of happy felt like.

But as I gazed down the sidewalk where he'd just been, I realized I *was* genuinely happy. It was good to see my friend so excited, and, for that moment, that was enough for me too.

My father (or my dream subconscious?) had reminded me that everything happens for a reason. Absolutely everything. So maybe time and place *did* matter after all. But maybe not to an exacting degree; perhaps fate gave us more than one chance at the right time and place.

But, as Benjamin Franklin pointed out, God helps those who help themselves.

I'd learned that companionship was really important to me. More so than I'd ever admitted, to myself or to anyone else. So it was time I took matters into my own hands.

CHAPTER THIRTY-ONE

IT DOESN'T TAKE LONG TO SIGN UP FOR A MATCHMAKING SER-
vice online. I was able to sit there, at that beautiful little coffee
shop, and become disheartened by countless men in just a matter
of about forty-five minutes.

I know plenty of people have had really good luck with those
services, so it's not that I think there's anything inherently wrong
with them, but something about my list of likes and dislikes
seemed to bring up a bunch of young men looking for cougars.

What *is* that?

For men, that would be a dream come true. A bunch of much
younger women coming on to them, perhaps openly eager for
gratuitous sex. No romance. No commitment. It was perfect.

For some.

For me, it was discouraging. I think I'd been hoping, still, that
fate was alive and well and working its butt off for me, and that
whoever that man in my dreams was, my opening myself to

online dating would call him in immediately. The angels would sing and God Himself would whisper in my ear, *I've been* waiting *for you to take just one tiny step forward so I could help you! Welcome to your own Paradise!*

I'm saying this like I'm joking, but, actually, I think part of me really thought it might go that way.

And I wasn't giving up; I didn't shut down the account, but after CallMeMaybe178 sent me a picture of his erect *self,* I decided I'd had enough for the day. I mean, for one thing, if 177 other people have chosen the handle CallMeMaybe before you, maybe you can come up with something more original? And, more importantly, if you're still in the "maybe calling" stage, perhaps that's not the time to go around showing your oddly bent dick to strangers.

That's how I see things, anyway.

So I closed my computer with a sigh, and then closed my eyes for a moment, trying to block out all I'd seen and wished I hadn't. Guys with twenty-eight nearly identical unattractive pictures, mostly taken shirtless in bathroom mirrors; guys with one single picture, in which they'd clearly cut out a woman, whose hand usually remained draped over his pictured (tuxedoed) shoulder; guys standing in front of a faded backdrop that pegged their picture as at least fifteen or twenty years old; and of course the ubiquitous Frat-Boy Guys with their mouths frozen in silent post-beer-bong roars of triumph.

There were a lot of those. More than any one of them probably thought.

Why weren't things the way I'd always thought they'd be? Why didn't people who were meant to be together just gravitate toward each other in real life and end up living happily ever after? It was so easy in high school and college; everyone was expected to be dating, and every classroom had a daily round of speed dating with no expectations and no real disappointments. When one person didn't work out, there was easily another. And another.

Often one of his friends.

Youth is all about constantly meeting people.

What was supposed to become of those who didn't meet their forever mate in youth? The whiny, petulant me wanted to complain that it wasn't fair. I'd been dating for over twenty years now and it was all miserable.

I took my wallet and went to the counter to order another coffee. This time I went all-out on a white mocha latté with sugar and full heavy cream. What did I care? It was one day, at my favorite coffee shop. Why not live a little?

As I waited for the coffee to be made, I looked around the crowded shop at the people. Many were tourists; this was a historic part of town, so it drew a lot of tourists, whether or not they'd read in the guidebook how great the coffee was. Most of those people were coupled up.

There were also artsy types. Multipierced college students who looked impossibly young. A pair of lesbian couples, one of which looked seriously happy and the other looking like one was ready to bitch-slap her partner. Love always had its bad days, I supposed.

I went back to my table. No one had disturbed my computer, so I sat down and opened it up again. Maybe I'd been too hasty.

The minute I pulled up the Web site, though, my discouragement came back.

"Excuse me. Miss?"

At first I didn't realize the voice was talking to me, but then I felt a tap on my shoulder.

I looked up and was instantly blinded by the sun. A looming figure was next to it. I moved to try and position the sun behind him so I could see. "Yes?" Spots dangled before my eyes from the glare.

"I'm really sorry to interrupt, and I know this is going to sound like a come-on, but it's not. . . . Do we know each other?"

I looked up into the face of a very good-looking man. "I don't think so," I said. Unfortunately. Then again, if it was a come-on, then maybe it didn't matter. Maybe I should let him come on.

"Sorry." He gave an embarrassed smile and I had a momentary twinge of thinking maybe he *did* look familiar. "I know it sounds stupid, and definitely sounds like a lie, but I had the strongest feeling. But it would have been from years ago."

I smiled. "Oh, well, there you go. I haven't lived here that long. Only about five years."

"Yeah? Where were you from before that?"

I laughed. "You're pretty good at this!"

"No, it's not that." He gave a very embarrassed smile. "It's just—you're not from Maryland, are you?"

The air rushed into my lungs, like I'd been hit. No way. "Actually I am."

"Potomac?"

"Yes." I shaded my eyes and looked closer, but the sun was too much. "Have a seat," I offered, indicating the empty chair in front of me.

"If you're sure. . . ."

"Why not? We're in public. You can't mug me easily." I gave a laugh.

"Oh, no, I'd never try anything like that. It's just that I'm working a job here and I would never have expected to see *anyone* familiar, and there you were. I almost didn't even come here, but something told me . . ." He shook his head. "This all sounds dumb. I'm sorry. So you're from Potomac, huh?"

"I am." He came into focus, and, sure enough, I *knew* I knew his face. I watched him sit down, marveling at how familiar his movements were, the way he held himself. "Joe?" I asked, disbelieving.

He blinked and half glanced over his shoulder. "Me? No, my name is Jeremy. Jeremy Norton." He put his hand out.

"No *way!*" Jer! It was him. It was *Joe* from my dream. Joe the contractor who'd worked on the garage. It was completely unmistakable. Somehow I'd put a few years on Jer and put him into my dream, although I hadn't gotten his name right. Joe was Jer!

Somehow I'd had him right, even if I'd had his name wrong.

"I think we went to school together," I fumbled, so he wouldn't feel like he was hanging out there on a limb. "I'm Ramie. Ramie Phillips. We drank Zima together."

He snapped his fingers. "*That's* it. Ramie Phillips." He gave a laugh. "Twelfth grade. Man, I had *such* a crush on you."

"I know." I raised an eyebrow, but we both laughed.

"I wasn't too subtle."

"That's okay, I wasn't too smart."

The conversation took off from there. He'd been married for like three years out of college, but it hadn't worked out and they'd parted ways, no hard feelings. Since then he'd been working as a master craftsman, all up and down the coast. For a long time he'd been working in my mom's neighborhood, where he'd lived when I'd met him, but finally he realized—as I had, once upon a time—that he was self-employed and could live anywhere, so why was he living and spending winters in such a mercilessly cold (or hot, depending on the time of year) part of the country?

We finished our coffees and decided to walk along the waterfront, even though I had work to do and I was quite certain he did too. He'd said he'd just stopped for a quick cup of java before getting back to work on a large project, but as soon as we started talking, he made a call to someone and then asked if I had time to go for a walk.

It was perfect. Unexpectedly perfect. The weather, the timing, and, I knew now, the person. Because *this* was who I'd dreamed about all those times, the man whose face I could never see. It was Jeremy Norton. The whole time.

Even though we weren't touching, I knew from the feeling I had, walking by his side, that this was the guy.

Finally.

I wanted to catch his hand in mine, to tell him we had a lot to catch up on, because that's the way it felt. Like I'd known him forever. Like he was meant to be, *all* of this was meant to be, just like my father had said. I felt this strange sense of urgency, like we'd waited too long and I didn't want to waste even one more second.

But that would have seemed crazy. And, besides, I knew there was time now. That was the one thing I had learned for sure.

There is always time.

EPILOGUE

WE GET MORE CHANCES THAN PERHAPS YOU MIGHT THINK TO
go back and revisit our loved ones after we're gone. Generally
speaking, communication is difficult, and often goes unnoticed
or dismissed as "coincidence" or "imagination," and those who
know and tell the truth are too often called "frauds" and "op-
portunists."

But sometimes—some rare times—when a soul has left in
its own time, it leaves a loved one wholly unprepared. Unrud-
dered. Missing some of the most important lessons that were
meant to be shared.

And in those cases, sometimes—some very rare times—a soul
can find its way back to communicate in a less subtle way. To
remind their loved one of those things they must know in order
to find their own fate, rather than running around in pointless
circles, only to have to start over again.

And so the soul that was Robert watched his daughter walk

away, down a brightly sunlit Florida sidewalk, with the man she had been longing for in her soul for all of her life. Finally her life was beginning in earnest, her purpose destined, and sure to be fulfilled. There was love in her future. So much love.

He concentrated on her for a moment, and sent one last signal to her. It was an easy one. Anyone could have done it. Elementary.

He smiled when he saw her stop, frown, and look around. She'd gotten his sign. Smelled it.

The faintest waft of Aqua Velva on the warm breeze.